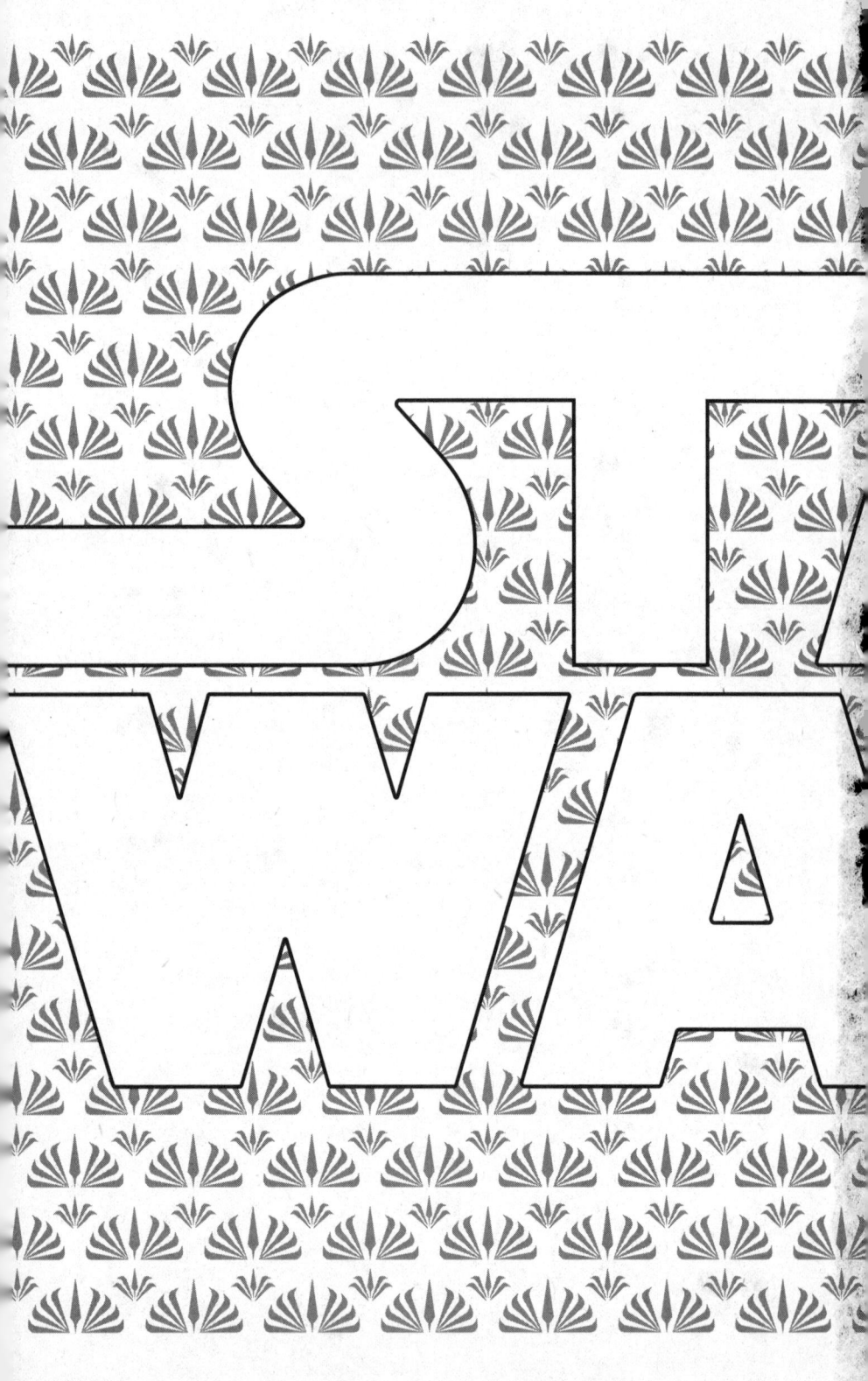

BY CAVAN SCOTT

Star Wars: The High Republic: Tempest Breaker
Star Wars: The High Republic: Path of Vengeance
Star Wars: The High Republic: Tempest Runner
Star Wars: The High Republic: The Rising Storm
Star Wars: The High Republic: The Great Jedi Rescue
Star Wars: Dooku: Jedi Lost
Star Wars: Life Day Treasury (with George Mann)
Star Wars: Adventures in Wild Space—The Escape
Star Wars: Adventures in Wild Space—The Snare
Star Wars: Adventures in Wild Space—The Heist
Star Wars: Adventures in Wild Space—The Cold
Star Wars: Choose Your Destiny—A Han & Chewie Adventure
Star Wars: Choose Your Destiny—A Luke & Leia Adventure
Star Wars: Choose Your Destiny—An Obi-Wan & Anakin Adventure
Star Wars: Choose Your Destiny—A Finn & Poe Adventure

TEMPEST BREAKER

TEMPEST BREAKER

Cavan Scott

RANDOM HOUSE
WORLDS

NEW YORK

Random House Worlds
An imprint of Random House
A division of Penguin Random House LLC
1745 Broadway, New York, NY 10019
randomhousebooks.com
penguinrandomhouse.com

Copyright © 2025 by Lucasfilm Ltd. & ® or ™ where indicated.
All rights reserved.

Penguin Random House values and supports copyright. Copyright fuels creativity, encourages diverse voices, promotes free speech, and creates a vibrant culture. Thank you for buying an authorized edition of this book and for complying with copyright laws by not reproducing, scanning, or distributing any part of it in any form without permission. You are supporting writers and allowing Penguin Random House to continue to publish books for every reader. Please note that no part of this book may be used or reproduced in any manner for the purpose of training artificial intelligence technologies or systems.

RANDOM HOUSE is a registered trademark, and RANDOM HOUSE WORLDS and colophon are trademarks of Penguin Random House LLC.

Hardback ISBN 978-0-593-72341-8
Ebook ISBN 978-0-593-72342-5

Printed in Canada

randomhousebooks.com

2 4 6 8 9 7 5 3 1

First Edition

The authorized representative in the EU for product safety and compliance is Penguin Random House Ireland, Morrison Chambers, 32 Nassau Street, Dublin D02 YH68, Ireland. https://eu-contact.penguin.ie.

For Alyssa, Charles, Claudia, Daniel, George,
Justina, Lydia, Mike, Tessa, and Zoraida

Thank you for being Luminous

THE STAR WARS NOVELS TIMELINE

THE HIGH REPUBLIC

Convergence
The Battle of Jedha
Cataclysm

Light of the Jedi
The Rising Storm
Tempest Runner
The Fallen Star
The Eye of Darkness
Temptation of the Force
Tempest Breaker
Trials of the Jedi

Wayseeker: An Acolyte Novel

Dooku: Jedi Lost
Master and Apprentice
The Living Force

I — THE PHANTOM MENACE

Mace Windu: The Glass Abyss

II — ATTACK OF THE CLONES

Inquisitor: Rise of the Red Blade
Brotherhood
The Thrawn Ascendancy Trilogy
Dark Disciple: A Clone Wars Novel

III — REVENGE OF THE SITH

Reign of the Empire: The Mask of Fear
Catalyst: A Rogue One Novel
Lords of the Sith
Tarkin
Jedi: Battle Scars

SOLO

Thrawn
A New Dawn: A Rebels Novel
Thrawn: Alliances
Thrawn: Treason

ROGUE ONE

IV — A NEW HOPE

Battlefront II: Inferno Squad
Heir to the Jedi
Doctor Aphra
Battlefront: Twilight Company

V — THE EMPIRE STRIKES BACK

VI — RETURN OF THE JEDI

The Princess and the Scoundrel
The Alphabet Squadron Trilogy
The Aftermath Trilogy
Last Shot

Shadow of the Sith
Bloodline
Phasma
Canto Bight

VII — THE FORCE AWAKENS

VIII — THE LAST JEDI

Resistance Reborn
Galaxy's Edge: Black Spire

IX — THE RISE OF SKYWALKER

Cast List

ARGAZ: Ereesi. One of Marchion Ro's elite guards known as She'ar.

AVAR KRISS: Human. Former Jedi marshal of Starlight Beacon. Still known to many as the Hero of Hetzal.

BARON BOOLAN: Ithorian. Nihil minister of advancement and scientist of dubious morals.

BELIN: Ugnaught. Rhil Dairo's partner and pilot.

CARANA-VEY TRANA: Aki-Aki. Jedi Master.

CATKIT: Alzarian. She'ar warrior.

CERET: Kotabi. Jedi Knight who shares a mind with their troubled bond-twin, Terec. Survived a Nameless attack before Starlight Beacon's destruction.

LINA SOH: Human. Chancellor of the Galactic Republic. Regal. Wise. Desperate to do well by her people.

DR. GINO'LE: Anacondan. Former chief of medical operations on Starlight Beacon.

ELZAR MANN: Human. Jedi Master. Trying his best to step into the shoes of a friend more suited to great office.

FARIS KARAN: Theelin. Padawan.

GABB: Muun. Pirate. Wouldn't know cunning if it bashed him over his elongated head.

GREYAMINA TISS: Iktotchi. Wheeler, dealer, and associate of Kradon Minst.

KEEVE TRENNIS: Human. Jedi Master.

KESKAR: Human. She'ar warrior.

KING SOKIDHARAN: Ruler of Waskiro.

KRADON MINST: Villerandi. Owner of the Enlightenment bar on Jedha and an old friend of Tey Sirrek.

LOURNA DEE: Twi'lek. Former Tempest Runner. A former lot of things, to be honest. Mostly bad. Recently has fallen in with her enemies, the Jedi.

MARCHION RO: Evereni. The Eye of the Nihil.

MÔR: Sledfrid. Bodyguard of Straan Valgar.

MUGLAN TARANTYNE: Gloovan. Lourna's former friend and Tempest member.

ORBALIN: Ugor. Gelatinous former Jedi archivist of Starlight Beacon. Thought to have been lost in the disaster but actually survived.

Q-4: Droid. Formerly the property of Lourna Dee, recently reprogrammed by the Jedi. A little prissy to say the least.

QUIN CARREE: Bivall. Lourna's former confidant, Tempest member, and ... something more.

RENGA: Clantanni. Pirate. Shrewd and cunning.

RHIL DAIRO: Human. Reporter and war correspondent who spent time in the Occlusion Zone, where she was forced to make propaganda for Marchion Ro while secretly working for the resistance.

SK-0T: Tey Sirrek's scout droid.

SSKEER: Trandoshan. Disgraced Jedi Master suffering from a rare condition that hinders his connection to the Force. And his sanity.

STRAAN VALGAR: Gloovan.

T-9: Rhil Dairo's cam droid.

TEREC: Kotabi. Jedi. Troubled bond-twin to Ceret. Secretly yearning for more independence.

TEY SIRREK: Sephi. Former Guardian of the Whills turned freedom fighter.

TIA TOON: Sullustan. Republic senator.

VULAX: Harch. A member of Marchion Ro's elite guard, the She'ar.

YACOMBE CHILD: Yacombe. Eight-year-old child strong in the Force, rescued from the clutches of the Nihil by Sskeer. In keeping with her religion, never speaks to outsiders unless through a proxy.

TEMPEST BREAKER

ANNOUNCER:
A long time ago in a galaxy far, far away....

CUE THEME

ANNOUNCER:
Star Wars: The High Republic

Tempest Breaker

By Cavan Scott

ANNOUNCER:

The galaxy is in turmoil. A year after the destruction of Starlight Beacon, the Nihil Stormwall has cut off a vast swath of the Republic, the civilizations within the Occlusion Zone at the mercy of Marchion Ro and his Nihil hordes.

With the Jedi unable to stand against Ro's Nameless, a foe that feeds on the Force itself, a new danger has inexplicably appeared through Republic and Nihil space alike, an unstoppable blight that is turning people and planets into stone. The race is on to find a way to halt its dreadful progress, a solution that Marchion Ro has promised to deliver.

As the various crises continue, holoreporter and war correspondent Rhil Dairo has secured an interview with one of the only people in the galaxy who can claim to know what the murderous Eye of the Nihil has in store. . . .

Part One
TEMPEST NO MORE

SCENE 1. INT. THE *BLUE RANGE*.

FX: The background thrum of a ship. Beeps and bloops of computer systems. The high-pitched buzz of Rhil's cam droid, T-9, hovering nearby.

RHIL DAIRO:
(TAKES A DEEP BREATH, STEADYING HERSELF AND HER NERVES)

BELIN: (DISTORT/COMMS)
How are you doing down there, Rhil?

RHIL:
How do you think?

T-9:
(DROID WHISTLES)

RHIL:
(TO THE DROID, A LITTLE ANNOYED) Yes, yes. I know.

BELIN: (DISTORT/COMMS)
What was that?

RHIL:
Just Tee-Nine reminding me that I was the one who set this up.

BELIN: (DISTORT/COMMS)
Well, that's true enough.

RHIL:
Back in front of the cam droid...

BELIN: (DISTORT/COMMS)
As much part of the war effort as secret broadcasts behind the Stormwall.

RHIL:
Is it? Really? That felt important. This interview... this *person*...

BELIN: (DISTORT/COMMS)
The chancellor wants the galaxy to know that the Nihil haven't already won.

RHIL:
That people can change. Yes, yes. I remember the meeting. Chancellor Soh was very persuasive. And here we are.

BELIN: (DISTORT/COMMS)
So... can we proceed?

RHIL:
Take us in, Belin.

BELIN: (DISTORT/COMMS)
You have spoken.

RHIL:
(SPOKEN, BUT WITH AFFECTION) Ha ha.

BELIN: (DISTORT/COMMS)
Stand by.

FX: A sudden burst of maneuvering thrusters. The creak of the ship's superstructure as it moves into position.

BELIN: (CONT, DISTORT/COMMS)
Bringing us alongside. (BEAT) Holding position.

FX: The beep of Belin opening a channel over the comm.

BELIN: (CONT, DISTORT/COMMS)
(TO THE OTHER SHIP) This is the *Blue Range*, awaiting docking sequence.

FX: The clang of the boarding tube connecting to the ship, followed by the hiss of hydraulics and various clunks as it attaches.

BELIN: (CONT, DISTORT/COMMS)
(TO RHIL) And we're locked in.

RHIL:
(SOTTO) Ain't that the truth? (STEADIES HERSELF) Okay. Let's go.

BELIN: (DISTORT/COMMS)
Opening air lock.

FX: Another clunk and a hiss of rushing air as the hatch slides slowly aside.

RHIL:
No going back now.

FX: Footsteps clang, boots on metal, as Rhil steps into the boarding tube and walks between the ships. T-9's buzz pitches up as the droid hovers with her.

RHIL: (CONT)
Okay, I'm in the docking tube. Let's make some final checks. Tee-Nine? Data connection secure?

T-9:
(DROID BLEEPS IN THE AFFIRMATIVE)

RHIL:
Excellent. Belin? You still there?

BELIN: (DISTORT/COMMS)
With you every step of the way.

RHIL:
Good to know.

FX: Her footsteps stop.

RHIL: (CONT)
Okay, I'm at their air lock. (BEAT, THEN TO HERSELF) Knock, knock. Let me—[in].

FX: *The air lock opens, cutting her off. There is the hum of another droid hovering on the other side, its repulsorlift louder than T-9's constant buzz.*

RHIL: (CONT)
Ah. Hello.

BELIN: (DISTORT/COMMS)
Rhil?

RHIL:
Welcoming party. Well, welcoming scout droid. (TO THE DROID) Hello there. Rhil Dairo, with GoNet News. I believe your . . . commander is expecting me.

SCOUT DROID:
Zet-zet-zet!

FX: *The droid hovers off abruptly.*

RHIL:
And I guess that's our cue to follow.

FX: *Footsteps on deck plates as she follows the scout droid hovering just ahead. T-9 buzzes nearby.*

BELIN: (COMMS, STATIC, BREAKING UP)
Rhil . . . Rhil, the signal's— (STATIC)

RHIL:
Belin?

BELIN: (COMMS, STATIC, WORSE THAN EVER)
(STATIC) losing the feed . . . (STATIC) data stream . . . (STATIC)

FX: *Rhil stops walking. Ahead, the scout droid halts, too.*

SCOUT DROID:
(IMPATIENT) Zet-zet-zutt?

RHIL:
I've lost comms with my technician. Some kind of interference.

SCOUT DROID:
Zut-zet-zut.

RHIL:
(RESIGNED, IF A LITTLE ANNOYED) Your captain has installed signal inhibitors. Of course she has. Guess we're on our own, Tee-Nine.

T-9:
(EVER SO SLIGHTLY WORRIED BLEEP)

SCOUT DROID:
(IMPATIENT) Zet-zet!

T-9:
(AFFRONTED BEEP)

FX: The scout droid continues.

T-9: (CONT)
(DROID EQUIVALENT OF BLOWING A RASPBERRY)

FX: Rhil starts following again.

RHIL:
(VOICE LOW) Keep it professional, Tee. We're the guests, remember.

CUT TO:

SCENE 2. INT. STAR CRUISER. MAIN QUARTERS—CONTINUOUS.

FX: Doors slide open. The scout droid sweeps in, followed by Rhil and T-9. A chair swivels to face them.

LOURNA DEE:
Ah. Good. You're here.

RHIL:
(COLDLY PROFESSIONAL) It's good to see you again.

LOURNA:
I'm sure it is.

RHIL:
Where would you like us to set up?

LOURNA:
Anywhere you like. You're the expert, after all.

RHIL:
Here will be fine.

FX: Rhil takes a seat.

RHIL: (CONT)
Good for you, Tee-Nine?

T-9:
(AFFIRMATIVE BEEP)

RHIL:
Excellent. (TO LOURNA) Let's start with your name.

LOURNA:
(AMUSED) My name?

RHIL:
For the recording.

LOURNA:
(AMUSED) You tell me.

RHIL:
I'm sorry?

LOURNA:
For the recording. Tell me my name.

FX: A creak of a chair as Lourna Dee leans forward.

LOURNA: (CONT)
(SAVORING THE MOMENT) Tell me who I am.

RHIL:
I—

Rhil takes a beat to gather herself, attempting to regain control of the situation.

RHIL: (CONT)
You're Lourna Dee.

FX: The chair creaks again as Lourna sits back, satisfied.

LOURNA:
Yes. Yes, I am.

RHIL:
(TAKES CONTROL AGAIN) Your name is important to you, isn't it, Lourna?

LOURNA:
I have always enjoyed a certain . . . reputation.

RHIL:
You like being feared.

LOURNA:
I like being *respected.*

RHIL:
But it was more than that. Back then. After the Republic Fair.

LOURNA:
Where we first met.

RHIL:
(NOT RISING TO THE BAIT) When you were blamed for the massacre on Valo, for the attack on Chancellor Soh.

LOURNA:
I don't see how this is relevant.

RHIL:
We're setting the scene. People knew your name back then. When you were first identified as the Eye of the Storm, supreme leader of the Nihil.

LOURNA:
That was their mistake. Not mine.

RHIL:
Whose?

LOURNA:
Republic "Intelligence." The Jays.

RHIL:
Jays?

LOURNA:
Sorry. Force of habit.

RHIL:
Nihil . . . slang? For the Jedi?

LOURNA:
For the Jedi, yes.

RHIL:
The Jedi who erroneously thought of you as the Eye, an assumption you didn't contradict or challenge. In fact, I'd go so far as to say that you leaned into the role you had been given. Reveled in the... infamy.

LOURNA:
I'd be careful if I were you, Dairo.

RHIL:
But this is why we're here. A chance for you to tell your side of the story. To explain what happened. And how you've... changed?

LOURNA:
I was falsely accused. That's what happened.

RHIL:
You weren't the Eye.

LOURNA:
No.

RHIL:
But you *were* Nihil.

LOURNA:
Yes.

RHIL:
One of Marchion Ro's most trusted lieutenants.

LOURNA:
I was... (CHOOSES HER WORDS CAREFULLY)... a Tempest Runner.

RHIL:
And your ship...

LOURNA:
The *Lourna Dee*.

RHIL:
Named after yourself.

LOURNA:
Naturally.

RHIL:
To further build your legend.

LOURNA:
You tell me.

RHIL:
I can only go on what was said at the time. What we reported on GoNet.

LOURNA:
And what was that . . . exactly?

RHIL:
That the battle was already lost the moment the *Lourna Dee* swung into view.

LOURNA:
Well . . . you got that right, at least.

CUT TO:

**SCENE 3. INT. THE *LOURNA DEE*. FLIGHT DECK—
THEN.**

Atmos: The deep thrum of the Lourna Dee*'s engines. The sounds of its turbolasers firing, blasting the Sullustan fighters out of the stars.*

MUGLAN TARANTYNE:
Entering Sulon's atmosphere, Tempest Runner.

LOURNA:
Was there any doubt, Muglan?

MUGLAN:
Not from me.

FX: A proximity alarm sounds.

QUIN CARREE:
More fighters coming in, Lourna.

LOURNA:
How many, Quin?

QUIN:
(SMILING) Not enough.

LOURNA:
Dispatch scav droids. Let the swarm deal with them.

FX: A comm unit beeps.

MUGLAN:
Incoming message.

LOURNA:
(DISPLEASED) Let me guess. The Eye.

MUGLAN:
He wants an update.

LOURNA:
And he can wait.

QUIN:
SoroSuub facility straight ahead, Lourna.

LOURNA:
Defenses?

FX: Beeps from the computer.

QUIN:
As we expected. Ground-to-air turbolasers. Deflector shields.

LOURNA:
Nothing we can't handle.

TIA TOON: (DISTORT/COMMS)
Unidentified Nihil cruiser, you are violating Sullustan airspace. Discontinue your approach or face the consequences.

LOURNA:
Unidentified? Insulting. Give me a channel.

FX: Muglan activates the comm with a bleep.

LOURNA: (CONT)
Senator Toon, this is Lourna Dee.

TIA: (COMMS)
(OBVIOUSLY SHAKEN) Lourna Dee?

LOURNA:
I assume that means you know the name of this vessel and what is about to happen.

TIA: (COMMS)
(TRIES TO SOUND BRAVE) We have advised Starlight Beacon of your presence, but your ship will be slag long before the Jedi arrive.

LOURNA:
(AMUSED) Is that right?

TIA: (COMMS)
This is your last warning, Dee.

LOURNA:
No, Senator. It's yours. (TO MUGLAN) Cut transmission.

FX: The channel is cut off with a beep.

MUGLAN:
He's gone.

FX: Distant explosions.

QUIN:
As is most of the defense force.

LOURNA:
These scav droids are better than ever. Remind me to congratulate Zeet next time I see the old wrench grinder.

MUGLAN:
Really?

LOURNA:
(SCOFFING) What do you think?

FX: A creak of the chair as Lourna stands up.

LOURNA: (CONT)
Prepare my shuttle for launch. Quin, you're with me.

QUIN:
Always.

CUT TO:

SCENE 4. INT. STAR CRUISER—NOW.

Atmos: As before.

RHIL:
What can you tell me about your crew at that time?

LOURNA:
They were loyal to me.

RHIL:
And that's it?

LOURNA:
There is little else to say.

RHIL:
Muglan Tarantyne, a Gloovan enforcer you sprung from the Republic correctional vessel *Restitution,* later to become a Storm commander in your Tempest.

LOURNA:
Correct.

RHIL:
Then there was Quin Carree. Another inmate from the *Restitution,* a ship that you eventually captured and renamed. Another ship, another *Lourna Dee.*

A beat.

LOURNA:
Are you asking me or telling me?

RHIL:
Quin was a slicer. A Bivall from Protobranch. And she, too, joined your Tempest, becoming . . . *important* to you.

LOURNA:
They were *all* important. They were my crew.

CUT TO:

SCENE 5. INT. SOROSUUB RESEARCH FACILITY—THEN.

FX: A fierce battle is under way outside the facility. Lasers are firing, muffled by thick walls. A squadron of soldiers charges in, boots tramping.

SULLUSTAN SERGEANT:
Move it. Move it. Defend the facility from the invaders. Defend— (SCREAMS)

FX: A massive explosion kills the sergeant and many of his soldiers. The dust has no chance to settle as lasers burst through the hole, followed by Lourna and her Nihil. There is an exchange of fire and the hiss of gas as a Nihil war cloud fills the base.

SULLUSTAN SOLDIER #1:
Sergeant. Sergeant Mund!

SULLUSTAN SOLDIER #2:
Leave him. He's dead.

SULLUSTAN SOLDIER #1:
(CHOKING) What in Triakk's name is that?

SULLUSTAN SOLDIER #2:
(CHOKING) Nihil war cloud! Don't breathe in the gas.

SULLUSTAN SOLDIER #1:
Aah! My eyes! Burns!

SULLUSTAN SOLDIER #2:
Visors down! Visors—

FX: Both soldiers are cut down in a barrage of blaster bolts.

SULLUSTAN SOLDIERS #1 and #2:
(SCREAM)

FX: Running feet as Lourna and Quin enter, firing.

QUIN: (MASKED)
This is too easy.

FX: She fires again. Another body goes down.

QUIN: (CONT, MASKED)
Like shooting mynocks in a power core.

LOURNA: (MASKED)
So much for Toon's Defense Force Program.

FX: More blasterfire.

LOURNA: (CONT, MASKED)
Pathetic.

SULLUSTAN SOLDIER #2:
(WEAK BUT DEFIANT) Then why are you here, gashead?

LOURNA: (MASKED)
Who said that?

QUIN: (MASKED)
This one. He's still alive.

LOURNA: (MASKED)
Excellent.

FX: She grabs the dying Sullustan.

SULLUSTAN SOLDIER #2:
(CRIES OUT IN PAIN)

LOURNA: (MASKED)
You have something to say, soldier?

SULLUSTAN SOLDIER #2:
Scum! [SULLUSTESE—Reko Numar!]

LOURNA: (MASKED)
Such language. Do you kiss your mother with that mouth? Come here!

FX: She grabs him, causing pain.

SULLUSTAN SOLDIER #2:
(SCREAMS IN AGONY)

LOURNA: (MASKED)
Where are the experimental weapons?

SULLUSTAN SOLDIER #2:
Experimental? I . . . I don't know.

LOURNA: (MASKED)
Wrong answer. Concussion warheads. Plasma shields. We've seen the manifest, Sullustan. We know what's here.

QUIN: (MASKED, OFF MIC)
Lourna! We've found them! Over here!

LOURNA: (MASKED)
Oh, will you listen to that? Looks like I won't be needing you anymore.

SULLUSTAN SOLDIER #2:
(THROUGH HIS PAIN) You won't get away with this. The Republic . . . (GRUNTS IN PAIN) the Republic . . .

LOURNA: (MASKED)
Sorry. What was that? The Republic?

FX: She shoots him at point-blank range. His body slumps back.

LOURNA: (CONT, MASKED)
The Republic will do nothing.

CUT TO:

SCENE 6. INT. STAR CRUISER—NOW.

Atmos: As before.

RHIL:
Was it worth it?

LOURNA:
The raids?

RHIL:
The blood on your hands.

LOURNA:
It was the way of the Nihil.

RHIL:
Take what you want...

LOURNA:
And destroy what you don't.

RHIL:
And what if you were caught?

LOURNA:
It happened from time to time.

RHIL:
And you escaped. Only to fall back into the same cycle. Violence and betrayal. Hunter and hunted. Over and over.

LOURNA:

I thought you were a reporter, not a psychologist.

RHIL:

I'm trying to understand why you did what you did. So I can help those watching understand. Was it all for Ro?

LOURNA:

(TAKEN ABACK) I'm sorry?

RHIL:

Marchion Ro, the actual Eye of the Storm. Was it all for him?

LOURNA:

I did it for *myself*. Ro was . . . a means to an end. Whatever you *think* you know about him . . . Whatever lies you've swallowed—

RHIL:

He never had you under his control.

LOURNA:

No. At least . . . at least that's what I told myself.

CUT TO:

SCENE 7. INT. SOROSUUB RESEARCH FACILITY—THEN.

FX: The skittering of more scav droids. Metal clanking as they gather supplies.

FX: A comlink beeps as it's activated.

LOURNA: (MASKED)
We're gonna need more scav droids, Muglan.

MUGLAN: (DISTORT/COMMS)
That good, huh?

LOURNA: (MASKED)
More than they can carry. Weapons, supplies.

FX: The sounds of the droids gathering items.

LOURNA: (CONT, MASKED)
An embarrassment of riches.

QUIN: (MASKED)
You'll be announcing a feast next. Like the good old days.

LOURNA: (MASKED)
Why not?

FX: Lourna grabs Quin, pulling her close.

LOURNA: (CONT, MASKED)
We deserve a party.

QUIN: (MASKED)
(MOCKS OUTRAGE) Tempest Runner! Get your hands off me!

LOURNA: (MASKED)
You got a problem, Storm?

QUIN: (MASKED)
Only that we're both still wearing these masks.

LOURNA: (MASKED)
Easily rectified.

FX: Lourna pulls off her helmet.

LOURNA: (CONT)
Better?

QUIN: (MASKED)
Let's see.

FX: Quin removes her own helmet, and they kiss passionately, not caring one bit who is watching... or listening.

MUGLAN: (DISTORT/COMMS)
(SIGHS) At least you could close the channel first.

QUIN:
(SMILING, LOOKING DEEP INTO LOURNA'S EYES) Such a prude.

LOURNA:
(CLOSE, MORE PLAYFUL THAN WE'VE HEARD HER) Maybe she's jealous.

MUGLAN: (DISTORT/COMMS)
In your dreams. Those droids are on the way. Try not to make them blush. Muglan out.

FX: The channel beeps shut.

QUIN:
(INTIMATE) We could leave them to it. Head back to the ship. There's no one else to kill anyway.

LOURNA:
Ride the Storm?

QUIN:
Promises, promises.

FX: The moment is broken by blaster bolts nearby.

LOURNA:
(SNAPS BACK TO BUSINESS) I thought you said everyone was dead.

QUIN:
They were. *Are!*

FX: More blasts, nearer still.

LOURNA:
Then who's attacking?

QUIN:
Reinforcements? The RDC?

LOURNA:
You're afraid of the Republic Defense Coalition?

FX: A familiar sound amid the battle: a lightsaber igniting.

QUIN:
No. But I *don't* like the sound of that.

FX: A lightsaber swings off mic.

NIHIL: (OFF MIC)
(SCREAMS)

LOURNA:
Jedi!

CARANA-VEY TRANA: (OFF MIC)
Drop your weapons. I do not wish to harm you.

FX: More blasters fire. More bolts sent flying back.

NIHIL:
(SCREAMS)

FX: *A body hits the floor.*

LOURNA:
He has a funny way of showing it!

QUIN:
We should get out of here.

LOURNA:
Like that's going to happen.

FX: *She fires a blaster.*

QUIN:
What are you doing?

LOURNA:
Testing the merchandise.

FX: *The sound of a plasma shield generating—a personal energy field that is generated from a strap around Lourna's wrist. It hums whenever in use. The sound should be distinct from a lightsaber to help navigate the fight.*

LOURNA: (CONT)
SoroSuub's finest plasma shield. Guaranteed to withstand anything.

QUIN:
Including a lightsaber?

LOURNA:
Only one way to find out. (SCREAMS A BATTLE CRY AS SHE CHARGES TOWARD THE JEDI)

CARANA-VEY:
What? Lourna Dee!

LOURNA:
The last name you will ever utter, Jedi.

FX: *Carana-Vey brings his lightsaber around. The blade clashes against the plasma shield.*

LOURNA: (CONT)
(EFFORT)

CARANA-VEY:
Starlight Beacon, this is Jedi Master Carana-Vey Trana. I have located the Eye of the Storm.

FX: The fight continues, lightsaber blade against humming shield. I've marked the points where the strikes happen so we can match the FX with the dialogue. They are breathing heavily throughout. This is a fight to the death... at least for Lourna.

LOURNA:
Good luck getting through to them. [STRIKE]

CARANA-VEY:
Starlight! Are you receiving me?

LOURNA:
My comm blocker says no. [STRIKE]

CARANA-VEY:
You will lower your weapon.

LOURNA:
And you [STRIKE] will get the hell out of my head. Mind tricks don't work on me, Jedi. [STRIKE]

CARANA-VEY:
Then I will have to disarm you. [STRIKE] This is not a fight you can win. I have the light on my... (NNG—)... on my...

The Jedi suddenly seems confused... a weakness Lourna exploits.

LOURNA:
What's the matter, Jay? Struggling to keep up? [STRIKE]

CARANA-VEY:
(SUDDENLY UNSURE, ON THE DEFENSIVE) The Force... it...

LOURNA:
The Force won't help you now.

FX: Lourna slams the shield into the Jedi's face.

CARANA-VEY:
Aah!

FX: *The Jedi goes down, and the lightsaber splutters out.*

LOURNA:
Can't even keep hold of his pretty sword. Shame. Looks like I won't be needing a shield anymore.

FX: *The shield deactivates.*

LOURNA: (CONT)
Only my fists.

FX: *Lourna punches down with her free hand, her fist mashing into the Jedi's face. Pak!*

CARANA-VEY:
(GRUNTS)

LOURNA:
That's the problem with lightsabers.

FX: *Pak.*

LOURNA: (CONT)
Take them away and what do you have left?

FX: *Pak.*

LOURNA: (CONT)
A coward in fancy robes.

FX: *Pak.*

LOURNA: (CONT)
So much for the light.

FX: *Pak.*

LOURNA: (CONT)
So much for the Force!

FX: *Pak.*

FX: *Lourna stops, breathing heavily. The Jedi is unconscious.*

LOURNA: (CONT)
See what I mean? Unconscious. Where's the fight, Jedi? Where's the challenge?

FX: There's a sudden hum of another lightsaber nearby.

FARIS KARAN: (OFF MIC)
I'll give you a challenge!

LOURNA:
Hmm?

FX: The lightsaber is held by Faris Karan, the fallen Jedi's Padawan, the plasma blade across Quin's throat. Faris tries to appear calm, but there is a tremor in her voice. She is nervous... and worried about her master, Carana-Vey Trana, not to mention unaware that she is being affected by the Nameless, making it even harder for her to be the Jedi she wants to be.

LOURNA: (CONT)
Well, well, well. What have we here?

FARIS:
Step away from him.

LOURNA:
Let me guess. You're his Padawan. A brave one, too, considering you have your lightsaber at my friend's throat.

QUIN:
I'm sorry, Lourna. She snuck up on me.

FX: The lightsaber buzzes.

QUIN: (CONT)
(REACTS, FEARFUL)

FARIS:
(MORE FORCEFUL DESPITE THE WAVES OF ANXIETY FLOWING THROUGH HER, MAYBE *BECAUSE* OF THAT)
Step *away* from him!

LOURNA:
Why?

FARIS:
What?

LOURNA:
Why should I do what you say? You're a child with a toy. Whereas I...

FX: *A click of Lourna's blaster.*

LOURNA: (CONT)
... have a blaster at your master's head.

QUIN:
(WARNING) Lourna.

LOURNA:
She's not going to hurt you, Quin. Look at her. She couldn't hurt a fly. Whereas, I ... I'm a murderer, aren't I, little Jay? A killer. That's what they've told you, isn't it?

FARIS:
(NERVOUS) Drop the weapon.

LOURNA:
Even that wouldn't help you. Any minute now, this facility will be swarming with scav droids. You've seen what they do to ships. All those pincers. Those saws. Imagine what they'll do to a fleshy little Padawan like you. Imagine what they'll do to your master.

FARIS:
Drop. The. *Weapon!*

FX: *And we're at a standoff. The only sounds are the hum of the Padawan's lightsaber and Lourna's breathing.*

QUIN:
Lourna. *Please.*

Beat.

LOURNA:
(SNORTS IN FRUSTRATION) Very well.

FX: *She throws the blaster aside, and it clatters on the ground.*

LOURNA: (CONT)
There. Better?

QUIN:
(SOTTO) Thank the stars.

FARIS:
(EMBOLDENED) Now, call off the attack.

LOURNA:
(LAUGHS AT THE AUDACITY, THEN HER TONE HARDENS) Not until you release Quin.

FARIS:
This isn't a negotiation. Call off the droids.

A beat as Lourna considers this, reluctantly making the decision.

FX: A beep of a comlink.

LOURNA:
Muglan, this is the Runner. Recall the scav droids.

FX: Static crackles over the link.

LOURNA: (CONT)
Did you hear me? Recall the droids.

FARIS:
What is happening?

LOURNA:
The signal isn't getting through.

FARIS:
Then boost it!

FX: Beeps as Lourna tries to do as she's asked.

LOURNA:
I'm trying.

QUIN:
The comm blocker?

LOURNA:
It shouldn't affect our channels.

FX: Faris starts to panic slightly. She doesn't realize that she's being affected by the presence of a hidden Nameless. Maybe we can use something, almost the rushing of blood in Faris's ears, her heartbeat amplified.

FARIS:
It's a trick. You're testing me. Everyone's always testing me. Master Trana. The Force.

QUIN:
Lourna. Something isn't right here. The Jedi. She's . . . she's losing it!

FARIS:
(MORE PANICKED) The Force is testing me!

LOURNA:
(TRYING TO TALK HER DOWN) Look, kid. You need to calm down. I did what you asked. Threw away my blaster. Called off the droids. Now lower your damned saber!

QUIN:
(*REALLY* CONCERNED) Lourna?

FARIS:
(LOSING IT) How are you doing this? The Force . . . the Force is gone . . . It's abandoned me . . . (SHOUTS) How are you doing this?

LOURNA:
It's not me! I don't know what's wrong with you!

QUIN:
Oh, for Storm's sake.

FX: Quin drives her elbow into the Padawan's stomach.

FARIS:
(REACTS)

QUIN:
And that's how you get a Jedi to drop their saber. An elbow to the stomach . . .

FX: Quin punches Faris, and the Padawan hits the floor.

FX: The lightsaber splutters out as the hilt hits the floor alongside Faris's body.

QUIN: (CONT)
. . . and a right hook to the jaw.

LOURNA:
Quin?

FX: Lourna rushes to her side.

LOURNA: (CONT)
Are you all right? Let me see.

QUIN:
It's nothing.

LOURNA:
You had a lightsaber to your throat. (SUCKS IN AIR) She burned you.

QUIN:
Nothing I can't handle. (BEAT) What the void was wrong with her anyway? She was shaking enough when she snuck up on me, but at the end... Did you see her?

Lourna turns, not happy, her eyes searching the shadows of the facility.

LOURNA:
Oh, I saw her, all right. And there I was, thinking I got the upper hand on Master Trana. (CALLS OUT) Where are you? Show yourself!

QUIN:
Who are you talking to?

LOURNA:
No one else could block our comms. No one else could do *that* to a Jedi.

FX: A terrifying growl nearby. The growl of a Nameless.

FX: Debris crunches under heavy boots as a figure emerges from the shadows, the Leveler prowling beside him.

MARCHION RO:
Quite so, Lourna. Quite so.

QUIN:
The Eye!

LOURNA:
(WITH ILL-DISGUISED HATRED) Marchion.

CUT TO:

Part Two

THE EYE OF THE STORM

SCENE 8. INT. STAR CRUISER—NOW.

Atmos: As before.

RHIL:
Marchion Ro.

LOURNA:
Yes.

RHIL:
The true head of the Nihil. The mastermind behind the attack on Starlight.

LOURNA:
"Mastermind" is a stretch.

RHIL:
No? He's conquered great swaths of the Outer Rim, enslaved billions behind his Stormwall.

LOURNA:
What are you? His publicist?

Ouch! That one stings. Rhil tries not to be rattled.

RHIL:
Never. (REGAINING HER COMPOSURE) But *you* were his decoy. While the Republic thought *you* were the Eye of the Storm, they weren't searching for him.

LOURNA:
We had an agreement. An understanding.

RHIL:
You had his respect?

Beat.

LOURNA:
Ro respects nothing and no one.

CUT TO:

SCENE 9. INT. SOROSUUB RESEARCH FACILITY—THEN.

Atmos: As before.

LOURNA:
What are you doing here?

MARCHION:
I wished to see your victory for myself.

LOURNA:
That's right. *My* victory. My haul.

MARCHION:
Indeed.

LOURNA:
So there was no need to block my comms to the *Lourna Dee*.

MARCHION:
The scav droids are still on the way. I saw no need to . . . disrupt them while I dealt with your Jedi.

LOURNA:
With your little pet.

FX: The Leveler trills.

MARCHION:
The Leveler has such a dramatic effect on them.

LOURNA:
I had it covered.

MARCHION:
So it appears. Curious that you were so quick to disarm yourself . . . to call off the droids . . . all to save one of your own.

LOURNA:
I was playing for time.

MARCHION:
The old Lourna would have let the Bivall die. *Pan Eyta* would have let the Bivall die.

LOURNA:
There was no need.

MARCHION:
Because you had it covered.

LOURNA:
Yes.

MARCHION:
Because you'd already beaten one Jedi to a pulp.

FX: He walks toward Carana-Vey Trana's prone body.

MARCHION: (CONT)
An Aki-Aki no less. The Jedi really do accept anyone into their number these days.

FX: Marchion turns on his heel.

MARCHION: (CONT)
And what about the Padawan, Lourna? What about the Theelin? You would've what? Rushed her? Snatched the lightsaber from her hand?

LOURNA:
She's unconscious, isn't she? Quin dealt with her.

MARCHION:
Like you knew she would.

FX: He stalks toward Quin, staring directly in her eyes.

MARCHION: (CONT)
Your washed-out, addled junkie of a Storm.

QUIN:
(FRIGHTENED BREATH)

LOURNA:
That is enough!

FX: Marchion snaps back around to Lourna.

MARCHION:
Enough? Quin would be dead—*you* would be dead—if it wasn't for me. If it wasn't for the Leveler.

FX: The Leveler growls.

LOURNA:
That thing had nothing to do with it.

MARCHION:
So the Aki wasn't feeling its effect when you fought? Wasn't caught off-balance?

CARANA-VEY:
(GROANS)

MARCHION:
Ah, he's coming around.

FX: Marchion marches toward the Jedi. The Leveler comes with him.

MARCHION:
Let's ask him whom he fears the most. Tempest Runner—

CARANA-VEY:
(GASPS IN FEAR)

MARCHION:
—or Nameless?

FX: *The Leveler growls. Hungry. We hear the Nameless effect as before. The throb. The heartbeat.*

CARANA-VEY:
(TERRIFIED) No. Please . . .

MARCHION:
I believe we have our answer.

CARANA-VEY:
(SCARED, BABBLING) The Force surrounds us. The Force dwells in us.

LOURNA:
But that still doesn't explain—

MARCHION:
Hush now. This is the part I've been looking forward to.

CARANA-VEY:
The Force flows . . . flows through us. The Force protects us.

MARCHION:
(TO THE LEVELER) He's all yours.

FX: *The Nameless's growl intensifies . . .*

CARANA-VEY:
The Force is strong. The Force is . . . is . . .

FX: *The Nameless roars . . . and pounces.*

CARANA-VEY: (CONT)
(SCREAMS)

FX: *The Nameless feeds—we hear flesh calcifying into stone, like ice forming on a lake.*

CARANA-VEY: (CONT)
(SCREAMS BECOME STRANGLED BEFORE CUTTING OFF SHARPLY)

FX: *The calcification process completes.*

MARCHION:
There. Shame the other one is already dead. But you've had your fill, haven't you?

QUIN:
Dead? She's not—

FX: Marchion pulls a blaster and shoots the Padawan.

FX: The Nameless bays, almost a disappointed whine.

QUIN: (CONT)
(SOTTO) Stars' end.

LOURNA:
Best to keep your creature hungry, eh?

MARCHION:
Always.

FX: He walks toward the calcified Jedi.

MARCHION: (CONT)
And that, Lourna, is how you kill a Jedi.

FX: The Nameless bays again, the sound drowned out by the sudden whoosh of the scav droids entering the facility, rushing past them. We hear them working in the background for the rest of the scene: chittering, gathering, scraping.

MARCHION: (CONT)
And your scav droids *finally* arrive.

The characters have to raise their voices slightly to be heard over the rushing droids.

LOURNA:
I *assume* I can contact my ship now?

MARCHION:
Be my guest.

FX: A channel opens.

LOURNA:
Muglan. Come in.

MUGLAN: (DISTORT/COMMS)
Thank the Storm! Lourna! The *Gaze Electric* is here! Marchion R—

LOURNA:
I know. Have the droids deliver the merchandise to cargo bay two.

MARCHION:
(SNORTS QUIETLY IN AMUSEMENT)

MUGLAN: (DISTORT/COMMS)
Um . . .

LOURNA:
Is there a problem?

MUGLAN: (DISTORT/COMMS)
We've already had orders—

MARCHION:
To deliver the weapons to the *Gaze Electric.*

LOURNA:
To *your* ship? Marchion, this is *my* raid.

MARCHION:
And the spoils belong to the Nihil. They belong to the Eye.

FX: Lourna takes a step toward Marchion, threatening him, trying to intimidate him.

LOURNA:
This is unacceptable.

FX: The Nameless growls, stopping her in her tracks, taking the intimidation up at least five levels!

MARCHION:
It is the way things are. Unless you'd like to take your chances against the Leveler.

FX: Another standoff. The Nameless growls at the back of its throat.

LOURNA:
(SNORTS, KNOWING SHE'S BEATEN)

MARCHION:
(SMILES LIKE A SHARK) I didn't think so.

FX: Marchion turns and marches away. The Leveler slinks alongside him.

MARCHION: (CONT, STRIDING OFF MIC)
Make sure you dispose of the remains. The last thing you want is another Jedi sniffing around. Next time, you might not be so . . . lucky.

QUIN:
(UNSURE) Lourna?

LOURNA:
(SEETHING) Do it.

QUIN:
But the scav droids . . . the *haul* . . .

LOURNA:
(SNAPS) You heard the Eye!

FX: Quin marches off.

LOURNA: (CONT)
(BITTER) It all belongs to the Eye.

FOCUS ON THE NOISE OF THE DROIDS AT WORK BEFORE CUTTING TO:

SCENE 10. INT. STAR CRUISER—NOW.

Atmos: As before.

FX: Lourna stands suddenly.

LOURNA:
You know, this was a mistake. We're done.

RHIL:
(SHOCKED) We are?

LOURNA:
I didn't agree to this to talk about Ro.

RHIL:
That's very much what you agreed to do.

LOURNA:
This is my story. Not his. You can return to your ship. We won't be seeing each other again.

FX: Rhil stands.

RHIL:
But the interview—

LOURNA:
There is no interview. Your droid will surrender its recording.

RHIL:
We had an agreement. The Republic... The *chancellor*...

LOURNA:
The chancellor can go hang.

FX: Lourna storms toward the door.

LOURNA: (CONT)
I *never* agreed to be humiliated.

RHIL:
Lourna, wait.

FX: She grabs Lourna's arm. They both freeze.

LOURNA:
(LOW, DANGEROUS) Tell me you didn't touch me.

RHIL:
I'm sorry. (BEAT) Look, I didn't mean to dredge up painful memories.

LOURNA:
You didn't!

RHIL:
(URGENT) But painful memories are pretty much all we have these days. (BEAT) And I know that includes you.

FX: Creak of Lourna's armor as she pauses.

LOURNA:
You know nothing.

RHIL:
Then this is your chance to tell me. To tell *everyone*. (BEAT) Look. The galaxy has . . . preconceptions about you. *I* have preconceptions. Hardly surprising given how we met. When you tried to kill me on Valo.

LOURNA:
I tried to kill a lot of people. You're nothing special.

RHIL:
Point taken. But whatever happened back then, the chancellor wants us to tell your story *now*, which means we have to go through this, however difficult it might be.

LOURNA:
Not to mention incriminating.

RHIL:
A candid conversation, that's what we discussed. No more masks. No sugarcoating the truth.

LOURNA:
(MOLLIFIED SLIGHTLY) No more masks.

RHIL:
But if this is going to work, I need you to be honest with me. Only then will people understand. (BEAT) Do you still want us to leave?

Beat.

LOURNA:
No.

RHIL:
We can continue?

LOURNA:
(BLOWS OUT) You better sit down.

RHIL:
Thank you.

FX: They return to their seats. Rhil sits first. Lourna hesitates before sitting herself.

LOURNA:
Okay. (BEAT, GATHERS HERSELF) Okay.

FX: T-9 buzzes back into position.

LOURNA: (CONT)
(LOOKS UP AT T-9) Is that thing still recording?

RHIL:
Tee-Nine? Sure.

LOURNA:
Then we need to move things along. You say the Republic wants to hear my story *now*? That they want to hear the truth?

RHIL:
Yes.

LOURNA:
Then you... then *we* need to stop thinking of me as a Tempest Runner. The events we've been discussing, yes, they are all true.

RHIL:
And in the public record.

LOURNA:
But all that happened long before Ro established the Occlusion Zone. Long before he destroyed Starlight Beacon. But Starlight changed everything—who I am and where I belonged.

What you said was correct. The people of the Republic... your viewers... were sold a lie that the Nihil was mine to command. A lie that served Marchion very well indeed, swallowed in every regard by the Jedi, specifically the woman who made it her business to track me down. To hunt me.

RHIL:
Avar Kriss, the Hero of Hetzal.

LOURNA:
Hero of Hetzal. Marshal of Starlight. I don't care what you call her. All I know is that I was her obsession. And yes, before you point it out, she had good reason to hate me.

RHIL:
Jedi don't hate anyone.

LOURNA:
It didn't look like that to me—not when she led an assault against my Tempest, when she cut off my hand.

RHIL:
She immobilized you, as per Jedi methods.

LOURNA:
She would've murdered me if she hadn't been stopped.

RHIL:
Avar... Avar Kriss tried to kill you?

LOURNA:
(SNORTS) The record doesn't show *that*, does it? The "Hero of Hetzal" stormed the Nihil's Great Hall, slaughtering my people in cold blood.

FX: Under this, the sound of Avar's lightsaber cutting through bodies. Blasterfire. Explosions.

Wild track: Nihil screams.

LOURNA: (CONT)
I tried to stop her. Tried to hold the line, but—

AVAR KRISS: (SLIGHT DISTORT TO SHOW THIS IS THE PAST)
For light and life!

KEEVE TRENNIS: (SIMILAR DISTORT)
Avar! *No!*

FX: The sounds of the past cease.

RHIL:
(SHAKEN) I had no idea. I knew that she was driven to the edge, but—

Lourna continues, although this is difficult for her to admit.

LOURNA:
It was a young Jedi called Keeve Trennis who stopped her. Who saved my life. I was taken prisoner on board the Jedi's flagship, the *Ataraxia,* and transported to Starlight Beacon with what was left of my Tempest to stand trial, when . . .

FX: A massive explosion in the past, tearing Starlight Beacon apart.

RHIL:
Starlight Beacon was destroyed.

LOURNA:
They left me on the *Ataraxia* as they rushed to save their friends. Avar. Trennis. (SLIGHT PAUSE) Trennis's mentor, Sskeer. They thought I couldn't get out, that they'd left me safe behind an energy field.

FX: The sound of that energy field in the past.

LOURNA: (CONT)
And then the energy field failed.

FX: The sound of an energy field shorting out.

LOURNA: (CONT)
I stood in the grandeur of their flight deck, watching Soh's Great Work tear itself apart. Watching all those people die.

FX: We hear the groans of Starlight's superstructure as the station drifts and twists. More explosions. They carry on below the following.

VOICE: (DISTORT/COMMS)
Please. Please help us. We can't get off the Beacon. It's drifting toward Eiram. The Jedi can't help. We're all going to die!

Wild track: Screams continue throughout the following.

LOURNA:
(ALMOST WISTFUL) He'd done it. Ro. He'd won. Without me. Without any of the Tempest Runners. And soon everyone would hear his voice . . .

MARCHION: (DISTORT/COMMS)
Our entire galaxy has watched Starlight Beacon splinter, crash, and burn.

FX: We hear the remains of Starlight Beacon racing across Eiram's sky, burning up.

MARCHION: (CONT, DISTORT/COMMS)
By now, most understand that the Nihil are responsible. Until this hour, however, very few have understood who is responsible for the Nihil. In other words—it's high time I introduced myself.

FX: Tumbling. Breaking up.

MARCHION: (CONT, DISTORT/COMMS)
I am Marchion Ro. I am the Eye of the Storm. (BEAT) I am the Eye of the Nihil.

FX: The station crashes into the sea, cutting off the screams forever. There's a moment of silence, and then . . .

RHIL:
And after that? You didn't go back to him. Didn't go back to the Nihil.

LOURNA:
No. I knew Marchion would be unbearable. Knew he would have no need for the likes of me. (FORCES HERSELF TO SOUND MORE CONFIDENT) Besides, I had a ship. And not just anyone's ship. *Her* ship.

RHIL:
The *Ataraxia.*

LOURNA:
Marshal Kriss took something of mine...

RHIL:
So you took something of hers.

LOURNA:
For the first time in years, the future seemed bright. For Lourna Dee, at least. The rest of the galaxy... not so much.

RHIL:
And for your Tempest?

Beat.

RHIL: (CONT)
Lourna?

LOURNA:
(FACE DARKENS) They were still in holding cells, aboard the *Ataraxia,* waiting to be rescued, waiting for their Runner.

CUT TO:

SCENE 11. INT. THE *ATARAXIA*. HOLDING CELLS—THEN.

Atmos: The elegant hum of the Ataraxia, *powerful yet calm. And nearby... energy fields on multiple holding cells. Muglan is behind one, Quin behind another.*

MUGLAN:
(WHIMPERING, CRITICALLY INJURED)

FX: A door swishes open. Lourna enters.

QUIN:
Lourna. Thank the stars. What was going on out there?

LOURNA:
(STRANGELY SUBDUED) You don't want to know.

QUIN:
You need to check on Muglan. She was hurt. Badly hurt.

LOURNA:
So I can see.

QUIN:
That Jedi witch cut her in two.

LOURNA:
But Gloovans are difficult to kill.

MUGLAN:
(WHIMPERING)

LOURNA:
She'll be fine. The Jedi have a stasis machine.

QUIN:
She should be in a bacta tank! Well? Aren't you going to let us out?

LOURNA:
Hm? Yes. Yes, of course.

FX: Beeps of a control pad. The energy fields drop. The Nihil rush out.

QUIN:
Stars. Is this all that's left of us?

LOURNA:
Look after Muglan.

FX: Lourna starts to leave. The door swishes open.

QUIN:
Why? Where are you going?

FX: Lourna stops.

LOURNA:
We're coming up on Valtos. I know a guy who can help Mug. Gen'Dai doctor by the name of Emorson. Wandering tentacles, but he knows his way around a cybernetic surgery.

QUIN:
Valtos? That's light-years from anywhere.

LOURNA:
Exactly. Muglan can get patched up, and the rest of you can scatter.

QUIN:
Scatter? What do you mean?

LOURNA:
Ro's taken down Starlight Beacon.

Wild track: Nihil gasps. Muttering.

LOURNA: (CONT)
They'll be looking for us. It's not safe to stay together. Not for now.

QUIN:
But if the Nihil have won . . .

LOURNA:
Marchion has won. There's a difference.

FX: Again Lourna goes to leave. Quin moves to her quickly.

QUIN:
Lourna, wait.

FX: Scuffing of feet as Lourna stops.

LOURNA:
Quin. We haven't time.

QUIN:
(SOTTO) I get it, okay? And you're right. If Ro's taken out Starlight—

LOURNA:
(SOTTO) There's no telling what happens next.

QUIN:
(SOTTO) But *we'll* stay together, won't we? You and me. The rest of the Tempest can scatter, but not us . . . We can look after Muglan. Get her back on her . . . her . . .

LOURNA:
Her feet?

QUIN:
Don't.

The briefest of beats.

LOURNA:
(EMOTIONLESS) Sure. We'll stay together.

FX: Lourna pulls away.

LOURNA: (CONT)
I'll set course for Valtos.

FX: The door slides shut.

CUT TO:

SCENE 12. INT. STAR CRUISER—NOW.

Atmos: As before.

RHIL:
And that's where you took them—to Wild Space.

LOURNA:
Where no one would ask any questions.

RHIL:
And Muglan?

LOURNA:
She was taken care of.

RHIL:
By you and Quin. (BEAT) Lourna?

CUT TO:

SCENE 13. INT. VALTOS. TOVEY'S CANTINA—THEN.

Atmos: The sounds of a busy bar. Music playing in the background. Drinks pouring. Tankards clanking on tables.

Wild track: General barroom hubbub.

QUIN:
(KEEPS HER VOICE DOWN) Lourna. Can you hear me?

LOURNA: (DISTORT/COMMS)
I hear you, Quin.

QUIN:
The doc says it's touch and go with Muglan. Says it's going to be *pricey*!

LOURNA: (DISTORT/COMMS)
I'm sure it will be.

QUIN:
But it'll be okay, won't it? The *Ataraxia* must be full of Jedi treasure or what have you. The Jedi do have treasure, right?

LOURNA: (DISTORT/COMMS)
And the rest of the Tempest—?

QUIN:
What?

LOURNA: (DISTORT/COMMS)
The Tempest. Have they—

QUIN:
Scattered. Like you said. Most will scurry back to Ro if you ask me, but more fool them. But what about the doc, Lourna? Can you bring down some credits?

CUT TO:

SCENE 14. INT. THE *ATARAXIA*. FLIGHT DECK—CONTINUOUS.

Atmos: As before—the hum of the Ataraxia.

QUIN: (DISTORT/COMMS)
Lourna?

LOURNA:
Sure, Quin.

QUIN: (DISTORT/COMMS)
(GLADDENED) I'm in a place called Tovey's Cantina, off the main strip. A real dive, but needs must and all that. (BEAT) Lourna? Can you hear me? Are you still the—

FX: A beep as Lourna kills the comms channel.

LOURNA:
Yeah. I'm here, Quin. I'm here.

FX: Another beat and then... Controls are pressed. The navicomp burbles. Lourna pulls down hard on the hyperdrive. The Ataraxia *bursts into hyperspace with a whoosh.*

CUT TO:

SCENE 15. INT. STAR CRUISER—NOW.

Atmos: As before. We hang on T-9's buzz for a moment and hear Lourna breathing.

RHIL:
You left them. Just like that. Flew off into hyperspace.

LOURNA:
Yes.

RHIL:
Left Quin.

Beat.

LOURNA:
I had places to go . . .

RHIL:
Planets to oppress?

LOURNA:
The *Hutts* oppressed the planets.

RHIL:
And you did their dirty work.

LOURNA:
I *worked* for them.

RHIL:
As an enforcer.

LOURNA:
As a facilitator. The galaxy was in chaos. Marchion Ro had won.

RHIL:
His Stormwall annexed hundreds of systems to create Nihil space.

LOURNA:
A territory you know all too well.

RHIL:
(IGNORES THE GIBE) And you, like your Hutt overlords...

LOURNA:
My Hutt employers.

RHIL:
You took advantage of the chaos, your "employers" illegally occupying numerous worlds along the border...

LOURNA:
Gambling that the Jedi would be occupied dealing with Ro and his motley band of maniacs.

RHIL:
A gamble that didn't pay off.

LOURNA:
That's one way of looking at it.

RHIL:
Above the planet Ballum, you encountered Keeve Trennis once again. The Jedi you claim saved you from Avar Kriss.

LOURNA:
It's not a *claim*. It's what happened.

RHIL:
And can you explain what happened here? On board the ship you'd stolen from the Jedi?

LOURNA:
What is there to tell? I had the *Ataraxia,* and Trennis wanted it back.

RHIL:
She took it from you.

LOURNA:
(UNCOMFORTABLE) Yes.

RHIL:
And captured you.

LOURNA:
Along with my droid. Kew-For.

RHIL:
To stand trial for your crimes.

LOURNA:
We came to an arrangement. Keeve Trennis wanted to enter Nihil space and needed a guide.

RHIL:
For the war effort?

LOURNA:
(LAUGHS) You'd like it to be that, wouldn't you? The story you always spin. The noble Jedi, risking all, rescuing people from Nihil tyranny, liberating planets. The thing you forget is that the Jedi—for all their self-sacrifice, for all their doctrines—are just people, like you and me, with their own needs and desires, with their own attachments.

You said you want me to tell you the truth, Rhil. Then here it is: Keeve Trennis did not fly into the Occlusion Zone for the sake of the Republic. Keeve Trennis flew into the zone for love.

CUT TO:

Part Three
THE ENEMY OF MY ENEMY

SCENE 16. INT. STAR CRUISER—CONTINUOUS.

Atmos: As before.

RHIL:
(TAKEN ABACK) I'm sorry... "love"? You mean—

LOURNA:
(LAUGHS) Ah, your face. I can imagine where your head is going right now. Jedi romance novels. Holodramas. Imagine the scandal. Imagine the ratings!

RHIL:
I am not—

LOURNA:
Relax. It was nothing that... salacious. But it was love, nonetheless. A terrible, aching, heartbreaking love.

RHIL:
I'm going to have to ask you to be slightly less cryptic.

LOURNA:
Sskeer.

RHIL:
Keeve Trennis's... mentor?

LOURNA:
Her master. For all intents and purposes, her parent, because that is what a Jedi Master is for a Padawan. They don't like to admit it, but it's true all the same.

RHIL:
And you have much experience with Jedi Masters?

LOURNA:
More than you know. And I'd crossed paths with Sskeer before. When I was arrested. When I was hunted by Avar Kriss.

Looking back, Sskeer was like no other Jedi I'd ever met.

RHIL:
Because he was a Trandoshan?

LOURNA:
Because he had wildness to him, a ferocity I... well, I have to admit I respected. What I didn't know at the time was that Sskeer was sick.

RHIL:
Sick?

LOURNA:
Magrak syndrome. I'm sure it's in that little datapad of yours.

FX: Several beeps as Rhil accesses her datapad.

RHIL:
"A condition that targets a Trandoshan brain, making the victim ... unstable."

LOURNA:
Uncontrollable. Imagine what that's like for a Jedi. Full of rage, of instinct. Sskeer was becoming an animal, barely able to function, let alone perform "magic." A Jedi who could no longer commune with the Force, could no longer bend it to his will. It must've been like losing a limb. (BEAT) Like losing your hand.

FX: Rhil's datapad beeps.

RHIL:
According to the records, Sskeer was listed as lost on Starlight.

LOURNA:
He was on it when the station went down, all the way to Eiram. Sacrificed his life for Trennis by all accounts, so she could survive.

RHIL:
But he didn't die.

LOURNA:
Trandoshans are tough. They regenerate. New arms, new legs, new scales—new everything. But when your mind is at war with itself...

Trennis received word that Sskeer was alive and in the Occlusion Zone but wasn't himself. Not anymore.

RHIL:
And that's why she wanted to enter Nihil space—to find him.

LOURNA:
To bring him home. And find him we did, on a planet called Kindosorn and—ho ho ho—were the reports true. He was *wild*. Feral. But still, after everything he'd gone through, still a Jedi.

RHIL:
He'd regained his abilities to manipulate the Force?

LOURNA:
No. That was gone. Along with his wits. You should have seen him. Snarling, salivating, ready to tear his former friends apart. And I would've let him if I'd had the chance. Pulled up a chair to watch. But there was something of the old Sskeer still in there.

Even in his wildest state, Jedi Master Sskeer was protecting a young girl he'd found on his... travels. A little lost soul, no more than eight or nine, but tough nonetheless.

RHIL:
And what was he protecting her from?

LOURNA:
The servants of Baron Boolan.

RHIL:
The Nihil's minister of advancement?

LOURNA:
If that's what you want to call him. Personally I'd go for butcher. Or lunatic. Probably both. The baron was searching for children... How do the Jedi describe it?... Children "strong in the Force."

RHIL:
Why?

LOURNA:
To experiment on them. To turn them into monsters.

RHIL:
Then this girl...

LOURNA:
Had abilities. She belonged to some weird Force cult I'd never heard of. The Yacombe, I believe they call themselves. Or they would, if they talked.

RHIL:
They don't talk?

LOURNA:
Not to anyone outside their order. Creepy as hell most of the time, if you ask me. This kid... she was as pretty as a lompop flower... but as silent as a grave.

RHIL:
But I hear you struck up quite the friendship.

LOURNA:
That's what you heard, is it? Well, did you also hear that I helped Sskeer regain a semblance of his wits? That I went willingly with the Jedi when Baron Boolan's lackeys snatched the child from beneath Sskeer's nose and spirited her away to his secret laboratory? At the heart of an asteroid of all places. Hidden away from everyone.

RHIL:
But you found her?

LOURNA:
Oh, we found her, all right. Her and the baron. Who we captured, nearly dying in the process.

RHIL:
But a victory nonetheless.

LOURNA:
Oh yes. A "great" victory. We had the girl. We had Boolan. We even had his research and the Nameless he'd been experimenting on.

RHIL:
And you had Sskeer. Who you'd brought back from the brink.

LOURNA:
More or less. He still had a long way to go . . .

CUT TO:

SCENE 17. INT. ASTEROID BASE. OCCLUSION ZONE—THEN.

Atmos: A base built into an asteroid. Industrial, the structure constantly groaning.

FX: Equipment is thrown across a room, smashing into a metal wall.

SSKEER:
(ROARS IN FURY)

FX: Running footsteps. It's Jedi Master Keeve Trennis finding her former teacher, the Trandoshan Sskeer, wrecking a lab, tearing the place apart.

KEEVE:
Sskeer! Sskeer, stop!

SSKEER:
(BELLOWS)

FX: Sskeer rips a bolted table from the floor—the bolts shrieking as they are pulled free—and throws it in anger. Whoosh!

KEEVE:
(FIRM) I. Said. Stop. (BEAT) Put the table down. Now.

SSKEER:
(A MOMENT OF COARSE BREATHING AND THEN A FRUSTRATED GRUNT)

FX: He does as he is told, the table clattering to the floor.

SSKEER: (CONT)
Happy?

KEEVE:
Hardly.

SSKEER:
I am . . . sssorry you have to sssee me like thisss . . .

FX: Footsteps as Keeve walks toward him.

KEEVE:
(GENTLER NOW) You have *nothing* to be sorry about.

SSKEER:
I wasss your teacher.

KEEVE:
You were more than that, and you know it.

SSKEER:
It isn't right for an apprentice to witness their master in sssuch disarray, unable to control themself, unable to control the Force.

KEEVE:
It doesn't matter.

SSKEER:
It does to me! (CALMS HIMSELF AGAIN) Do you remember what I told you . . . before Ssstarlight was destroyed?

KEEVE:
You told me to follow my own path.

SSKEER:
And here you are, ssstill chasing after me. Ssstill cleaning up my mess.

KEEVE:
That's not what this is.

SSKEER:
(YELLING) You don't know what this is!

KEEVE:
(QUIET, SAD) Master.

SSKEER:
You're the master now. And I'm . . . I'm a monster. That's never going to change.

FX: Heavy footsteps as he storms past her.

KEEVE:
Sskeer. Wait.

SSKEER:
I need to be alone.

KEEVE:
There isn't time. We'll be leaving soo—

SSKEER:
Alone!

FX: The doors open. He thunders out.

KEEVE:
(SIGHS, THEN TO HERSELF) It wasn't supposed to be like this.

CUT TO:

SCENE 18. INT. STAR CRUISER—NOW.

Atmos: As before.

RHIL:
And what about you, Lourna?

LOURNA:
Hmm?

RHIL:
Where were you when all this was happening? How did you even know what was going on?

LOURNA:
Oh, you could hear. The walls of that station echoed with Sskeer's rage. And the rest of us just had to get on with it.

CUT TO:

SCENE 19. INT. ASTEROID BASE. OCCLUSION ZONE—THEN.

Atmos: As before, but now the structure is constantly groaning, water drip, drip, dripping.

FX: Beeps of a computer as buttons are pressed.

LOURNA:
Any joy, Kew-For?

Q-4: (COMMS)
Unfortunately not, Mistress Lourna.

LOURNA:
There's *no* way of piggybacking a signal?

Q-4: (COMMS)
Not on the encrypted channels, no. The Nihil have encoded them in such a way—

LOURNA:
That piggybacking is impossible. Of course they have.

Q-4: (COMMS)
It really is quite ingenious. The use of tabulation alone...

LOURNA:
Yes. Yes, Kew-For. No need to gush. (TO HERSELF) Quin, if only you were here...

Q-4: (COMMS)
What's that?

LOURNA:
Nothing. Just someone I used to know. A slicer who would have done this in half the time.

Q-4: (COMMS)
Maybe if I flew down to the asteroid.

LOURNA:
No, we need you on the *Ataraxia*. Our getaway driver.

Q-4: (COMMS)
I'm not sure I understand the reference.

LOURNA:
You would've before the Jedi got their claws into your programming. Okay, let's try again. Play the message.

FX: A click and then a whir as a message plays.

KEEVE: (RECORDING)
Jedi Council, Republic Senate, this is Jedi Master Keeve Trennis of the Jedi cruiser *Ataraxia*. We have apprehended Baron Boolan, who seems to have been experimenting on the Nameless.

LOURNA:
(TO HERSELF) That's one way of describing it.

KEEVE: (RECORDING)
My crew are currently attempting to duplicate the baron's research in the hope that it will provide a solution to the Nameless problem. If all else fails, we will attempt to transport his... augmented Nameless back to Coruscant for study, along with the baron himself, who can be questioned by the defense coalition.

FX: A beep as Lourna stops the recording.

LOURNA:
Yes. And that's not all you'll bring back to Coruscant, is it, Trennis?

Q-4: (COMMS)
Mistress?

LOURNA:
Haven't you worked it out yet, Kew-For? Baron Boolan isn't the only prisoner that will be delivered to the defense coalition. What do you think will happen to you and me?

CUT TO:

SCENE 20. INT. STAR CRUISER—NOW.

Atmos: As before.

RHIL:
You've mentioned Keeve's crew. Who exactly was there?

LOURNA:
Don't you know?

RHIL:
I'd rather hear it in your own words. You were there, not me.

LOURNA:
Yes. I was there. As were others who had joined Trennis on her quest to find the lizard...

RHIL:
Such as...

LOURNA:
(SIGHS) Such as Ceret and Terec.

RHIL:
Both Jedi, originally from the planet Sagamore. Bond-twins who share the same thoughts.

LOURNA:
For all intents and purposes.

RHIL:
Bond-twins you tortured in the past. Fracturing their once-symbiotic union.

LOURNA:
And how exactly are these *my* words? I know what you're trying to do, Dairo. You want me to break down, to admit I had a history with all these people. A *violent* history. And yes, you're right. I tortured Terec and Ceret when I was a Tempest Runner. I tortured Trennis, for that matter. Sskeer, too, probably. It's hard to remember. And let's not forget about dear old OrbaLin. You remember OrbaLin, don't you? From Valo.

RHIL:
You know I do.

LOURNA:
Jedi OrbaLin, former archivist of Starlight Beacon who Lourna Dee shot in the head while stealing the *Ataraxia*. But he doesn't have a head, does he? Because he's a giant ball of slime. He survived. They *all* survived. And what about the members of the crew I'd never tried to kill, hmm? The ones I barely knew. Shall we go through them, too? For the people at home?

RHIL:
Lourna.

LOURNA:
Let me see. There's Chit-Chit. Oh, you'll like him, you and your sponsors. Cute little monkey thing Terec picked up on Kindosorn. Perfect for a family demographic, but even he's not the main event. Oh no, because you've yet to meet Tey Sirrek. Talk about leaving the best for last. Wild man of the woods. Beard as white as snow and ears as sharp as his tongue. He has it all: banter, a wisecracking droid, tragic backstory. And that's before we get onto the power glove hidden beneath his cloak, the one capable of flash-frying a Nameless.

Is that enough for you, Rhil? Know who everyone is? Feeling up to speed?

RHIL:
You've made your point.

LOURNA:
My *point* is that none of us made easy bedfellows. But we didn't have a choice. We'd been thrown together like the rest of the galaxy, and like the rest of the galaxy, we had to make the best of a bad deal.

A deal that was about to get a hell of a lot worse...

CUT TO:

SCENE 21. INT. ASTEROID BASE. MAIN LAB. OCCLUSION ZONE—THEN.

Atmos: Similar to the other rooms, other than the chattering of computers, the buzz of an energy field, and the earsplitting alarm.

Terec and Ceret are rushing from computer bank to computer bank, the bond-twins identical in just about every way, including voices, although there is a slight electronic buzz every time Ceret speaks due to their new artificial vocal cords. Ceret never uses contractions, although Terec has become more informal in their speech patterns, a clue that the twins are growing apart.

Note for performers: All characters strong in the Force—the Jedi and, to a lesser extent, Tey and the Yacombe child—are operating under heightened conditions because the Nameless are nearby.

FX: Doors slide open and Lourna enters. Everyone is shouting to be heard.

LOURNA:
What the hell is happening?

CERET:
We tripped an alarm, Lourna Dee.

TEREC:
(TERSE) That much is obvious, Ceret.

CERET:
The lady did ask, Terec.

TEY SIRREK:
(SNORTS) Lady.

LOURNA:
What was that, Sirrek?

TEY:
Nothing, my old dear. Just clearing my throat.

FX: An animal, Terec's pet krinnan, chitters excitedly.

CERET:
This would be a lot easier if your krinnan could be kept under control, Terec.

TEREC:
Our krinnan, Ceret. And Chit-Chit is just agitated by the noise.

LOURNA:
He's not the only one. What did it?

TEREC:
Sorry?

TEY:
What were you doing when you tripped the alarm?

CERET:
We were attempting to access Baron Boolan's notes.

FX: We hear a laugh from behind the buzzing energy field. This is Baron Boolan, the Nihil's top scientist. Like most Ithorians, his speech is translated by a vocalizer. Beneath his words, we can hear the Ithorian's guttural language.

BARON BOOLAN:
(LAUGHS) You can try, Kotabi.

TEY:
And you can shut your vocabulator, Boolan.

LOURNA:
Just ignore him.

TEY:
If only I could. Sitting there behind his energy field.

BOOLAN:
An energy field you encaged me within, Jedi lover.

TEY:
No more than you deserve. Experimenting on people. One sick game after another. But now it's all come back to bite you, hasn't it, matey boy? All the torture, all the pain. We're going to take your work right back to the Republic, your Nameless, too. They're going to be the key to winning this war, just you wait and see.

BOOLAN:
Such an emotional response, don't you think, Lourna?

LOURNA:
It has nothing to do with me.

BOOLAN:
But don't you find it fascinating, watching them scurry back and forth, struggling to operate under the effect of the Nameless? Where have you put them, by the way? What remains of my pack?

TEREC:
They're safe. In their pens.

LOURNA:
But still near enough to shred your nerves?

CERET:
Unfortunately.

TEREC:
But nothing we can't handle.

CERET:
Through the Force.

BOOLAN:
You keep telling yourself that, Kotabi. Wouldn't it be easier if you just killed them?

TEY:
Put them out of their misery, you mean? I never thought I'd feel sorry for a Force Eater, but what you've done to them... replacing their limbs with cybernetics... fitting them with controls.

BOOLAN:
A control device that Sskeer now possesses. A feral Jedi in command of creatures that could kill you all. What could go wrong?

TEY:
He's stronger than you think.

BOOLAN:
Is he now?

SK-0T:
Zut-zut-zut!

LOURNA:
Listen to your scout droid, Tey. You're supposed to be helping, not baiting the Ithorian.

FX: The door opens and Keeve enters.

TEY:
You're right. The Nameless effect is a gift that just keeps on giving, eh? Sorry, Skoot. Where were we?

KEEVE:
A good question. I turn my back for five minutes...

TEREC:
It is good to see you, too, Keeve.

FX: Terec's krinnan chitters.

KEEVE:
(WEARY) What happened?

CERET:
Where would you like us to start?

FX: Beeps as Lourna presses buttons.

LOURNA:
The twins got themselves locked out of the computer.

KEEVE:
Where's OrbaLin?

TEREC:
Inside the computer.

LOURNA:
Inside?

FX: A slimy, squelching sound as OrbaLin emerges through a vent and forms in front of them. He's a giant ball of continually squirming gelatinous slime with the voice of a refined professor, albeit one that is constantly gargling jelly! In his first appearance he sounded like someone with a head cold, since he's talking through mucus!

ORBALIN:
Ah, Master Trennis. The gang's all here, so to speak.

LOURNA:
(DISGUSTED) I preferred you when you wore an environment suit.

ORBALIN:
But my natural form is far more flexible, Miss Dee. Unless you'd like to crawl into the terminal's cooling vent.

CERET:
Did you find anything of use, Archivist OrbaLin?

ORBALIN:
I'm afraid not, Ceret. The problem is definitely system related.

LOURNA:
Couldn't you just force Boolan to tell you how to deactivate the damned thing?

TEY:
A mind trick! Now you're talking. What do you say, Keeve? Time for a bit of hand-waving. (PUTS ON VOICE) "You waaant to tell us the access codes. You waaant to tell us right now."

KEEVE:
That's not how it works, Tey.

LOURNA:
That's *exactly* how it works.

BOOLAN:
But they can't, can they, Lourna? Our enemies. It's taking everything they have not to curl up into a ball and hide, not with my Nameless on the base. Even the Sephi. You can feel it, can't you, Tey? Gnawing at the edge of your consciousness. Knowing what they would do to you if they were free.

ORBALIN:
While I hate to agree with the baron, he does have a point. Perhaps if the Nameless could be moved away from their pens... farther from the laboratory? Maybe Master Sskeer could oblige?

KEEVE:
I... I don't know where he is.

LOURNA:
Again?

KEEVE:
He's not himself.

LOURNA:
He has the control unit for the Nameless!

BOOLAN:
My point exactly.

KEEVE:
I'll find him.

LOURNA:
No, I'll go. I'm the only one who isn't affected by the Nameless. You stay here and— (REALIZES) Where's the kid?

TEREC:
Who?

LOURNA:
The Yacombe child.

TEY:
I thought she was here.

CERET:
And we assumed the child was with you.

LOURNA:
How you lot protected the galaxy for so long I'll never know.

TEY:
I'll look for the kid. You find the big guy.

LOURNA:
Fine.

CUT TO:

SCENE 22. INT. ASTEROID BASE. CORRIDOR. OCCLUSION ZONE.

Atmos: As per the rest of the base, the alarm is blaring not far away. Sskeer is sitting against the wall, wrapping a long bandage around his arm, reciting an ancient mantra as he does.

SSKEER:
"We call upon the Three: Light, Dark... and Balance True. One... isss no greater than the others. Together, they unite, ressstore, center, and... renew."

FX: There's a scuff of a boot against deck plates nearby. We hear breathing against cloth.

SSKEER: (CONT)
Who's there? Show yourself.

FX: A child's footsteps as the Yacombe child tentatively steps out of the shadows. The rustle of her long robes.

SSKEER: (CONT)
Ah. Little one. It isss you. There is no need to hide in the ssshadows. (A BEAT WHEN SHE DOESN'T MOVE) Unless... unless you are ssscared of me. I can sssee why that would be the case, even after everything we've been through. But when we met... when I found you on Kindosorn... I was not myself, and yet you ssstill trusted me, did you not? I looked

after you. Protected you from the Nihil. (TO HIMSELF) Even though I couldn't ssspeak, could barely think. (TO THE GIRL) But you didn't mind, did you? Because you didn't ssspeak, either. The first Yacombe I've ever met. All those nights, sssitting around the fire. You helped me. Gave me sssomeone to protect, to look after. And these help, too. These bandages. You remember, don't you? The wraps Tey gave to me, teaching me how to use them. Remember the wordsss weaved into the fabric?

FX: *The girl shuffles nearer, intrigued.*

SSKEER: (CONT)
Here. Let me ssshow you. The ssscript is old. A language used by the Jedi of long ago. And this is their balm. The Balm of the Luminousss. It calms my mind... wrapping the fabric around my arm... reciting the words. Like this.

FX: *A rustle of fabric as she moves nearer.*

SSKEER: (CONT)
See. I take the end of the bandage and wrap it around my scales. Once. Twice. That's it. "We walk in the Light, acknowledge the Dark... and find Balance in ourselves. For the Force is strong. For the Force is strong."

(SIGHS) I wish you could ssspeak the words with me, little one... but your presence is a comfort. One I don't deserve. They shouldn't have followed me. Ssshould have gone back to the Republic, to their duty. (GETTING MORE AGITATED) But Keeve... Keeve just can't help herself. Running after me, putting herself in danger. She ssshouldn't be here. She ssshouldn't be anywhere near me!

FX: *Sskeer gives in to a feral roar, punching the floor, hard. The girl scuttles back.*

YACOMBE CHILD:
(GASPS)

SSKEER:
(GENUINELY AGHAST AT HIS OUTBURST) No. I'm sssorry. Don't back away. I won't hurt you. (SUDDENLY ANGRY AGAIN) I said I won't hurt you!

LOURNA:
What are you doing?

SSKEER:
Dee! I—

LOURNA:
Stay away from her.

YACOMBE CHILD:
(SOBS)

FX: Lourna sweeps the girl up into her arms, showing the same rare warmth we've recently seen in the comic books.

LOURNA:
(SOOTHING) It's okay, little lady. I've got you. I've got you.

SSKEER:
You don't understand. I was just... just...

LOURNA:
I don't care what you were doing. She's a child, for void's sake.

SSKEER:
Sssays the Nihil.

LOURNA:
And look who I'm protecting her from.

TEY: (OFF MIC)
(CALLING) Lourna?

LOURNA:
(CALLING BACK) Over here, Sirrek!

TEY: (COMING UP ON MIC)
Have you—

FX: Tey comes running around the corner. SK-OT is with him, both of them skidding to a halt.

TEY: (CONT)
—found him? Ah. Yep, so you have. (SPOTS GIRL) And our little friend, too! Hey, there, sweetie. You okay?

YACOMBE CHILD:
(SOBS)

TEY:
What happened?

LOURNA:
Just take her back to the others.

TEY:
Are you sure? Is that safe?

LOURNA:
Safer than staying here. She shouldn't be around when we move the Nameless.

SSKEER:
Move the Nameless?

LOURNA:
Tey?

TEY:
Of course, of course. (TO GIRL) What do you say, little one? Fancy a carry from Uncle Tey? Of course you do.

FX: Lourna passes the child to him.

TEY: (CONT)
(SLIGHT EFFORT AS HE TAKES HER) There. That's better.

SK-0T:
Zet-zet!

TEY:
And my back is fine and dandy, thank you, Skoot. (TO THE GIRL) You're as light as a feather, aren't you, Bright Eyes? As light as a feather.

LOURNA:
Just get her out of here.

TEY: (GOING OFF MIC)
We're going. We're going. (HIS TONE HARDENS) You two play nice.

FX: They leave, and SK-OT zips after Tey.

LOURNA:
Wouldn't have it any other way.

SSKEER:
Why do we need to move the Nameless? Are we leaving?

LOURNA:
Not yet, but your friends can't operate with them nearby.

SSKEER:
But I can. Thanks to my . . . condition. Because I no longer feel the Force.

LOURNA:
Every cloud has a silver lining, eh?

SSKEER:
(GRUNTS) I meant what I said, Lourna . . . I didn't mean to ssscare the girl.

LOURNA:
Do you really think I care one way or another? I just want to get off this rock as soon as possible. So let's take a pair of Force-sucking nightmares for a walk, shall we? Before anything else goes wrong.

CUT TO:

SCENE 23. INT. ASTEROID BASE. MAIN LAB. OCCLUSION ZONE.

Atmos: As before, the alarm is still wailing.

FX: The doors open, and Tey enters, carrying the Yacombe child. SK-0T bobs behind them.

TEY: (COMING UP ON MIC)
Look who I found. One bundle of joy present and correct. (WINCES AT THE SOUND) No luck with the alarm, eh?

TEREC:
Obviously.

BOOLAN:
(CHUCKLES)

KEEVE:
As soon as we try to open a file, it locks.

TEY:
Corrupting the data?

KEEVE:
There's no way of knowing. (CRIES IN FRUSTRATION)

FX: She slams her hand down on the terminal.

YACOMBE CHILD:
(WHIMPERS)

TEY:
Hey there. Remember what I said about the bundle of joy. I get you're all on edge because of the Nameless, but—

KEEVE:
But so is she. And so are you, Tey. I . . . apologize. But this, this is hopeless. Maybe we should just head back to the *Ataraxia* and—

BOOLAN:
Run back to your precious Temple, where you belong.

FX: The scrape of a chair as Keeve jumps to her feet, her lightsaber igniting.

FX: Terec's krinnan shrieks in alarm.

KEEVE:
You smug, sanctimonious—

TEY:
Whoa, whoa, whoa, whoa!

ORBALIN:
Master Trennis, we must remain calm. As Tey says, it is the presence of the Nameless. Once Sskeer moves them—

KEEVE:
(ANGRY) He'll what? Run away again? Lead us on another wild-gargol chase to Force knows where?

TEREC:
(TRYING TO CALM HER) Keeve.

KEEVE:
(BARELY KEEPING HER COOL) I'm sorry. It's just so much. *Too* much—

FX: The alarm suddenly stops.

TEY:
But at least that's better.

KEEVE:
(GENUINELY RELIEVED) It is. Ceret?

CERET:
We are not out of the proverbial woods just yet, Keeve Trennis. We have managed to deactivate the alarm—

TEREC:
But the files are still locked.

FX: Another alarm activates, a smaller one this time. Beep, beep, beep, beep, continuing throughout the scene.

FX: The krinnan cries out.

ORBALIN:
And vanishing!

KEEVE:
What?

TEREC:
Some kind of virus in the system.

CERET:
The files are being deleted, one by one. All the research.

KEEVE:
Then stop it!

TEREC:
We're trying.

TEY:
Keeve, your people know what they're doing.

KEEVE:
(DESPERATE) Tey, if there's something here that can destroy the Stormwall or find a defense against the Nameless, we have to find it. We just *have* to!

TEY:
Yes we do. We do. (TO THE CHILD) Tell you what, little one. How about I put you down over here, away from all the silly arguing adults, eh?

FX: *Footsteps as he carries her to the side of the room.*

TEY: (CONT)
Uncle Tey has to help them from losing their minds. Is that okay?

FX: *A rustle of fabric as he puts her down.*

TEY: (CONT)
Good girl. Good girl.

TEREC:
Files ten percent deleted.

FX: *A surge of Keeve's lightsaber as she turns back to the energy cage.*

KEEVE:
You *could* stop this, Boolan! You could help us!

BOOLAN:
And why would I do that? The Eye will prevail.

KEEVE:
Not if we stop him. Not if we stop *you*!

FX: *Small footsteps run back in.*

ORBALIN:
Tey! The girl!

TEY:
What? No. What did I say, kiddo? It's better you stay out of the way for a minute.

CERET:
Fifteen percent.

TEY:
Auntie Keeve is busy.

FX: *The child scoots around him.*

TEY: (CONT)
Come back.

SK-0T:
Wep-wep!

KEEVE:
(YELLING) Tell us how to stop it!

ORBALIN:
Keeve! Look out! The Yacombe child!

KEEVE:
(GASPS) What does she think she's doing? I could have...

FX: The lightsaber buzzes as Keeve brandishes it.

KEEVE: (CONT)
This isn't a toy. I could've hurt you!

FX: The lightsaber extinguishes.

KEEVE: (CONT)
(QUIETER) I could've hurt you.

TEY:
(TRIES TO CALM) But you wouldn't. She knows that, and she wants to help.

TEREC:
Twenty percent.

KEEVE:
I don't understand. The sash from her gown?

TEY:
Why is she holding it out to you? Looks like someone has been spending time with the big guy. Is that right, sweetheart? You been talking to Sskeer? How you wrap the cloth around your arm? A reminder for Auntie Keeve to keep her head in a crisis...

KEEVE:
And trust in the Force.

ORBALIN:
The Balm of the Luminous.

KEEVE:
(TO THE CHILD) Thank you, little one. I'll try not to forget again.

BOOLAN:
(TO HIMSELF) Pathetic.

FX: A comlink beeps, a channel opening. We hear the sounds of the Nameless, snarling, slobbering.

LOURNA: (DISTORT/COMMS)
Main laboratory, this is Lourna. We're moving the Nameless as far as we can. Hope it helps.

KEEVE:
It already is.

ORBALIN:
Like a fog lifting.

KEEVE:
Thank you. And to Sskeer, too. For everything.

CUT TO:

SCENE 24. INT. ASTEROID BASE. OUTLYING CORRIDOR. OCCLUSION ZONE—CONTINUOUS.

Atmos: As before, now with added Nameless. Boolan has experimented on these two, adding copious cybernetic implants that whir and clank. One is even missing its head, but that doesn't seem to be holding it back. The monster is still stalking along. Its partner growls. For ease of use, we'll describe the creature with the head "cybernetic Nameless" and its cranially challenged packmate "headless Nameless." We can also hear the whir of Boolan's Nameless control device softly in the background.

KEEVE: (DISTORT/COMMS)
Keeve out.

SSKEER:
Thank me. Why would ssshe thank me?

LOURNA:
Your guess is as good as mine.

FX: Cybernetic Nameless howls.

LOURNA: (CONT)
(TO THE NAMELESS) And you can shut up. Typical Ro. Take something as freakish as the Nameless and then make them worse.

SSKEER:
They disssturb you?

LOURNA:
They don't you? Look, I was the first to see the ... advantage they'd bring against you lot, but the cybernetics Boolan has added? That one's missing a head, for stars' sake ... It's ghoulish ...

SSKEER:
Obssscene.

LOURNA:
And you're sure you have them under control?

SSKEER:
Their implants bend them to my will as long as I wear Boolan's device.

LOURNA:
Just like the old days, huh? More mind tricks.

SSKEER:
I am *trying* to concentrate.

LOURNA:
Good. Because if your pets get free ...

SSKEER:
(GETTING ANGRY) They have *nothing* to do with me! You're the one who unleashed them on the galaxy! You and Ro!

FX: When Sskeer gets angry, the Nameless get angry, too, snapping and growling. The whir of the control device gets louder.

LOURNA:
(WARNING) Careful. They're reacting to your mood.

SSKEER:
(BREATHING HEAVILY TO CONTROL HIMSELF ... AND THE NAMELESS) I am in control.

LOURNA:
Well, that would make a pleasant change. Looks like an air lock up ahead. We could stash them in there. Unless, of course, you want to shove them out onto the asteroid's surface. See how they do with no oxygen.

SSKEER:
They are to be taken back to Corussscant to be studied.

LOURNA:
Of course. Back to Coruscant.

FX: Beeps as Lourna tries to open the air lock. There's a stubborn buzz.

LOURNA: (CONT)
That's odd.

SSKEER:
Problem?

LOURNA:
Only if you want to get out in a hurry. The doors are jammed. Some kind of interference.

SSKEER:
Let me try.

LOURNA:
You keep those two under control. This might be another of Boolan's traps. Unless . . .

FX: She opens a comm channel.

LOURNA: (CONT)
Trennis? Respond.

KEEVE: (DISTORT/COMMS)
Keeve here . . . seeing as how you asked *so* nicely.

LOURNA:
We haven't time for niceties. We have a problem.

CUT TO:

SCENE 25. INT. ASTEROID BASE. MAIN LAB. OCCLUSION ZONE—CONTINUOUS.

Atmos: As before.

KEEVE:
Just the one?

FX: A computer beeps.

TEREC:
Keeve.

LOURNA: (DISTORT/COMMS)
It's the air lock to the asteroid's surface.

TEREC:
Keeve, you really need to see this.

LOURNA: (DISTORT/COMMS)
Are you listening to me?

TEY:
Give them a minute, Lourna. Something's up.

LOURNA: (DISTORT/COMMS)
We might not *have* a minute.

KEEVE:
What is it, Terec?

TEREC:
This cluster of records here. Do you see them?

KEEVE:
Yes. But I don't recognize—

CERET:
It is Ithorese.

KEEVE:
Of course it is. But what does it say?

TEREC:
"Blight research."

KEEVE:
What?

CERET:
The reports of ... calcification affecting planets across the Republic. Flora, fauna, even sentient beings.

ORBALIN:
Marchion Ro promised the people of the galaxy he'd find a solution to the problem.

KEEVE:
And you think this is it?

CERET:
Or maybe the malady's cause.

LOURNA: (DISTORT/COMMS)
Hello? Is this a private panic attack, or can anyone join in? Say, someone with information vital for our survival?

KEEVE:
Not now, Lourna.

FX: Keeve walks toward Boolan. The sound of the energy field comes up in volume.

KEEVE: (CONT)
What are those files, Boolan? What have you got to do with the blight?

BOOLAN:
Nothing.

KEEVE:
But Ro instructed you to investigate...what? How to stop it? Or is Ceret right? Did you manufacture the...the...

BOOLAN:
Infection?

KEEVE:
Yes.

BOOLAN:
You'll never know, will you? Unless you release me.

KEEVE:
Not going to happen. Not yet.

ORBALIN:
We may not have a choice. The baron's files are still deleting.

TEY:
Faster than ever by the look of things. Cluster after cluster.

BOOLAN:
Cascading into oblivion.

KEEVE:
And the blight research?

CERET:
Bound to go the same way.

TEREC:
Unless we can stop the deletion.

ORBALIN:
Which, at present, seems beyond even our abilities.

BOOLAN:
All that data, lost forever. A lifetime's work. Medical advancements, quantum leaps in biological engineering, cures for ailments...large and small.

KEEVE:
How large?

BOOLAN:
You'll never know.

LOURNA: (DISTORT/COMMS)
(FRUSTRATED) Unless you make a backup.

KEEVE:
What?

LOURNA: (DISTORT/COMMS)
Copy the files before they're deleted!

KEEVE:
(TO THE OTHERS) Can we do that?

ORBALIN:
I'm rather embarrassed we haven't thought of it before.

CERET:
So busy trying to dam the flood—

TEREC:
We forgot we could siphon off the water. Tey, can we borrow Skoot?

TEY:
Be my guest. Go help, Fruit Face.

SK-OT:
Zep-zep-zet.

FX: SK-OT buzzes over.

CERET:
Archivist OrbaLin, if you could attach a data cable to the droid.

ORBALIN:
Gladly.

FX: The squelchy sound of OrbaLin manipulating one of his pseudopods followed by the clunk of a connector being slotted into a dataport.

FX: A positive trill from the computer.

TEREC:
We have a connection!

SK-OT:
Zet-zet-zet!

TEY:
Safe? Of course it's safe. (LOWERS VOICE) It *is* safe, isn't it?

SK-OT:
(WORRIED) Zeeeep...

FX: Data starts copying over. Click, click, click.

CERET:
The data is copying into the droid's databanks. Fifteen percent. Sixteen.

KEEVE:
Including the blight research?

TEREC:
Stand by.

FX: The krinnan trills.

KEEVE:
How did I know you were going to say that?

CERET:
Nineteen percent.

LOURNA: (DISTORT/COMMS)
Meanwhile, some of us are still waiting...

KEEVE:
Kriff. Sorry, Lourna. What is it?

LOURNA: (DISTORT/COMMS)
Finally. Glad to have your full attention.

CERET:
Twenty-four percent.

KEEVE:
We're juggling a lot here.

LOURNA: (DISTORT/COMMS)
And it might be about to get a lot worse. We wanted to stash the Nameless in an air lock.

KEEVE:
Makes sense. Good plan.

LOURNA: (DISTORT/COMMS)
It would be, if the air lock wasn't locked. More than that. The entire system is jammed. Overridden by a remote code.

TEY:
Remote?

LOURNA: (DISTORT/COMMS)
We had a similar device back in the good old days. Lock the doors—

KEEVE:
So your victims couldn't run. I remember. And you're saying that's what's happening here?

LOURNA: (DISTORT/COMMS)
Looks that way to me.

KEEVE:
Which means—

TEY:
Someone's on the way.

ORBALIN:
The Nihil?

KEEVE:
A safe assumption.

TEY:
And another ticking time bomb.

KEEVE:
How are we doing on that data?

CERET:
Forty-five percent copied.

KEEVE:
Including the blight research?

ORBALIN:
Not yet, I'm afraid.

TEY:
Can't we ... prioritize it?

TEREC:
It's all we can do to stop it being deleted. Every time we block the virus—

CERET:
It adapts, taking more files with it.

BOOLAN:
(CHUCKLES)

TEREC:
Sixty-three percent copied.

FX: Another bleep sounds from Keeve's comlink, shrill and repeating. Blip. Blip. Blip. Blip.

TEY:
Do I want to know what that is?

KEEVE:
Lourna's droid, signaling from the *Ataraxia*. (INTO COMLINK) Kew-For, we hear you.

Q-4: (DISTORT/COMMS)
Ah, Jedi Keeve, (STATIC) thought you'd like to know. A (STATIC) has come around the asteroid.

KEEVE:
Sorry, can you repeat that, Kew-For? A what has come around the asteroid?

Q-4: (DISTORT/COMMS)
A ship.

KEEVE:
A ship has come around the asteroid.

LOURNA: (DISTORT/COMMS)
What kind of ship?

FX: The base is barraged by laserfire. Deep reverberating booms. The entire base shakes. Dirt falling from the ceiling. The cast reacts every time there's a boom.

TEY:
A hostile one?

FX: Boom.

KEEVE:
Kew-For, report. Is it the Nihil?

FX: No response but static.

TEREC:
We've lost him.

ORBALIN:
But I believe I can access the station's external cams. One moment, please.

FX: A slurpy, slimy noise as OrbaLin manipulates controls that bleep and bloop.

FX: A screen activates.

KEEVE:
There.

TEY:
That doesn't look like a Nihil ship.

KEEVE:
It's hard to tell these days. Pirates?

FX: Boom.

TEY:
I don't think it's more Jedi.

ORBALIN:
They're landing. Near the forward air lock.

KEEVE:
Lourna, where are you?

LOURNA: (DISTORT/COMMS)
Where do you think?

KEEVE:
Of course you are. Fall back. Meet us at the shuttle.

LOURNA: (DISTORT/COMMS)
We're abandoning the base?

KEEVE:
As soon as we have the data, yes.

TEREC:
Thirty-five percent to go.

CERET:
Including the blight research.

KEEVE:
Come on. Come on.

FX: Boom.

FX: The comlink fizzes and goes out.

KEEVE: (CONT)
Lourna? Lourna, are you there? Kriff!

TEY:
Do you think we can trust her?

KEEVE:
With the pirates or whoever is out there? No. Not really. But Sskeer is with her.

TEY:
True. But can we trust *him*?

CUT TO:

SCENE 26. INT. ASTEROID BASE. OUTLYING CORRIDOR. OCCLUSION ZONE—CONTINUOUS.

Atmos: As before, the Nameless baying, the control device buzzing.

FX: The air lock clunks. It's about to open.

FX: A blaster bolt slams into the unlocking mechanism, which explodes in a blaze of sparks.

LOURNA:
(GRUNTS AS SHE FIRES) That should slow them down.

FX: The sound of cutting gear on the other side of the air lock.

SSKEER:
But not for long.

LOURNA:
Then we leave a welcoming committee. How far is the range of that thing?

SSKEER:
The Nameless control? I am not sssure.

LOURNA:
You wanted to study how these things operate. Here's your chance.

CUT TO:

SCENE 27. INT. ASTEROID BASE. MAIN LAB. OCCLUSION ZONE.

Atmos: As before. The data continues to click over.

KEEVE:
How much longer?

CERET:
Eighty-three percent has been transferred.

TEREC:
And the blight research is in the next cluster.

TEY:
Finally, some good news.

KEEVE:
OrbaLin, can you get internal cams working?

ORBALIN:
I can try.

FX: More slimy sounds of OrbaLin manipulating controls.

FX: The screens click.

ORBALIN: (CONT)
There.

KEEVE:
Show us the forward air lock.

FX: The image changes, bringing with it the sound of the pirates' cutting device slicing through the air lock and the baying of the Nameless.

TEY:
No sign of Lourna and Sskeer.

KEEVE:
Doing what they're asked for once.

ORBALIN:
But they've left guard hounds.

TEY:
Will the Nameless be able to hold them back?

TEREC:
Whoever "they" are.

KEEVE:
We're not waiting to find out. Ceret?

CERET:
Ninety-two percent.

KEEVE:
Close enough.

FX: Keeve ignites her lightsaber.

KEEVE: (CONT)
Baron Boolan, I'm going to lower the energy field. You're coming with us.

BOOLAN:
Am I, now?

TEY:
OrbaLin, you look after the kid.

ORBALIN:
Why? What are you going to do?

TEY:
Lend a helping hand.

FX: The sound of a large metal gauntlet being pulled from Tey's canvas bag—an ancient Sith artifact known as the Hand of Siberus.

KEEVE:
Oh no. You're not putting that gauntlet on.

BOOLAN:
(TRYING NOT TO SHOW HOW NERVOUS HE IS) Ah yes. The Sephi's ever-intriguing lightning glove. The Hand of Siberus. A relic of a darker time, no less.

TEY:
That's right. It's old. So old. Older than me.

FX: Tey puts it on and it crackles with Eldritch energy. Tey's voice echoes ominously now that he's wearing the artifact.

TEY: (CONT, ECHOING)
Older than you.

BOOLAN:
Is this how the Jedi treat their prisoners, threatening them with relics from the Sith Wars?

KEEVE:
No. No, it is not! Tey, things are bad enough as it is. That thing is lousy with the dark side.

TEY: (ECHOING)
The Balm of the Luminous protects me from its influence.

KEEVE:
We don't know that!

FX: Threatening crackles.

TEY: (ECHOING)
But it won't protect the baron.

KEEVE:
Kinda proving my point, Tey!

BOOLAN:
(OBVIOUSLY SCARED) It's fine! It's fine. I'll go with you.

TEY: (ECHOING)
See? I knew he'd see sense. Lower the energy field.

KEEVE:
Only if you lower your hand first.

TEY:
(SNARLS) Very well.

FX: A crackle as the glove lowers, but Tey does not remove it.

TEY: (CONT)
But I'm not taking it off. Just in case.

KEEVE:
(TO HERSELF) Light preserve us.

FX: Keeve hits a control, and the energy field deactivates.

KEEVE: (CONT)
Okay, the energy shield is down. On your feet, Baron.

FX: The rustle of Boolan's robes and the whir of his apparatus.

BOOLAN:
It would be easier to walk without the binders.

TEY: (ECHOING)
Easier to escape, you mean.

KEEVE:
(WARNING) Tey.

CERET:
The blight data is copying over.

BOOLAN:
Then you should stand back.

KEEVE:
What does that mean?

TEREC:
Copying over ... now!

FX: Terec's "now" is accompanied by a small explosion, the computer console sparking.

SK-0T:
Zeeeeee!

ORBALIN:
(GASPS)

YACOMBE CHILD:
(CRIES IN ALARM)

KEEVE:
Another booby trap.

TEY: (ECHOING)
Little one?

ORBALIN:
The girl is unharmed.

KEEVE:
And the data?

CERET:
Safe in the droid's memory banks.

TEREC:
And just in time.

TEY: (ECHOING)
Are you sure? What's that? Within the terminal?

ORBALIN:
A glass vial!

TEREC:
Smashed by the explosion.

CERET:
When the transfer reached a specific record, maybe.

ORBALIN:
(ANGRY WITH HIMSELF) Saber's Grace, how did I miss it?

TEREC:
It is not that glass that we should be worried about, Archivist.

KEEVE:
That dust.

FX: Terec has spotted blight forming on the terminals, with the sound of spreading ice.

FX: The krinnan chirps in alarm.

TEREC:
The blight, we can assume.

CERET:
Spreading across the equipment.

KEEVE:
But I thought it affected only organics?

CERET:
Usually, yes. But if it has been adapted . . . experimented upon . . .

TEY:
Maybe leave the theorizing for now? Disconnect Skoot! Quick!

SK-0T:
Zet-zet!

FX: Terec pulls out the data cable with a clunk. He drops it as if it's red hot, and it clatters to the floor.

TEREC:
It's on the data cable. (TO HIS KRINNAN) Chit-Chit, keep back.

FX: The krinnan chirps.

KEEVE:
Everyone step back. Don't let it touch you.

CERET:
Do you think that is how it spreads?

KEEVE:
I'd rather not find out.

TEY: (ECHOING)
This was you, wasn't it, Baron? Experimenting with the blight. Weaponizing it.

FX: The gauntlet crackles.

TEY: (CONT, ECHOING)
So much for Ro's promise to find a solution!

BOOLAN:
An insurance policy, nothing more. And a rather ingenious one, don't you think?

FX: A slimy noise as OrbaLin checks SK-OT.

ORBALIN:
But one that failed.

KEEVE:
Skoot is okay?

ORBALIN:
No sign of damage. The Force has been good to us.

CERET:
But for how long?

TEY: (ECHOING)
The monitor! Look!

FX: The tinny sound of the air lock door falling in with a crash.

FX: The Nameless jump back, snarling, as the metal stomp of multiple droids is heard over the comm, servos whirring.

TEREC:
Enforcer droids.

KEEVE:
Lots of enforcer droids.

FX: On the screen, the Nameless attack, snarling and clawing.

TEY: (ECHOING)
But the Nameless will be able to hold them back. Right?

KEEVE:
Let's not wait to find out. Move!

CUT TO:

SCENE 28. INT. ASTEROID BASE. SOUTH CORRIDOR. OCCLUSION ZONE.

FX: The control device pulses. Sskeer stops running and:

SSKEER:
(ROARS IN PAIN)

LOURNA:
Sskeer?

SSKEER:
(PAINED) Feedback from the control unit. The Nameless. Under attack.

LOURNA:
Well, that's why we left them behind, isn't it?

SSKEER:
(MORE DISCOMFORT)

FX: As Sskeer moans, we hear distorted blaster shots, along with the droid's tramping feet and relentless servos, all experienced through his connection to the Nameless, as if in a dream. Or a nightmare.

ENFORCER DROIDS: (DISTORTED)
Advance. Advance.

SSKEER:
Droidsss.

LOURNA:
Is that all?

FX: The distorted cries of the Nameless.

RENGA: (DISTORTED, AGAIN AS IF IN A DREAM)
Captain, the creatures are falling back.

SSKEER:
No. There are . . . organicsss.

MUGLAN: (HEAVILY DISTORTED)
Do *not* kill them.

SSKEER:
Piratesss.

RENGA: (DISTORTED)
Did you hear that? Stun. Stun only.

FX: A slight change in the sounds of the blasters to indicate the change in setting.

ENFORCER DROIDS: (DISTORTED)
Stun. Stun.

FX: The distorted cry of the stunned Nameless.

SSKEER:
(ROARS IN SYMPATHY)

LOURNA:
We need to keep going.

SSKEER:
No. You. You keep going. The Namelessss. The Namelessss are down.

FX: Heavy footsteps as he starts to run the other way.

LOURNA:
That's the wrong way, Sskeer.

SSKEER: (OFF MIC, CALLING BACK)
You get the others to sssafety. I'll hold the droids back.

CUT TO:

SCENE 29. INT. ASTEROID BASE. NORTH CORRIDOR. OCCLUSION ZONE.

FX: Six sets of footsteps hurrying down the corridor, plus OrbaLin sliming along. SK-0T follows behind. We can hear Tey's gauntlet crackling.

SK-0T:
Zet-zet-zep!

TEY: (ECHOING)
Now isn't the time to panic, Skoot.

FX: An explosion sounds in the distance. The base shakes.

YACOMBE CHILD:
(CRIES OUT)

TEY: (ECHOING)
Then again . . .

YACOMBE CHILD:
(WHIMPERS)

ORBALIN:
Hush now, little one. It's not far to the shuttle.

KEEVE:
Any word from Sskeer or Lourna?

TEREC:
Nothing. Our comlinks are being disrupted.

CERET:
Another jamming device.

BOOLAN:
You must protect me.

TEY: (ECHOING)
Protect you? How do we know this isn't a rescue mission?

BOOLAN:
For me? Those droids were *not* Nihil. The markings, the weapons—they're all wrong.

KEEVE:
You're telling me.

FX: The Yacombe child suddenly stops and doubles over.

YACOMBE CHILD:
(CRIES OUT IN PAIN)

TEY: (ECHOING)
What's wrong with the kid?

ORBALIN:
I'm not sure.

TEY: (ECHOING)
Why's she holding her hand like that?

FX: A slurping noise as OrbaLin compresses himself down to the Yacombe child's height.

ORBALIN:
Let me see, little one.

YACOMBE CHILD:
(WHIMPERS)

ORBALIN:
That's it. Nothing to be afraid of.

FX: A rustle of her sleeve.

CERET:
(SHOCKED) Saber's Grace.

TEY: (ECHOING)
Nothing to be afraid of? That's the blight on her skin!

KEEVE:
No.

ORBALIN:
It's affected only the tips of her fingers. Ah. And the palm of her hand.

FX: Tey's gauntlet crackles.

TEY: (ECHOING)
(TO BOOLAN) This is your doing!

BOOLAN:
(GASPS IN FEAR)

TEY: (ECHOING)
You hid the blight in the terminal! You knew this would happen!

FX: More crackling.

BOOLAN:
(CRIES OUT)

KEEVE:
Tey! Don't! We need him alive.

TEREC:
The files in Skoot's memory . . . they're still locked.

TEY: (ECHOING)
Then we'll force him to *unlock* them.

BOOLAN:
(SCARED, BUT DEFIANT) So you can kill me the moment I reveal the key? I think not.

YACOMBE CHILD:
(WHIMPERS AGAIN)

TEREC:
We need to get the child to the shuttle. We will carry her.

CERET:
And risk infection ourselves?

TEREC:
We have no choice!

FX: Terec picks her up.

TEREC:
There. Hold on tight. That's it. Look at Chit-Chit. He needs you to keep him calm.

FX: The krinnan trills.

FX: Ahead, in the distance, there's a whump of something being fired from a projectile weapon.

ORBALIN:
Incoming!

TEY: (ECHOING)
What now?

FX: A small metallic sphere bounces down the corridor in front of them. Clink, clink, clink . . . hissssss. Gas bursts from the sphere, filling the corridor, continuing through the rest of the scene.

KEEVE:
Gas! Rebreathers on!

FX: Tey's gauntlet crackles.

TEY: (ECHOING)
(CHOKING) And you said it wasn't the Nihil! (MORE CHOKING)

KEEVE: (DISTORT, THROUGH REBREATHER)
Tey! I said, "Rebreathers."

TEY: (ECHOING)
(CHOKING) I don't have one.

KEEVE: (REBREATHER)
Crik.

FX: Keeve removes hers.

KEEVE: (CONT)
Take mine.

TEY: (ECHOING)
I can't see ...

FX: He grabs the rebreather from her.

TEY: (CONT, ECHOING)
Got it!

FX: Tey puts it on.

FX: Blaster bolts come from ahead, zipping through the smoke. The stomp of approaching enforcer droids.

CERET: (REBREATHER)
Ahead!

FX: Ceret and OrbaLin ignite their lightsabers, already blocking the shots.

TEY: (REBREATHER)
Where's Boolan? Can anyone see him? We mustn't let him escape.

CUT TO:

SCENE 30. INT. ASTEROID BASE. SOUTH AIR LOCK. OCCLUSION ZONE.

FX: The stomping of the enforcer droids' feet continuing into the base and the whimpering of the Nameless.

FX: A comlink activates.

RENGA:
The creatures are subdued, Captain. Droids advancing. Me and Gabb are going to get these... whatever they are back on the ship.

GABB:
Do we have to, Renga? That one hasn't even got a head! Surely the droids could—

RENGA:
Belay that, do you hear, mister? The captain gave me an order, and now I'm giving one to you. Put your back into it.

FX: In the distance, Sskeer's thundering feet come running in, accompanied by:

SSKEER: (COMING UP ON MIC)
(BATTLE ROARS)

ENFORCER DROIDS:
Engage the enemy.

SSKEER: (OFF MIC)
Engage this! (ROARS AGAIN)

FX: Droids start firing. A lightsaber snaps on and blocks the first bolts, slicing through the first line of the droids.

RENGA:
Of course, you could stay and fight *that*.

GABB:
You're right. Creatures it is.

FX: More blaster bolts. One hits Sskeer.

SSKEER: (OFF MIC)
(CRIES OUT IN PAIN)

FX: One of the Nameless wails in unison.

GABB:
Ha ha! That's it, boys! Zap that Jedi do-gooder!

RENGA:
Did you see that?

GABB:
See what?

RENGA:
The Nameless. It . . . it cried out. When the Jedi was hit.

GABB:
Who cares? They're weird, and you said it yourself . . . the last place we want to be is here.

FX: Sskeer's lightsaber rends droid metal.

SSKEER: (OFF MIC)
For light and *life*!

CUT TO:

SCENE 31. INT. ASTEROID BASE. SOUTH CORRIDOR. OCCLUSION ZONE—CONTINUOUS.

FX: The sound of the battle—Sskeer's lightsaber, bolts fired, droids scrapped—moves behind us.

SSKEER: (DISTANT)
(ROARS)

FX: Lourna's footsteps come running and then stop.

LOURNA:
I'll say one thing about you, Sskeer . . . you would've made a damned good Nihil.

FX: The sounds of battle continue.

LOURNA: (CONT)
The question is, do I keep running or go back and help?

SSKEER: (DISTANT)
(GRUNTS AND ROARS)

A beat of the distant fight as she considers. A very short beat.

LOURNA:
Who am I kidding? You're on your own, Trandoshan.

FX: A sudden explosion knocks Lourna from her feet.

LOURNA: (CONT)
(CRIES OUT)

FX: Lourna hits the floor.

FX: Mechanical legs approach, clattering on the deck plates, hydraulics hissing.

MUGLAN: (MASKED, COMING UP ON MIC)
Good to see nothing's changed, Lourna. Always putting yourself first.

LOURNA:
What the—who?

FX: The heavy metallic legs come to a halt.

MUGLAN: (MASKED)
Who? Who am I?

FX: The mask opens with a click.

MUGLAN: (CONT)
How soon we forget, Tempest Runner.

LOURNA:
Muglan.

MUGLAN:
Surprise, Lourna. Miss me?

FX: Lourna picks herself up.

LOURNA:
Looking good, Mug. No need to thank me.

MUGLAN:
Thank you?

LOURNA:
For taking you to Valtos.

MUGLAN:
Dumping us, more like.

LOURNA:
Dumping you, dropping you off—what's the difference? All that matters is that you're alive. New legs, new crew . . .

FX: A comlink buzzes.

RENGA: (COMMS)
Captain, the creatures are on board the *Gloovan Moon*.

LOURNA:
Your crew, by the sound of it, "Captain."

RENGA: (COMMS)
But they're not like the others. All kinds of implants. And then there's the Trandoshan...

FX: Muglan grabs the comlink.

MUGLAN:
What Trandoshan?

RENGA: (COMMS)
A Jedi. At least, I think he's a Jedi. There's something odd going on between them.

MUGLAN:
Then take him with them.

RENGA: (COMMS)
What?

MUGLAN:
Get the lizard on the ship.

LOURNA:
He won't like that. And neither will your crew.

RENGA: (COMMS)
And how in the living kriff are we supposed to do that?

MUGLAN:
Just do it!

FX: Muglan kills the comlink channel.

LOURNA:
Not easy being in charge, is it?

MUGLAN:
How would you know?

FX: Lourna draws a sword.

MUGLAN: (CONT)
A new sword, Lourna? Phrik blade?

LOURNA:
With a few optional extras.

FX: She thumbs a control, and the blade crackles with energy.

MUGLAN:
An *energized* phrik blade! I stand corrected. Wasted on a washed-up old hag like Lourna Dee, of course. I'll try not to break it when I break you.

LOURNA:
We don't have to do this, Muglan. We could come to an arrangement.

MUGLAN:
For old times' sake?

LOURNA:
Something like that.

MUGLAN:
Let me think . . .

FX: The sudden roar of a chainsword.

MUGLAN: (CONT)
Nah!

LOURNA:
Don't say I didn't warn you.

FX: Both Lourna and Muglan bellow as they clash—electrified blade meeting chainsword again and again.

CUT TO:

SCENE 32. INT. ASTEROID BASE. NORTH CORRIDOR. OCCLUSION ZONE.

FX: Lightsabers slice through droids, batting back blaster bolts. These sounds of the fight continue through the scene.

CERET AND ORBALIN:
(GRUNT AS THEY FIGHT)

ORBALIN:
How many are there?

TEREC: (REBREATHER)
Hard to tell. Keeve?

KEEVE:
I'm here.

FX: Keeve destroys another droid.

KEEVE: (CONT)
(COUGHS) Does anyone have eyes on Boolan?

CERET: (REBREATHER)
There!

FX: A bolt whizzes past.

BOOLAN:
(GASPS)

FX: Heavy footsteps as Boolan makes a break for it.

CERET: (REBREATHER)
He is running.

TEY: (REBREATHER)
Not for long!

FX: Tey lets loose with the Hand of Siberus, destructive energy striking Boolan like lightning.

BOOLAN:
(SCREAMS IN AGONY) Please! The lightning!

KEEVE:
Tey, stop!

FX: Another surge of the lightning. Boolan hits the ground, unconscious.

TEY: (REBREATHER)
Not so light on his feet now.

KEEVE:
Is he . . . ?

TEREC: (REBREATHER)
Unconscious, but still alive.

CERET: (REBREATHER)
Alive and a dead weight.

TEY: (REBREATHER)
We'll just have to carry him.

ORBALIN:
While holding back droids?

CERET: (REBREATHER)
We cannot do both!

TEY: (REBREATHER)
(GROWLS TO HIMSELF) If you need a job done—*yaah!*

FX: A huge crack of lightning as Tey takes out all the remaining droids at once. Circuits burst, and joints explode.

ENFORCER DROIDS:
(MASS SCREAMS)

FX: The wrecked droids tumble to the ground, rolling and then stopping. The odd cog or wheel tinkers on the floor as the battle—suddenly—comes to a halt.

TEY: (REBREATHER)
There. No bloody droids.

SK-0T:
(INDIGNANT) Zep-zep!

TEY: (REBREATHER)
Present company excluded.

KEEVE:
One day soon, you and I are going to have a serious conversation about that gauntlet!

TEREC: (REBREATHER)
Where's the girl?

ORBALIN:
Here. She's safe.

TEY: (REBREATHER)
Show me.

YACOMBE CHILD:
(WHIMPERS)

TEY: (REBREATHER)
What's wrong? Is it the blight?

TEREC: (REBREATHER)
She's scared.

TEY: (REBREATHER)
Hardly surprising.

CERET: (REBREATHER)
Of the Hand of Siberus!

TEY: (REBREATHER)
Oh.

FX: Tey removes the gauntlet.

TEY: (CONT, REBREATHER)
Look. I've taken it off. No more Hand.

KEEVE:
If only. The gas is clearing. We should get moving before reinforcements arrive.

FX: Ceret removes their rebreather.

CERET:
And the baron?

ORBALIN:
I can carry him.

FX: A slimy noise as OrbaLin picks him up.

KEEVE:
(EXHAUSTED) Great. Who wants to carry me?

CUT TO:

SCENE 33. INT. PIRATE SHIP.

FX: The sound of Sskeer fighting the droids is being played over a screen. This sound continues underneath the following dialogue.

ENFORCER DROID: (ON-SCREEN)
Surrender. Surrender.

SSKEER: (ON-SCREEN)
Not today!

FX: Sskeer slices the droid in two on-screen.

ENFORCER DROID: (ON-SCREEN)
Aieeeeee!

RENGA:
"Get him on the ship," the captain says. Like it's that easy! Look at him go.

FX: Nearby, the headless Nameless thrashes against its restraints.

GABB:
Forget the monitor. Look at this thing. Missing a head and still putting up a fight.

RENGA:
Are the clamps secure?

GABB:
Yeah. Nothing's getting out of these babies. And if they do...

FX: Renga thrusts an electroprod into the cybernetic Nameless. It cries out as it's shocked.

GABB: (CONT)
(LAUGHS) Want some more, do you?

FX: He thrusts the prod into the creature again, prompting more wails, as on-screen:

SSKEER: (ON-SCREEN)
(WAILS IN UNISON)

RENGA:
There it is again. Like before.

GABB:
What?

RENGA:
Do it again. Zap the Nameless.

GABB:
Which one?

RENGA:
It doesn't matter.

FX: Another thrust of the electroprod into the cybernetic Nameless. It wails in pain, as does...

SSKEER: (ON-SCREEN)
(CRIES OUT)

RENGA:
I knew it. There, on the side of the lizard's head.

FX: Renga taps the screen.

RENGA: (CONT)
See?

GABB:
Some kind of... what? Transmitter?

RENGA:
And maybe receiver. (WITH MORE URGENCY) Turn that thing up. The electroprod. Maximum setting.

FX: Renga takes off at a run.

GABB:
Where are you going, Renga?

RENGA:
(CALLING BACK) Wait for my signal!

GABB:
But—

RENGA: (OFF MIC)
Just wait for it!

CUT TO:

SCENE 34. INT. ASTEROID BASE. SOUTH CORRIDOR. OCCLUSION ZONE.

FX: The fight continues. As before, I've marked points in the dialogue when the blades hit with [strike] so the actors can react. We need to hear the effort of the fight—a lot of energy—throughout the dialogue. These two really want to kill each other.

MUGLAN:
You can't win this, you know. [STRIKE] I'll slice you in two.

LOURNA:
Yeah? You and whose army?

FX: Lourna fires her blaster . . . and misses.

MUGLAN:
Bringing a blaster to a sword fight? Shame on you.

FX: Muglan swings her chainsword, knocking the blaster from Lourna's hand.

LOURNA:
(CRIES OUT)

MUGLAN:
You're getting old, Lourna. Getting sloppy. [STRIKE]

LOURNA:
Says the woman who lost her legs to a Jedi!

MUGLAN:
Your new friends? [STRIKE] I've heard all about it. You and Trennis, the best of pals. She was there, Lourna! [STRIKE] When they took the Great Hall! Before you turned *traitor*!

FX: Their swords cross, Lourna's jamming the teeth of Muglan's chainsword for a moment.

LOURNA:
(EFFORT) You still don't get it, do you? (MORE EFFORT) Haven't a clue how the galaxy works. You need to keep moving, never staying still.

FX: She punches Muglan with her sword hand.

MUGLAN:
(GRUNTS)

LOURNA:
Because nothing lasts forever, Muglan.

FX: Another kick. Lourna's winning.

LOURNA: (CONT)
Crews. Tempests. They're all fleeting. Here one minute. [STRIKE] Gone the next. You have to look after yourself, be who you need to be, [STRIKE] *what* you need to be to survive. Running faster than those who want to bring you down. Staying one step ahead of the opposition. [STRIKE] No one can do it for you, because if you stop, even for a minute—

FX: Lourna slices through the chainsword, which sparks and clatters to the ground.

LOURNA: (CONT)
—you die.

MUGLAN:
(GRUNTS IN FRUSTRATION)

FX: Lourna's blade crackles as it points at Muglan's chest.

LOURNA:
Call off your crew. Let the Jedi go.

MUGLAN:
Let *you* go, you mean.

LOURNA:
Same difference. For now.

MUGLAN:
Until you need to run again. Like you ran from us. Like you ran from *Quin*.

LOURNA:
(EVER SO SLIGHTLY SHAKEN) Quin? She's... she's here? With you?

MUGLAN:
Would it matter if she was?

LOURNA:
No.

MUGLAN:
You broke her. You know that, don't you? When you left her behind. Me? I was ready for it. Never trusted you in the first place. But Quin, she thought she knew you. The *real* you.

LOURNA:
(MEASURED) Call off your crew, Muglan.

MUGLAN:
She loved you. But you broke that, too—

LOURNA:
(SHOUTING) Call off your crew!

FX: Muglan charges Lourna—

MUGLAN:
Like you break everything!

FX: Muglan slams Lourna against the bulkhead. Lourna's sword clatters onto the floor.

LOURNA:
(CRIES OUT)

CUT TO:

SCENE 35. INT. ASTEROID BASE. SOUTH AIR LOCK. OCCLUSION ZONE.

FX: Sskeer continues to slice through the enforcer droids. There are only three left.

ENFORCER DROID:
Advance. Advance.

SSKEER:
You're not getting anywhere.

FX: His lightsaber slices through two of the droids. They crash to the floor. The last remaining droid's servos whir.

SSKEER: (CONT)
(BREATHING HEAVILY) And then there was one.

FX: His lightsaber thrums as he faces the droid, ready for it to attack. It continues beneath the following. The droid's servos whine as it considers its options.

SSKEER: (CONT)
Well? Ready to make your move?

ENFORCER DROID:
Drop your weapon.

SSKEER:
And *that's it*? You've already lost. My friends will have gotten away. Your mission has failed.

RENGA: (OFF MIC)
It's not over yet.

FX: The buzz of Sskeer's lightsaber as he shifts slightly, reacting to the voice.

SSKEER:
Ssshow yourself.

FX: Renga approaches, his footsteps slow and cautious.

RENGA:
I'm right here, Jedi.

SSKEER:
Ssso I see.

RENGA:
Two against one, Jedi. This ain't going to go well.

SSKEER:
For you. Drop the blassster, Clantanni. Deactivate the droid.

RENGA:
And there won't be any trouble, I guess? Any bloodshed?

SSKEER:
You have my word.

RENGA:
The word of a Jedi. Controlling a pair of *Jedi killers*. How does that work, eh? Only one way to find out! (SHOUTING OUT) Gabb? Do it! Zap the Nameless now!

SSKEER:
What?

GABB: (COMMS)
This better work!

FX: Over the comm we hear Gabb ram the electroprod into the cybernetic Nameless. It shocks the creature harder than ever. The Nameless screams out, and with it:

SSKEER:
(ROARS IN AGONY)

RENGA:
I knew it! You're connected to those things!

SSKEER:
(MORE PAIN)

RENGA:
With me, droid! Fire!

FX: Both the droid and the pirate fire their blasters, hitting Sskeer.

ENFORCER DROID: (UNDER THE BLASTER BOLTS)
Attack! Attack!

SSKEER:
(SHARP CRY OF PAIN)

FX: Sskeer's body hits the deck, and his lightsaber extinguishes and rolls away.

ENFORCER DROID:
The Jedi is down!

RENGA:
And then some.

FX: Beep of comlink.

RENGA: (CONT)
Keep going, Gabb. Give those monsters hell.

FX: We hear the electroprod crack and the Nameless howl over the comm. The sound continues in the background for the remainder of the scene, Sskeer reacting to the pain of the Nameless.

GABB: (COMMS)
You sure, Reng? If they break their bonds ...

FX: Footsteps as Renga approaches the writhing, pained Sskeer.

RENGA:
That won't be a problem, will it, Jedi?

SSKEER:
Ssstop. Please.

RENGA:
You can feel it, can't you? Every stab of the electroprod. Zap. Zap. Zap.

SSKEER:
(GROWLS IN FRUSTRATION)

ENFORCER DROID:
Careful. The Jedi is attempting to retrieve his weapon.

RENGA:
But he can't. (TO SSKEER) Can you? Just out of reach.

SSKEER:
(EFFORT)

RENGA:
What kind of Jedi can't use the Force? Pathetic.

FX: Renga kicks Sskeer in the head, knocking him out.

SSKEER:
(GRUNTS AS HE LIES STILL)

CUT TO:

SCENE 36. INT. ASTEROID BASE. SOUTH CORRIDOR. OCCLUSION ZONE.

Atmos: Muglan grinds Lourna into the bulkhead, an armored arm pressing against Lourna's throat.

LOURNA:
(STRANGLED) Mug—lan.

MUGLAN:
It's over, Lourna. All the running. All the betrayal. It ends here.

FX: A comlink chimes.

RENGA: (DISTORT/COMMS)
Captain, we have the Trandoshan. Out for the count.

LOURNA:
(STRANGLED) Sskeer.

MUGLAN:
Ha. Like you care. (INTO COMLINK) Good work, Renga. Prepare for takeoff.

RENGA: (DISTORT/COMMS)
What about the third team?

MUGLAN:
They'll be with you as soon as they have the baron.

RENGA: (DISTORT/COMMS)
Right you are. Renga out.

FX: The channel deactivates.

LOURNA:
(STRANGLED NOISES)

MUGLAN:
And that's how you do it, Lourna. How you handle a crew. A little encouragement every now and then. A little praise. I suppose I *should* thank you after all. You see, I never set out to be a captain. Didn't think I had it in me, but whenever I hit a snag, whenever I face a... personnel problem, I just think, *What would Lourna do?*

LOURNA:
(STRANGLED) And do... the opposite.

MUGLAN:
Never fails.

LOURNA:
(STRANGLED) Then tell me this, Muglan, what would Lourna do in this situation? An arm to her throat. The life being crushed out of her. Sword gone. Blaster gone. No way out.

MUGLAN:
(REALIZING) She'd...

LOURNA:
(STRANGLED BUT FIRM) She'd have another trick up her sleeve.

FX: Lourna stabs Muglan in the side with a hidden vibroknife.

MUGLAN:
(CRIES OUT)

FX: Muglan releases her slightly, and Lourna reacts, kicking Muglan away. The vibroknife continues to buzz.

LOURNA:
(EFFORT) Another trick. Or another knife.

MUGLAN:
(GRUNTS, PAINED, BADLY INJURED)

FX: Muglan crashes back.

FX: Lourna steps toward the injured Gloovan, her vibroknife buzzing.

LOURNA:
Looks to me like you need another strategy, Muglan. You see, in that situation, in that very specific situation, when I'm staring death in the face, I live. I always live. Which means, if you're intent on doing the opposite—

MUGLAN:
(PAINED) Lourna. Don't.

LOURNA:
(CRIES OUT IN VICTORY)

FX: Lourna buries the vibroknife into Muglan's chest, the buzz muffling as it enters her body.

MUGLAN:
Hhk—

LOURNA:
Hope you enjoyed the lesson.

MUGLAN:
(A GARGLED SIGH AS SHE PASSES OUT)

FX: Lourna pulls the knife free. The buzz is loud again until she deactivates it.

LOURNA:
Don't mind if I take my sword, do you? And your blaster, for that matter. A DeathHammer 270. Nice.

FX: A scrape as she picks up the sword and holsters the blaster.

LOURNA: (CONT)
See you around, Muglan.

FX: She starts running, activating her comlink.

LOURNA: (CONT)
Trennis, if you can hear me, I've taken out the so-called mastermind behind the raid, but we're not out of trouble yet. Stay vigilant, do you hear? Are you receiving? (BEAT) Damn it!

CUT TO:

SCENE 37. INT. ASTEROID BASE. HANGAR BAY. OCCLUSION ZONE.

Atmos: As before. Running footsteps as Keeve's party races in.

TEY:
(RUNNING) The hangar bay! Finally!

FX: The krinnan trills excitedly.

KEEVE:
(RUNNING) Ceret, lower the shuttle ramp.

CERET:
(RUNNING) Of course.

FX: A beep as Ceret operates a remote control, followed by a clunk and the whine of the ramp lowering. The sound continues below the following.

TEREC:
(RUNNING) OrbaLin?

ORBALIN:
(SLIMING) Do not concern yourself with me, Terec. The baron is cumbersome, but the Force provides. Is the girl . . . ?

TEREC:
(RUNNING) Scared.

KEEVE:
We'll be able to help her soon enough.

TEY:
We hope.

KEEVE:
It's all we have, Tey.

CERET:
That hope will never become real unless Baron Boolan unlocks the files.

FX: The ramp hits the deck plates.

KEEVE:
One crisis at a time, Ceret. Help OrbaLin up the ramp.

ORBALIN:
I tell you, I can manage.

LOURNA: (OFF MIC)
Trennis!

FX: Keeve turns as Lourna runs in.

KEEVE:
Lourna? Lourna, where's Sskeer?

LOURNA: (COMING UP ON MIC)
We don't have time for that now. There's another boarding party after the baron.

KEEVE:
What? Where?

TEY:
I think I know. Incoming!

FX: A missile flies in from in front of the Jedi shuttle. It slams into the shuttle, destroying the craft and throwing everyone back.

EVERYONE:
(CRIES OUT)

FX: A high-pitched whistle that represents everyone's ears ringing. When the characters speak, their voices are muffled, as if heard through water, the effect of the blast. The only person we can hear properly is Keeve, as she is the POV here, but even then, her voice is nearer the mic.

KEEVE:
(GROANS)

LOURNA: (MUFFLED)
(STUNNED) Tried to warn you.

KEEVE:
(SLUGGISH) Is . . . is everyone . . . ?

FX: Muffled blaster bolts pour in, distorted beneath the white noise.

TEY: (MUFFLED)
Droids.

FX: Tey is hit.

TEY: (CONT, MUFFLED)
(CRIES OUT)

LOURNA: (MUFFLED)
They're going for the baron!

FX: Muffled blasts as Lourna fires back.

KEEVE:
(LOOKING AROUND) Saber . . . saber.

LOURNA: (MUFFLED)
Pull yourself together!

KEEVE:
I'm trying!

FX: A swoosh of the Force, and the lightsaber slaps into her hand, the blade snapping on, and with it—whoosh—the sound clears. The blaster bolts are now crystal clear, and fires are burning.

FX: Keeve blocks blaster bolts with her lightsaber.

KEEVE: (CONT)
(CALLING OUT) Do we have eyes on the baron?

FX: Lourna continues firing.

LOURNA:
Hard to have eyes on *anything* right now!

KEEVE:
OrbaLin? (NO RESPONSE) OrbaLin!

CERET:
The archivist took the brunt of the blast. He has been temporarily... dispersed.

FX: More blasterfire. More lightsabers.

LOURNA:
Stars! When I told you people to pull yourselves together, I didn't mean literally!

KEEVE:
Who has the baron? Ceret? Terec!

SK-0T:
Zet-zet-zep!

LOURNA:
Damn this smoke!

KEEVE:
Jedi, listen to me. War cloud dispersal tactic. On three. One, two, *three.*

FX: A whoosh as they use the Force in harmony.

LOURNA:
And *finally* you reach for the magic!

KEEVE:
It's not magic. Where is he? Do they have him?

FX: The roar of an engine.

TEREC:
There! A shuttle!

TEY:
(PAINED) A shuttle already taking off.

LOURNA:
Leaving the droids in its wake. *Exactly* what I would've done.

FX: More blasts from Lourna.

LOURNA: (CONT)
Maybe Muglan learned something from me after all.

TEY:
(WEAK) I can use the Hand . . . to bring them down.

KEEVE:
No, Tey! The baron might be on that thing.

ORBALIN: (MORE GLOOPY THAN EVER)
I would say that it is a distinct possibility.

CERET:
Good to have you back with us, Archivist. Just a pity we no longer have a vessel of our own to give chase.

LOURNA:
Yes, we do! Over there! Boolan's Cloudship!

FX: She shoots another droid.

LOURNA: (CONT)
The droids are almost done. Move!

FX: Everyone runs (except for OrbaLin, who slobbers). SK-OT bobs after them.

KEEVE:
What about Sskeer?

LOURNA:
Muglan's people have him.

KEEVE:
Muglan?

LOURNA:
I'll explain when we're out of here. On board now!

CUT TO:

SCENE 38. INT. CLOUDSHIP COCKPIT—CONTINUOUS.

FX: Feet on deck plates. The sound of a ramp being raised.

TEY:
(WEAK) Ugh. Do all Nihil ships smell this bad?

SK-0T:
Zet-zet-zet!

TEY:
Stop fussing, Fruit Face. It'll take more than a blaster burn to finish me off.

FX: The creak of a pilot's chair as Lourna drops behind the controls.

LOURNA:
Everyone, strap yourself in.

CERET:
With what exactly? There are no restraints.

FX: Lourna flicks the controls, powering up the engine.

LOURNA:
Just how I like it.

FX: She fires the engine.

CUT TO:

SCENE 39. EXT. SPACE—CONTINUOUS.

FX: The Cloudship rockets out of the asteroid, banking hard.

CUT TO:

SCENE 40. INT. CLOUDSHIP COCKPIT—CONTINUOUS.

Atmos: The ship in flight.

CERET:
There! Two vessels, straight ahead. The shuttle and the pirate ship!

LOURNA:
Yes, thank you, Ceret. I do have eyes.

TEREC:
They're already docking. If they make the jump to hyperspace...

TEY:
Where's the *Ataraxia*?

KEEVE:
(WARNING) Lourna?

LOURNA:
How am *I* supposed to know?

ORBALIN:
We left your droid in charge.

LOURNA:
A droid that the bond-twins reprogrammed! He has little to do with me anymore!

FX: The deep rumble of the Ataraxia *coming around the asteroid.*

TEY:
There! There it is!

KEEVE:
(RELIEVED) The *Ataraxia*.

TEY:
Large as life and twice as beautiful!

FX: The rumble of the Ataraxia*'s engines.*

KEEVE:
Can we talk to them?

FX: Terec presses the controls.

TEREC:
We can try, but if the jamming signal is still in range—

KEEVE:
Kew-For? This is Keeve. Can you hear me?

Q-4: (DISTORT/COMMS)
Master Trennis? Oh, thank the Maker. Where *are* you?

KEEVE:
Don't worry about us. We need to stop that ship from escaping.

Q-4: (DISTORT/COMMS)
And?

TEY:
And we thought you might be able to help?

Q-4: (DISTORT/COMMS)
What am *I* supposed to do?

LOURNA:
Target their propulsion. Knock out their engines.

Q-4: (DISTORT/COMMS)
I am a pacifist!

LOURNA:
You didn't use to be! Not until *someone* messed around with your processors.

KEEVE:
You can use your tractor beam. Are they still in range?

Q-4: (DISTORT/COMMS)
I believe so.

LOURNA:
Then activate it, you useless clanker!

Q-4: (DISTORT/COMMS)
Well. There's no need for *that* kind of language.

FX: A tractor beam activates.

KEEVE:
That's it.

Q-4: (DISTORT/COMMS)
Do I have them?

FX: The tractor beam locks on with a clunk.

TEY:
Now you do! Good work, fella!

Q-4: (DISTORT/COMMS)
Oh. Yay, me!

LOURNA:
I'm *so* embarrassed.

ORBALIN:
I wouldn't celebrate just yet if I were you.

KEEVE:
What do you mean?

FX: An alarm sounds. The krinnan squeals.

TEREC:
Proximity alert.

CERET:
Multiple signals coming in fast.

LOURNA:
From which heading?

ORBALIN:
All of them!

CUT TO:

SCENE 41. EXT. SPACE—CONTINUOUS.

FX: The chittering of hundreds of scav droids swarming toward the ships.

CUT TO:

SCENE 42. INT. CLOUDSHIP COCKPIT—CONTINUOUS.

Atmos: As before.

TEY:
Scav droids!

Q-4: (DISTORT/COMMS)
Hundreds of the things! Oh, Master Trennis, the *Ataraxia* is under attack!

FX: A small explosion followed by a shower of sparks as scav droids target the Cloudship, too.

KEEVE:
And it's not the only one.

FX: The Cloudship shudders. We can hear scraping on the hull.

EVERYONE:
(CRIES OUT)

TEY:
They're going for the thrusters.

FX: Another explosion, followed by a warning klaxon.

ORBALIN:
And the fuel lines!

LOURNA:
What do you expect? It's what they're for. Tearing apart any ship in Nihil space that doesn't have the right codes.

KEEVE:
Including the pirate ship, too, for that matter. Look.

CERET:
At least that proves Master Sskeer's abductors are not Nihil.

LOURNA:
I told you. They're not.

Q-4: (DISTORT/COMMS)
(CRIES OUT) I don't know what to do. They're slicing through the hull!

LOURNA:
See, this is why you shouldn't have reprogrammed him. Kew-For used to be good in a crisis.

Q-4: (DISTORT/COMMS)
You always called me a coward!

LOURNA:
I call everyone a coward!

FX: Another explosion.

CERET:
We are down to one thruster!

KEEVE:
Get us on board the *Ataraxia*. (INTO COMLINK) Kew-For, open the hangar bay doors.

Q-4: (DISTORT/COMMS)
I can't. The scav droids are jamming the mechanism!

LOURNA:
Then we'll have to scrape them off. Trennis, take the controls.

FX: The chair creaks as Lourna stands.

KEEVE:
Why? Where are you going?

FX: Lourna runs from the cockpit.

LOURNA:
(CALLING BACK) Gun turret!

CUT TO:

SCENE 43. EXT. SPACE—CONTINUOUS.

FX: The skittering of the scav droids. The rumble of the Ataraxia. *The Cloudship's damaged thrusters coming about.*

CUT TO:

SCENE 44. INT. CLOUDSHIP GUN TURRET—CONTINUOUS.

FX: Another explosion rocks the small ship. The scraping on the hull gets louder.

KEEVE: (COMMS, TINNY)
Lourna? Lourna, are you there?

FX: Lourna runs in.

LOURNA:
Okay. I'm here. I'm here.

FX: Lourna drops into the gunner's seat.

LOURNA: (CONT)
In the seat and headset on.

FX: Lourna pulls the headset on. The voices from the cockpit are clearer but still heard over the comms.

KEEVE: (COMMS)
Finally.

LOURNA:
You need to bring us about.

FX: The hydraulics of the gun turret whir.

KEEVE: (COMMS)
(EFFORT) Not the easiest . . . with only one thruster.

LOURNA:
The Force will provide, I'm sure.

CERET: (COMMS)
The scav droids are breaking through.

YACOMBE CHILD: (COMMS)
(WHIMPERS)

LOURNA:
How's the kid doing, Tey?

TEY: (COMMS)
Scared. But it's going to be all right. (TO THE CHILD) Isn't it, little one?

LOURNA:
Wish I had your faith.

ORBALIN: (COMMS)
We have more than faith, Miss Dee. You said it yourself.

TEREC: (COMMS)
The Force will provide.

ORBALIN: (COMMS)
Are you ready, my friends?

CERET: (COMMS)
Always.

FX: We hear the thrum of the Force.

LOURNA:
What's happening, people?

FX: The last scrabbling of the scav droids as they're pushed away.

TEY: (COMMS)
(LAUGHS) OrbaLin and the others used the Force. Pushed the droids from the hull.

ORBALIN: (COMMS)
(STRAINED) The trick is to stop them from reattaching.

KEEVE: (COMMS)
We haven't long before they're back. Are you ready, Lourna?

FX: Beeps as Lourna activates controls on the gun.

LOURNA:
And waiting.

KEEVE: (COMMS)
(STRUGGLING WITH CONTROLS) The drive unit's shot.

LOURNA:
Then point us at the bay and hope for the best.

KEEVE: (COMMS)
I hope you know what you're doing.

FX: More beeps.

LOURNA:
So do I. Kew-For, prepare to open the doors on my mark.

Q-4: (DISTORT/COMMS)
(STILL PUT OUT) Only if you think I can manage.

LOURNA:
Save me from self-righteous Jedi and petulant droids.

KEEVE: (COMMS)
It's now or never, Lourna.

LOURNA:
Copy that! Firing ... now!

FX: She fires repeatedly. Pew. Pew. Pew. Pew.

CUT TO:

SCENE 45. EXT. SPACE—CONTINUOUS.

FX: Scav droids squeal as they're blown free.

CUT TO:

SCENE 46. INT. CLOUDSHIP GUN TURRET—CONTINUOUS.

KEEVE: (COMMS)
You did it, Lourna. The doors are clear.

LOURNA:
Over to you, Kew-For. Don't let us down now.

FX: We hear Q-4 pressing controls over the comm.

Q-4: (DISTORT/COMMS)
Oh, this pressure is intolerable. If we ever get back to the Republic, I'm going to apply for a position more suited to my disposition. A nice quiet library. Maybe even a horticultural unit.

LOURNA:
Kew-For!

Q-4: (DISTORT/COMMS)
Yes, yes. I'm opening them. I'm opening them! No need to snap!

KEEVE: (COMMS)
Quicker. Open quicker.

Q-4: (DISTORT/COMMS)
You are coming in rather fast!

LOURNA:
Not much she can do about that! Everyone . . . brace!

CUT TO:

SCENE 47. INT. THE *ATARAXIA*. HANGAR BAY—CONTINUOUS.

FX: The Cloudship screams through the doors and crashes, scraping along the floor, knocking Vectors out of the way, all before hitting a wall.

CUT TO:

SCENE 48. INT. CLOUDSHIP COCKPIT—CONTINUOUS.

FX: The sound of small fires.

ORBALIN:
(GROANING) Not bad, Master Trennis. You hit only three Vectors.

KEEVE:
Felt like more. Is everyone all right?

FX: Lourna clambers into the cockpit.

LOURNA: (COMING UP ON MIC)
Stow that! What about Muglan's ship? Kew-For?

Q-4: (DISTORT/COMMS)
They are still being swarmed by scav droids.

KEEVE:
Open a channel. Offer them assistance.

LOURNA:
Like they'll listen.

KEEVE:
Anything to stop them from getting away.

Q-4: (DISTORT/COMMS)
Unidentified vessel, this is the Jedi cruiser *Ataraxia*. Stand by for assistance.

FX: There's a crackle on the line.

MUGLAN: (COMMS)
That won't be necessary, *Ataraxia*.

LOURNA:
Muglan?

MUGLAN: (COMMS)
Thanks for helping with the baron, Jedi. We couldn't have done it without you.

FX: A distant sound of a hyperjump alert over the comm.

Q-4: (DISTORT/COMMS)
They've made the jump, scav droids and all!

LOURNA:
(SOTTO) Why are Gloovans so hard to kill?

TEY:
What now?

LOURNA:
We get out of here.

TEREC:
Shouldn't we at least *try* to follow them?

LOURNA:
Follow them where, Terec? They've jumped to lightspeed. They could be anywhere.

KEEVE:
And they have Sskeer, too. But we have the data. And we have a Path drive.

LOURNA:
So?

KEEVE:
So I suggest we make a strategic retreat before the remaining scav droids attempt to finish us off.

LOURNA:
No more running after your master?

KEEVE:
This is bigger than both of us. Kew-For, set course for Coruscant.

LOURNA:
(TO HERSELF) Great.

FX: The engines swell in volume.

CUT TO:

SCENE 49. INT. STAR CRUISER—NOW.

Atmos: As before.

RHIL:
How did it feel? Another—

LOURNA:
Failure?

RHIL:
I was trying to be more... tactful.

LOURNA:
Made no difference to me. After all, capturing the baron had been the Jedi's mission, not mine.

RHIL:
But you had... invested in the group, in the fate of the child.

LOURNA:
Like I told Sskeer, why would I care what happened to her? These people meant nothing to me.

RHIL:
And yet there you were, speeding back to the Core in their company. To Coruscant, no less. Your first visit?

LOURNA:
Yes.

RHIL:
As a . . . prisoner of the Jedi again.

LOURNA:
An . . . associate.

RHIL:
Although technically you *were* still a fugitive, from the *Restitution*, from Starlight. Is that why you went with them? Why you didn't cut your losses and run?

LOURNA:
Again.

RHIL:
Yes. What was it, Lourna? A sense of duty? Of responsibility?

LOURNA:
I had little choice. Although Trennis told me to trust her, that we would receive—

RHIL:
A warm welcome?

LOURNA:
Clemency, all things considered. (BEAT) I should have known better . . .

CUT TO:

SCENE 50. INT. THE *ATARAXIA*—THEN.

FX: The Ataraxia *groans as it races through hyperspace.*

TEREC:
This ship is not what it was.

KEEVE:
It's been through a lot.

LOURNA:
Don't look at me! You're the one who took it into the Occlusion Zone.

ORBALIN:
The hyperdrive is holding—

Q-4:
By a thread. Although passing through the Stormwall was no picnic, even *with* a Path drive.

TEREC:
A Path drive that is in an even worse state than the hyperdrive.

YACOMBE CHILD:
(WHIMPERS)

FX: The krinnan chirps as well.

LOURNA:
You're scaring the kid.

CERET:
(SOTTO) Not to mention "our" krinnan.

ORBALIN:
The child is asleep. The sedative is holding.

KEEVE:
And the blight?

TEY:
Still on the advance.

KEEVE:
The Republic will be able to help.

LOURNA:
Yes. Because it's been doing *so* well recently.

TEY:
Way to poke the rancor, Lourna.

LOURNA:
Worried, Sirrek?

TEY:
About what?

LOURNA:
That we're about to meet a whole army of Jedi who might take offense to your little Sith "accessory."

ORBALIN:
The Jedi are *not* an army.

TEY:
And even if they were, the Hand of Siberus has *nothing* to do with them.

LOURNA:
Yeah. Let's see how that goes.

KEEVE:
That's *enough*, both of you. Tey, you will surrender the Hand of Siberus into our custody.

TEY:
The hell I will!

KEEVE:
So it can be cleared for use in the field.

LOURNA:
(LAUGHS) Never going to happen.

ORBALIN:
Actually, recent additions to the Guardian Protocols do speak of assessing all Force-related artifacts as potential tools, whatever the provenance.

KEEVE:
(UNCOMFORTABLE WITH THAT) Yes. Yes, they do.

LOURNA:
(LAUGHS) Marchion really has you on the run, doesn't he? (PLAYACTING) Oh, can you hear that?

KEEVE:
What?

LOURNA:
The sound of principles falling by the wayside. For. Light. And. Life.

Q-4:
We're coming up on Coruscant.

LOURNA:
About time.

KEEVE:
Just let us do the talking. We're going to have a lot of explaining to do. But they *will* listen, I promise you.

TEY:
The Republic or the Jedi?

LOURNA:
They're the same thing, aren't they?

Q-4:
Dropping out of hyperspace.

FX: The Ataraxia *drops into realspace with a whumph.*

TEY:
And there she is. The jewel of the galaxy.

KEEVE:
Coruscant.

FX: Proximity alarms sound.

ORBALIN:
And we have company. Multiple ships.

KEEVE:
Jedi?

TEREC:
RDC.

TEY:
Skyhawks *and* Skywings.

LOURNA:
Not to mention a Longbeam.

CERET:
Is that—

KEEVE:
(SUDDENLY WITH A LITTLE MORE TREPIDATION) It's the *Gios.*

ORBALIN:
We are being signaled to lower our defenses.

LOURNA:
Well, go on, then. Do the talking.

KEEVE:
(SIGHS) Republic Longbeam *Gios,* this is Jedi Master Keeve Trennis of the *Ataraxia.* We are requesting safe passage to Coruscant. Please respond.

FX: A hologram snaps on.

AVAR: (HOLO)
We hear you, *Ataraxia.* Loud and clear.

KEEVE:
(SHOCKED) Avar?

TEY:
(UNDER HIS BREATH TO LOURNA) Avar? As in Avar Kriss, the Hero of Hetzal?

LOURNA:
(ICY) Wonderful.

KEEVE:
(FLUSTERED) Avar, it's . . . it's good to see you after so long. I mean, after Eiram. After Starlight. I didn't know you were back. I have so much to . . . to tell you.

AVAR: (HOLO)
You will report to the Temple immediately, *Master* Trennis.

KEEVE:
The Temple? But we have information vital—

AVAR: (HOLO)
Immediately, Keeve. Kriss out.

FX: The holo shuts off.

LOURNA:
Well. That went well, didn't it?

CUT TO:

Part Four
REUNIONS

SCENE 51. INT. THE JEDI TEMPLE.

FX: The buzz of nearby air traffic.

FX: Footsteps as the heroes enter the Temple. SK-OT bobs behind.

KEEVE:
The Jedi Temple.

TEY:
(WHISTLES) Vildar always told me it was spectacular, but this is something else!

LOURNA:
(BROODING) Isn't it?

KEEVE:
I told you, Lourna—

LOURNA:
Everything is going to be fine. Yeah. Looks like it.

AVAR: (COMING UP ON MIC)
(ICY) Master Trennis.

FX: Two sets of footsteps approaching. Avar Kriss and Elzar Mann stride toward them, Avar's face like thunder, Elzar in his "trying to be Stellan Gios" diplomatic mode.

KEEVE:
Avar. Master Mann.

ELZAR MANN:
Keeve.

TEY:
Elzar Mann! I've heard all about you!

KEEVE:
(WARNING) Tey...

TEY:
Do you know what they call you on the frontier? Laser Mann! Not bad, eh? Now, that's a name to conjure with.

KEEVE:
Tey!

AVAR:
Guards!

KEEVE:
The Temple Guards? Really? Avar, there's no need.

LOURNA:
I knew this was a mistake.

KEEVE:
I know it's been a while. But this is me. It's Keeve.

FX: Multiple sets of additional footsteps approach them and come to attention.

AVAR:
Where are Ceret and Terec?

KEEVE:
They have gone straight to the medcenter. With OrbaLin.

ELZAR:
Archivist OrbaLin? He's alive?

AVAR:
I told you to report here.

KEEVE:
Yes, but it wasn't as easy as that.

TEY:
There's this young girl, you see. A Yacombe.

AVAR:
This gets better and better. An order known to have embraced the dark side.

ELZAR:
I don't think—

TEY:
It's been a long time since anyone's thought—

KEEVE:
Avar, what's wrong with you?

ELZAR:
I was wondering the same thing. (LOWERING HIS VOICE) Avar, I think we need to take a breath here. I know seeing Keeve after so long stirs things up, but—

AVAR:
Elzar, please. (TO THE OTHERS) You will surrender your weapons. All of you.

KEEVE:
Including me? Oh no. No, you don't.

TEY:
I'm not surrendering anything.

KEEVE:
You're not taking my lightsaber like you did Sskeer's.

ELZAR:
No one is taking *anyone's* lightsabers.

TEY:
But the rest of us are fair game.

ELZAR:
I'm sorry. Who *are* you?

LOURNA:
That's it. I'm leaving.

FX: Lourna goes to leave. Temple Guards ignite their lightsabers to stop her.

KEEVE:
No! Lower your sabers! Avar, tell the guards to stand down.

AVAR:
You're going nowhere, Lourna Dee.

LOURNA:
You remember my name, then? What are you going to do, Marshal? Chop off my other hand?

AVAR:
You are a prisoner of the Republic.

LOURNA:
(SNORTS) Unbelievable. What did I say, Trennis?

KEEVE:
Avar, I realize you have... history with Lourna, but she has proved herself to be a valuable asset in recent weeks.

AVAR:
An *asset*.

KEEVE:
Without her, we would never have survived the Occlusion Zone.

LOURNA:
Or got out of it again, for that matter.

AVAR:
And that's the problem, right there. You had a ship, Jedi Master Keeve... The *Ataraxia* of all things... able to zip in and out of the Occlusion Zone on a whim.

TEY:
It really wasn't that easy.

AVAR:
And all that time, we have been *desperate* to cross the Stormwall. Staging rescue missions in planet hoppers. Leaving all those people on Naboo.

ELZAR:
Keeve didn't know, Avar.

AVAR:
Did she even ask? Just think what we could've done with the *Ataraxia* if Keeve hadn't disobeyed orders. Think of the lives we could have saved.

LOURNA:
(QUIET) Trennis *has* saved lives.

AVAR:
And if that wasn't enough, to let Baron Boolan slip through your fingers. I knew you weren't ready when the Council made you a master, but this. This is unforgivable.

KEEVE:
(INCREDULOUS, HURT) *Unforgivable?*

ELZAR:
(WARNING) Avar . . .

AVAR:
This could've been the turning point—you see that, don't you, Elzar? After Naboo. After the blight—

LOURNA:
(SHOUTING ACROSS HER) She went to find her master!

AVAR:
(STOPPED IN HER TRACKS) She what?

ELZAR:
Sskeer? Sskeer is *alive?*

KEEVE:
Yes. Yes, he is.

LOURNA:
That's why Trennis disobeyed orders. To save one of your own. One of your own who was hurt. In pain. She has acted with more honor and loyalty than I've ever seen. She even saved me—her enemy—on numerous occasions. She is everything you people like to say you are. I would've thought that was something to be celebrated, Marshal Kriss.

AVAR:
Is this true, Keeve? Sskeer...

KEEVE:
He survived Starlight. But he's not well.

AVAR:
Then where is he? Is he on Coruscant?

KEEVE:
No. We lost him again. Along with Boolan.

LINA SOH: (OFF MIC)
But you didn't return completely empty-handed, I hear.

FX: The growl of two targons as Lina Soh strides purposely through the Temple, accompanied by Matari and Voru, her constant companions.

Elzar moves to intercept.

ELZAR:
Chancellor Soh, there was no need for you to come to the Temple, with your targons, no less. We would've come to the Senate...

LINA:
As soon as I read Jedi Master Trennis's preliminary report, I had to see it for myself, Elzar. A potential cure for the blight... within this scout droid, I presume?

SK-0T:
Zut-zut-zep!

LINA:
(SMILING) It's good to meet you, too.

TEY:
Skoot, Madam Chancellor.

LINA:
I'm sorry.

TEY:
His name's Skoot. And I'm Tey. You know Laser Mann, of course, and this is . . .

LINA:
(TONE COOLING) This is Lourna Dee. Yes, we met. On *Valo*.

LOURNA:
Chancellor.

ELZAR:
Perhaps we should find a more suitable place to confer. The Council Chamber, maybe. *Without* the guard.

AVAR:
Whatever you think best.

CUT TO:

SCENE 52. INT. STAR CRUISER—NOW.

Atmos: As before.

We hold on the silence for a moment, and then:

RHIL:
Lourna? Do you need a moment? We can take a break if you want?

LOURNA:
What? Why would I?

RHIL:
The conversation you just described. It must have been something, coming face-to-face with Master Kriss after all that time. After she defeated you. After she took your hand.

FX: A subtle creak of Lourna's mechanical hand as she looks at it.

LOURNA:
It meant nothing to me. I'm not intimidated by the likes of Avar Kriss.

RHIL:
Which is why you stood up to her. But not for yourself. For Keeve. For someone you once considered an enemy, and now was something else. An ally? Maybe even a friend?

LOURNA:
Trennis *needed* to stand up for herself, but couldn't. She was overwhelmed, out of her depth. Anyone could see that.

RHIL:
So you stepped in.

LOURNA:
Not that it did me any good. Me or anyone else, for that matter. That's the problem with Jedi: too much talking, not enough action.

RHIL:
And all the time Baron Boolan was still at large.

LOURNA:
Baron Boolan was *missing*. And so was Sskeer.

CUT TO:

SCENE 53. INT. MUGLAN'S SHIP—THEN.

Atmos: The buzz of an energy field, less sophisticated than the one we heard in Boolan's lab, pulsing, sparking, crackling. Behind it all is the deep, throaty rumble of the ship's hyperdrive, overpowered and as ragged as the energy field. Sskeer and Boolan are in separate energy cages, Boolan sitting on the floor, Sskeer unconscious but coming around.

SSKEER:
(GROANS)

BOOLAN:
Welcome back.

SSKEER:
(SLUGGISH) Where—

BOOLAN:
Are we? What do you remember, Sskeer?

SSKEER:
The asssteroid base . . . The droidsss . . .

FX: Sskeer jumps up as he remembers, agitated and growling.

SSKEER: (CONT)
(SUDDENLY URGENT) The Clantanni. Ssshot me.

FX: Sskeer looks around himself, grunting like the caged animal he resembles.

BOOLAN:
They did more than just shoot you. (TO HIMSELF) Snatched by pirates like a bounty to be auctioned on a flea-bitten waystation. The indignity.

SSKEER:
Thisss... will not... ssstand!

FX: Sskeer throws himself at the energy field with dramatic effect. The field almost screams with energy, the power surging through Sskeer, holding him in agonizing place like a fly caught in glue.

SSKEER: (CONT)
(ROARS IN PAIN, CONTINUING BENEATH BOOLAN'S DIALOGUE)

FX: Boolan jumps up.

BOOLAN:
Sskeer, stop it, you fool! These aren't standard energy fields. They won't repel you, only catch you in their web. The more you struggle, the worse it will get.

FX: Sskeer is writhing as the energy crackles around him.

SSKEER:
(CONTINUES TO ROAR IN AGONY) Need to be free. Need it to stop!

BOOLAN:
And it won't unless you relax! Stop struggling! Stop fighting it!

FX: Finally, Sskeer pulls himself free...

SSKEER:
(YAAAAHH!)

FX: Sskeer stands, swaying on his feet.

SSKEER: (CONT)
(PANTS ANGRILY)

BOOLAN:
If you're thinking of trying that again... don't. For both our sakes.

SSKEER:
Your... inssstruments...

BOOLAN:
You think I haven't tried to use them? How do you think I received these burns? It's hopeless.

SSKEER:
(STILL PANTING) There'sss... always hope.

BOOLAN:
Now, say it like you believe it.

FX: Heavy doors slide open. Muglan enters, her exosuit clanking.

FX: Sskeer's breathing is ragged and furious throughout.

MUGLAN:
I see you're up on your feet.

SSKEER:
You... will releassse usss...

MUGLAN:
(CHUCKLES) Trying that old Jedi magic. Sneaky. Very sneaky.

SSKEER:
(ROARS IN FRUSTRATION)

BOOLAN:
Sskeer, have a care.

MUGLAN:
No. No, this is interesting, Professor.

BOOLAN:
Baron. Baron Boolan.

MUGLAN:
I've seen Jedi before, this lump included. Back in the Great Hall on the battlefield, arms outstretched, hands out, calling on the Force. I should be, what? Dragged forward? Pulled into the pain field? And yet here I am, feet on the ground.

FX: Muglan takes a couple more steps toward Sskeer. Gloating.

SSKEER:
(SNARLS)

MUGLAN:
You want to, don't you? You want to break every bone in my body. But you can't, can you? A Jedi who can't use the Force. (SMILES EVILLY) My employer is going to love you.

BOOLAN:
Employer? Someone hired you to abduct us?

MUGLAN:
To abduct *you*, Professor. This one is a bonus.

BOOLAN:
If it's credits you want—

MUGLAN:
You have credits, yeah, yeah. I know the drill, but thanks, I value what's left of my skin.

SSKEER:
Ssslime-encrusted Gloovan *ssscum*!

MUGLAN:
And there he goes again. The most un-Jedi Jedi I've ever seen. What happened to you, I wonder?

SSKEER:
(THROUGH GRITTED TEETH) Lower the pain field and I'll ssshow you.

MUGLAN:
Tempting. Although I think even *I* would need a little more... protection if I did something that monumentally foolish. Something like this, maybe.

FX: Muglan brings out the Nameless control headpiece.

BOOLAN:
My control matrix.

MUGLAN:
You invented it, did you, Prof? Good work. I like it a lot!

FX: Muglan puts it on over her slime-covered forehead.

MUGLAN: (CONT)
There. How do I look? Shall we give it a try? (CALLING OUT) Come to Mommy!

FX: Boolan's Nameless slink into the room, snarling and slobbering.

MUGLAN: (CONT)
And here they are, the Shrii Ka Rai. So docile, so obedient. (TONE HARDENING) Forward. Approach the Trandoshan.

FX: The Nameless pad forward, growling low and dangerous.

SSKEER:
(THREATENING) You've been injured, pirate. I see the bacta patch on your chest.

MUGLAN:
(AMUSED) Stab wound. Survived worse.

SSKEER:
When I get out of here, I'm going to tear that throat out. I'm going to make you sssuffer as you've never sssuffered before. You'll wisssh you had *died* in the Great Hall.

FX: The Nameless growl.

FX: Muglan clanks forward.

MUGLAN:
(QUIET, CONTROLLED) You're no Jedi. If you were, you would be writhing on the floor, out of your tiny Trandoshan mind. You have no control over the Force. You barely have control over yourself.

SSKEER:
(HISSES)

MUGLAN:
What happened to you, Jedi? What broke you?

SSKEER:
(HISSING TURNS INTO A SHORT, SHARP ROAR)

MUGLAN:
(PLEASED WITH HERSELF) Maybe I'll leave these two with you. Just in case. What do you say, fellas? (AS IF TALKING TO A DOG) Sit!

FX: The Nameless snarl but do what they're told.

MUGLAN: (CONT)
Will you look at that? Good boys. Good boys.

FX: Muglan turns to leave, exosuit clunking.

MUGLAN: (CONT)
You all play nice, now.

FX: The doors clang shut.

FX: We hold the moment for a beat, hearing Sskeer's breathing and the Nameless's low trilling, and then:

BOOLAN:
(QUIET) Sskeer.

SSKEER:
Be quiet.

FX: He sits down hard, pulling the wrap from his arm.

BOOLAN:
What are you doing? That cloth. Is that what the Yacombe described back on the asteroid? The Balm ritual?

FX: Sskeer begins the Balm of the Luminous ritual again.

SSKEER:
(VOICE QUIET, CRACKING, FULL OF DISAPPOINTMENT IN HIMSELF) "We call upon the Three: Light, Dark, and Balance True . . . One is no greater than the others . . . Together, they unite . . . (SOBS) . . . restore . . . center, and renew."

BOOLAN:
(WITH GENUINE EMPATHY) Sskeer.

SSKEER:
(GENTLY WEEPS)

FADE TO:

SCENE 54. INT. JEDI TEMPLE. THE COUNCIL CHAMBER.

FX: Coruscant's sky traffic buzzes past a large window.

LOURNA:
And how long are we supposed to stay here?

ELZAR:
In the Council Chamber?

LOURNA:
In the whole bloody Temple!

AVAR:
As long as it takes.

LOURNA:
With those ... things looking at us.

FX: One of Chancellor Soh's targons growls deeply.

LINA:
You have nothing to fear from my targons, Miss Dee. Matari and Voru are merely ...

LOURNA:
Protecting you ... from me.

KEEVE:
Not that they need to. Isn't that right, Lourna?

LOURNA:
Of course not. How's the leg, Madam Chancellor?

KEEVE:
(SOTTO) You just can't help yourself.

AVAR:
Maybe we should make better use of time. We could question our—

LOURNA:
(QUICK) Prisoner?

ELZAR:
(EVEN QUICKER) Guest.

LINA:
Let's see what the data reveals, shall we?

TEY:
Yes. The data, in *my* droid. I want him back in one piece.

ELZAR:
And you'll get it.

FX: A door chime sounds.

ELZAR: (CONT)
Ah, here we are. Enter.

FX: The door opens, and a technician enters.

TECHNICIAN WEBLEY:
Masters. Chancellor.

LINA:
Technician Webley.

FX: SK-OT sweeps in.

SK-OT:
Zeb-zeb!

TEY:
Skoot! Did they look after you?

SK-0T:
Zep-zep-zep!

TEY:
(LAUGHING) Yeah, it's good to see you, too, mate!

LINA:
What have you found, Technician?

TECHNICIAN WEBLEY:
The datafiles stored in the droid are intact but remain locked.

AVAR:
There's no way to decrypt them?

TECHNICIAN WEBLEY:
Not without the correct key, no.

KEEVE:
A key that only Boolan knows.

ELZAR:
Which means we have no idea of what the files contain.

TECHNICIAN WEBLEY:
I'm afraid not. Although the labels do seem to relate to the different aspects of the baron's work: genetic manipulation, the Nameless, even the Force itself.

LINA:
And the blight? He *was* researching the blight?

TECHNICIAN WEBLEY:
It appears so, yes.

LINA:
I can almost hear Marchion Ro laughing at us.

LOURNA:
(SOTTO) Again.

KEEVE:
(SOTTO) Lourna.

ELZAR:
Of course, we have only the baron's word that there *is* a solution, Chancellor.

LINA:
Marchion Ro made a promise that he—and only he—would cure the blight.

ELZAR:
And for all we know, his scientists are as confounded as our own. More so, even.

AVAR:
Unless the files contain something else. A record of the blight's *creation.*

ELZAR:
Manufactured by Boolan himself, you mean? A biological weapon. Surely we don't believe that. Not even Ro would put the entire galaxy at risk.

TEY:
The guy does have form.

KEEVE:
And Boolan did seem to be experimenting with the blight. We saw it ourselves.

LINA:
We need to know what's in those files!

AVAR:
Maybe this is where Lourna comes in.

LOURNA:
Me?

AVAR:
You're Nihil.

LOURNA:
I *was* a Nihil. Past tense.

AVAR:
You might still be able to unlock the data.

LOURNA:
Because we all walk around with secret codes in our back pockets?

AVAR:
You were a Tempest Runner!

LOURNA:
Before Ro recruited Boolan! I didn't even know he existed before all this.

KEEVE:
But you could help find him, right?

ELZAR:
Keeve?

KEEVE:
Who has more experience with the Nihil? Avar said it herself. She was a Tempest Runner.

LOURNA:
And now you want me to be a bounty hunter?

KEEVE:
Why not?

AVAR:
Where do you want me to start?

KEEVE:
Avar . . .

AVAR:
Lourna Dee is an enemy of the Republic, Keeve. She is wanted for numerous crimes, not least her part in the destruction of Starlight—

LOURNA:
Which I had *nothing* to do with.

AVAR:
And will run back to Marchion Ro at the first opportunity.

LOURNA:
I'd rather stick probes in my eyes!

KEEVE:
This is Lourna's chance to prove she has changed.

LOURNA:
Trennis.

KEEVE:
That she wants to make amends.

AVAR:
And what then? She receives a pardon?

KEEVE:
Why not? She deserves a second chance. Everyone deserves a second chance.

AVAR:
And then a third? A fourth? A fifth? Where does it end?

KEEVE:
I can't believe you're saying this.

AVAR:
And I can't believe you're being this naïve.

LINA:
(FIRM) That's enough!

AVAR:
Madam Chancellor.

LINA:
If Lourna wishes to make amends, she can remain here on Coruscant—

LOURNA:
Now wait a minute . . .

LINA:
Under house guard.

LOURNA:
No. No way.

FX: One of the targons growls.

LINA:
It's all right, Matari. Lourna isn't going to try anything.

FX: The door opens again, and Republic Guards march in.

LOURNA:
I thought we said we weren't going to bring any guards.

ELZAR:
Madam Chancellor!

LINA:
I apologize for bringing Republic Guards into the Temple, Elzar, but these are extraordinary times.

TEY:
You're not kidding.

LINA:
Captain, take Lourna Dee to the accommodations we discussed. There she will tell us everything she knows about Marchion Ro and his government.

REPUBLIC GUARD CAPTAIN:
Chancellor.

LOURNA:
I've never been part of his "government." It has nothing to do with me.

LINA:
Then you will tell us about life *before* the Occlusion Zone. How the Nihil are structured. How Ro operates. Captain?

FX: The Republic Guard captain steps forward.

LOURNA:
Looks like I don't have much of a choice, do I?

GUARD CAPTAIN:
This way, please.

FX: Lourna is led from the room by the Republic Guards, passing Keeve.

LOURNA:
(SARCASTIC) Thanks for speaking up, Trennis.

KEEVE:
(EMBARRASSED) Lourna...

FX: They exit and the doors shut, leaving an uncomfortable silence.

TEY:
Well... this is fun, isn't it?

KEEVE:
I told her she would be listened to. Gave her my word.

LINA:
And we will listen to her, under our own terms.

ELZAR:
And what of the baron?

LINA:
I will speak to the Bounty Hunters' Guild.

AVAR:
Chancellor, the *Jedi* can recover Boolan—

ELZAR:
Along with the defense coalition.

LINA:
Not this time. We can't risk alerting Ro.

AVAR:
And we do that by hiring cutthroats and mercenaries?

LINA:
Professionals with specialized skill sets. My mind is made up, Master Kriss. We will locate Boolan, bring him to Coruscant, and compel him to provide the key to his research.

AVAR:
(NOT HAPPY) Madam Chancellor.

Lina goes to leave.

LINA:
And if that is all...

KEEVE:
Actually, there is one last thing...

ELZAR:
What's on your mind, Keeve?

KEEVE:
Sskeer. He was taken at the same time as Boolan. If the bounty hunters find the baron . . .

LINA:
They may also locate Master Sskeer.

FX: Lina takes a step toward Keeve.

LINA: (CONT)
We will do everything in our power to locate your teacher, Master Trennis. That I promise you. But Baron Boolan must remain the priority.

KEEVE:
Yes, Chancellor. Of course.

MUSICAL SEGUE:

SCENE 55. INT. MUGLAN'S SHIP.

Atmos: As before. There is the whirring and clanking of Boolan's many implements as he works silently in his energy cage. The Nameless sleep. And they're not the only ones...

SSKEER:
(SNORES THROUGH THE FOLLOWING)

FX: Sparks as Boolan works on the control box of his energy field.

BOOLAN:
(QUIET) Gently. Gent-ly.

FX: A louder spark.

SSKEER:
(STARTS AWAKE MIDSNORE) Boolan? Boolan, what are you doing?

BOOLAN:
(WHISPERS) Quiet. You'll wake the Nameless.

SSKEER:
(WHISPERS) You said your equipment was useless against the pain fields.

BOOLAN:
(WHISPERS) I indicated it had been thus far. That's the thing with science, you brute. One experiment fails and so you try...

FX: *Another spark, and Boolan's energy cube vanishes.*

BOOLAN:
(WHISPERS) Another.

SSKEER:
(WHISPERS) You've done it. You have deactivated your cube. Release me.

FX: *Boolan creeps away.*

SSKEER: (CONT)
(HISSES) Boolan!

BOOLAN:
(WHISPERS) I said, be quiet!

SSKEER:
(WHISPERS) You can't leave me here. Together we could—

BOOLAN:
(WHISPERS) Together? There is no *we*, Jedi. No *us*. You were always a . . . distraction. A puzzle to solve.

FX: *He continues to creep away.*

BOOLAN: (CONT)
(WHISPERS) But now is not the time for puzzles.

FX: *A deck plate creaks.*

FX: *The Nameless wake.*

SSKEER:
Tell that to your Nameless, Baron.

FX: *The Nameless rise, growling.*

BOOLAN:
(SHARP INTAKE OF BREATH) By the Path.

SSKEER:
They're awake. They see you.

BOOLAN:
Stay where you are. It is not me you want. Not me you have been instructed to guard.

FX: The Nameless stalk toward him.

BOOLAN: (CONT)
(PANIC RISING) I have nothing to offer you. No connection to the Force. It's the Jedi you should focus on. I *helped* you. Gave you new purpose.

SSKEER:
You *experimented* on them.

FX: The Nameless stalk toward Boolan.

BOOLAN:
No. Stay back. Remember what you have been commanded. Remem—

FX: The Nameless pounce, snarling and clawing, the sounds of the attack continuing throughout.

BOOLAN: (CONT)
(CRYING OUT) Help me. I won't be able to hold them back for long. Help me!

SSKEER:
I ssshould let them turn you inside out for what you did to me. To your *victimsss*! But . . . that isss not the Jedi way.

BOOLAN:
(SCREAMS IN AGONY AND FEAR)

SSKEER:
(THROUGH GRITTED TEETH, PREPARING HIMSELF) "We call upon the Three: Light, Dark, and—"

FX: Sskeer throws himself against the pain field.

SSKEER: (CONT)
(PAINED) "Balance True!" Aaagh!

FX: The pain field crackles around him, burning him.

BOOLAN:
(EFFORT) What are you doing?

SSKEER:
(PAINED) I thought you wanted my help. And to help, I need to get past the pain field.

BOOLAN:
(EFFORT) By pushing yourself through it? There'll be nothing left of you!

SSKEER:
(PAINED) I've lived through worse. For the Force is strong. For. The. Force. Is.

FX: He bursts through the energy field.

SSKEER: (CONT)
(TRIUMPHANT) Strong!

FX: Boolan struggles to hold back the Nameless.

BOOLAN:
(EFFORT) You made it through! Incredible!

SSKEER:
Tell me that when my scales have stopped burning!

BOOLAN:
Get them off me!

FX: Sskeer lunges for the cybernetic Nameless, grabbing it.

SSKEER:
You heard the man, Force Eater! (ROARS IN EFFORT) Let's see how those cybernetic implants cope with an energy field.

FX: He throws the Nameless against the pain field, which crackles, the Nameless screaming.

SSKEER: (CONT)
Badly, it ssseems.

Sskeer turns his attention to the headless Nameless.

SSKEER: (CONT)
And asss for your headless ghoul of a packmate.

BOOLAN:
Hurry!

SSKEER:
What the baron said was true, Nameless!

FX: Sskeer punches the Nameless in the side.

SSKEER: (CONT)
It's me you want! Not him!

FX: The Nameless attacks Sskeer, and he wrestles with it.

SSKEER:
Attack me all you like. You'll never win. We walk into the Light! Acknowledge the Dark! And find Balance—

BOOLAN:
Sskeer! Behind you!

FX: The cybernetic Nameless leaps onto his back, its claw raking his scales.

SSKEER:
(BELLOWS IN PAIN) Maybe your pet's implants coped better than I assumed.

FX: Both Nameless attack him now.

SSKEER: (CONT)
(MORE PAIN AND EFFORT) Maybe . . . it is I . . . who needs rescuing . . .

FX: The doors open, and Muglan and Renga rush in.

MUGLAN:
What in the name of Gloon!

RENGA:
The control unit, Captain!

FX: Muglan activates the Nameless control, and the now-familiar whine sounds.

MUGLAN:
Back!

FX: The Nameless hiss at her.

MUGLAN: (CONT)
Get back from him!

FX: The Nameless whimper . . . and retreat.

MUGLAN: (CONT)
If you've harmed the merchandise... (TO RENGA) See to him.

RENGA:
Me?

MUGLAN:
Don't make me set them on you!

FX: Renga scuttles over to Sskeer.

RENGA:
Jedi? Jedi, can you hear me?

SSKEER:
(REARING UP) Don't touch me!

FX: He backhands the pirate, sending him flying.

RENGA:
(CRIES OUT)

MUGLAN:
Stars preserve us! Renga! Stay down!

RENGA:
(MUFFLED, HOLDING HIS NOSE) He broke my nose!

SSKEER:
You're not putting me back in that cage.

FX: Sskeer roars as he charges at Muglan.

FX: Muglan fires at Sskeer, the stun bolt hitting him at point-blank range.

SSKEER: (CONT)
(GRUNTS)

FX: Sskeer collapses.

MUGLAN:
My stun bolt disagrees.

BOOLAN:
(QUIETLY, TO HIMSELF) He tried to save me. Even though I abandoned him. He tried to save my life.

MUGLAN:
More fool him. Do I need to shoot you as well, Baron?

BOOLAN:
(SCARED) No, Captain. I'm sorry. It won't happen again.

MUGLAN:
Damn right, it won't. (TO RENGA) Get them back behind the pain fields.

RENGA:
Yes, Captain.

FX: Muglan storms out, and the Nameless follow her.

MUGLAN:
And turn up the frequency!

CUT TO:

SCENE 56. INT. JEDI TEMPLE.

FX: The buzz of a holoprojector.

ORBALIN: (HOLO)
The repairs to the *Ataraxia* are going to be quite extensive, I'm afraid, Keeve. Jedi Tarinaa estimates it could be a complete refit.

KEEVE:
And the Path drive?

ORBALIN: (HOLO)
Oh, that's in pieces. The techs are all but pulling it apart to see how it works at such scale.

KEEVE:
And what about you?

ORBALIN: (HOLO)
I'm staying to lend a hand. Or at least a pseudopod. (CHUCKLES)

KEEVE:
And Ceret and Terec will be returning to help with the repairs—

ORBALIN: (HOLO)
After accompanying our young friend the Yacombe to Protobranch, yes.

KEEVE:
I can't believe she's being sent so far away.

ORBALIN: (HOLO)
The Yarvellian Institute is one of the best medcenters in the galaxy, Keeve. She will be quite safe until a cure is found.

FX: A burble of an astromech droid comes over the comm.

ORBALIN: (CONT, HOLO)
Hm? Oh yes. I'll be there presently, Kaysee.

KEEVE:
Kaysee? As in—

ORBALIN: (HOLO)
(DELIGHTED) Kaysee-Seventyate, yes! It's been quite the reunion up here, I can tell you. Little fellow is a positive boon.

KEEVE:
And all the time, I'm *kicking* my heels in the Temple.

ORBALIN: (HOLO)
The Force *will* find a role for you, Keeve.

KEEVE:
It already has. Sskeer is somewhere out there—*again*—and *no one* is looking for him. All I need is a Vector with a hyper-ring and—

FX: A door opens. Avar Kriss enters.

AVAR:
And?

KEEVE:
Avar!

ORBALIN: (HOLO)
Oh, Marshal Kriss! It is a pleasure to see you again.

AVAR:
Archivist OrbaLin, the feeling is mutual. It is good to have you back where you belong.

ORBALIN: (HOLO)
Yes, well. The shipyard isn't exactly a library, but I do so love a challenge. Speaking of which—

KEEVE:
Thanks for checking in, OrbaLin.

ORBALIN: (HOLO)
The Force will show you the way, Keeve. I promise you. OrbaLin out.

FX: The hologram deactivates.

AVAR:
He doesn't wear an environment suit anymore.

KEEVE:
You get used to it. After a while.

AVAR:
So much change forced upon us. Lives turned upside down.

KEEVE:
(TAKES A DEEP BREATH) Can I help you, Avar? Although, if you're spoiling for another fight...

AVAR:
A fight? (SIGHS) No. That is not my intention. Was never my intention. (BEAT) Ceret and Terec. I hear they are experiencing... difficulties.

KEEVE:
They'll pull through. But yes, they're not as... united as they once were.

AVAR:
And Sskeer? How was he when you found him?

KEEVE:
Honestly? He was a mess.

AVAR:
His Magrak syndrome.

KEEVE:
More advanced than ever, although he tries to hide it. Not very well, as it goes. His body regenerated after going down on Starlight, but his mind... his connection to the Force... Do you know the worst thing? When I found him, he was shedding.

AVAR:
Shedding?

KEEVE:
His skin. I mean, all Trandoshans do it, I know that. But Sskeer always took such pride in his appearance. To see him like that... Silly, I know, all things considered, but...

AVAR:
It doesn't sound silly at all. (BEAT) I never had a chance to tell him how sorry I was.

KEEVE:
Sorry?

AVAR:
About his condition, about how I treated him. I should've listened, should have tried to understand the changes he was going through.

KEEVE:
He wasn't exactly forthcoming back then.

AVAR:
Then I should've listened to the Force. Instead, I... reprimanded him.

KEEVE:
You took his lightsaber.

AVAR:
I'm not proud of the person I became before Starlight fell. Not proud of how I reacted yesterday when I saw you for the first time since Eiram. I've never forgotten how you comforted me after the crash... after Maru.

KEEVE:
You would've done the same.

AVAR:
Maybe once. And maybe again. Definitely again. But seeing you...

KEEVE:
Brought it all back.

AVAR:

Elzar has pointed out that I may have been a little . . . hypocritical in how I spoke to you. That I myself—

KEEVE:

Ran off into the Occlusion Zone at the first opportunity?

AVAR:

Yes. To help people. To be a light. Just like you. Keeve Trennis, a Jedi Master. (LAUGHS) When I think of the Padawan who stood in front of me on Starlight—

KEEVE:

Swearing her head off.

AVAR:

I've uttered a few choice phrases myself in recent days.

KEEVE:

Perhaps we should compare notes?

AVAR:

I shouldn't have said what I did. I shouldn't have suggested that your actions were unforgivable. That you weren't ready.

KEEVE:

I've suggested it enough myself.

AVAR:

The changes to the Order. The . . . things we've had to do. It's hard to take. Hard to . . . process. But if any of us can make sense of this, it's you. (TEARS PRICK HER EYES) The Light of the Jedi.

A single tear runs down Keeve's cheek. No sound effect to illustrate this, of course, but it is there all the same.

KEEVE:

(VOICE CATCHING) Avar.

AVAR:

I'm so proud of you. Of the Jedi you've become. (PULLING HERSELF TOGETHER) And what would she have us do, I wonder, the Light of the Jedi?

KEEVE:
About what?

AVAR:
About Lourna Dee.

KEEVE:
(LAUGHS) Seriously? (CONSIDERS IT, EVEN THOUGH SHE ALREADY KNOWS THE ANSWER) I'd give her what she wants.

AVAR:
A pardon?

KEEVE:
Or at least the chance to earn one.

AVAR:
You'd grant a former lieutenant of Marchion Ro a bounty hunter's charter...

KEEVE:
And send her after Boolan, yes.

AVAR:
Just Boolan.

KEEVE:
Boolan... and Sskeer.

AVAR:
The Republic would never allow such a thing to happen unless...

KEEVE:
Unless what? Avar, you can't keep me hanging like this.

AVAR:
Unless she wasn't alone.

CUT TO:

SCENE 57. INT. REPUBLIC SECURITY BUILDING. CORUSCANT—EVENING.

FX: A door chime buzzes.

LOURNA:
(CALLING OUT) Not today, thank you!

FX: It buzzes again.

LOURNA: (CONT)
I have nothing left to say!

FX: A beep, and the door slides open.

KEEVE:
That's a first.

FX: Lourna swivels on the chair she's been slouching in.

LOURNA:
Ever heard of privacy?

KEEVE:
Security override. Guardian Protocols.

LOURNA:
You must be so proud.

KEEVE:
Can I come in?

LOURNA:
Like I have a choice.

FX: Keeve enters, and the door slides shut behind her.

FX: Lourna scratches her arm: shrcc, shrcc, shrcc.

KEEVE:
That looks uncomfortable.

LOURNA:
A tracker band that monitors my position every hour of every day. Fashionable, don't you think?

KEEVE:
How many times have you tried to take it off?

LOURNA:
Four in the last hour. Maybe five. (BEAT AS SHE LOOKS KEEVE UP AND DOWN) You look different.

KEEVE:
Must be my hair.

LOURNA:
Or your clothes. What happened? Finally told the grand master where he could stick his robes?

KEEVE:
Grand master*s*. We know three at least.

LOURNA:
(SIGHS) What are you doing here, Trennis?

KEEVE:
I wanted to give you this.

FX: Keeve throws down a metal chip on the table in front of Lourna.

LOURNA:
What is it?

KEEVE:
Have a look and see.

FX: A scrape of metal on glass as Lourna picks up the chip.

LOURNA:
(GENUINELY SURPRISED) I don't believe it. A bounty hunter's charter?

KEEVE:
A *provisional* charter. On one condition.

LOURNA:
Which is?

KEEVE:
That you're accompanied by your sponsor ... a member of the Order.

LOURNA:
You? You're coming with me?

KEEVE:
If you want to get out of here, yeah, I am.

LOURNA:
It won't work. Look, Trennis. I like you—

KEEVE:
Really?

LOURNA:
(REALIZING SHE SLIPPED) *Tolerate* you. But you—

KEEVE:
Haven't got what it takes? I was undercover the first time we met, remember?

LOURNA:
And do *you* remember how well that went down?

FX: Keeve takes another step toward her.

KEEVE:
Look, Lourna, this is your chance to gain Chancellor Soh's trust ... to gain the *Republic's* trust ... as you gained mine.

FX: Lourna turns the token over and over in her hand, the metal clinking against the cybernetic fingers of her left hand.

LOURNA:
And what if I don't want that trust?

KEEVE:
Then you keep running for the rest of your life, never breaking the cycle. Remembered as a fugitive. A killer. A *pawn* of Marchion Ro.

LOURNA:
Careful.

KEEVE:
Well? Will you do it? Will you take control of your life?

LOURNA:
With you at my side.

KEEVE:
For now. If you'll have us.

That gets Lourna's attention.

LOURNA:
"*Us*"?

CUT TO:

SCENE 58. EXT. SPACEPORT. CORUSCANT—SOON AFTER.

Atmos: A busy spaceport. People and droids bustle around. Ships land and take off. Repulsorlifts whine. Close by, a holoprojector buzzes.

TEY:
Hello? Hello, can you hear me?

FX: A gonk droid waddles by.

GONK DROID: (BACKGROUND)
Gonk gonk. Gonk gonk.

TEY:
Are you there?

KRADON MINST: (HOLO)
Yes, Kradon hears you. Age has not mellowed you, has it, Tey Sirrek?

TEY:
I'm at the shipyard.

KRADON: (HOLO)
So Kradon can see.

TEY:
Unlike your contact!

KRADON: (HOLO)
Patience, my friend. She's just running a little late, that's all.

TEY:
It's not inspiring much confidence, Kradon.

KRADON: (HOLO)
What's the expression in the Core, hmm? Beggars can't be choosers. It isn't easy to procure a ship that can travel to the Occlusion Zone.

TEY:
Why do you think I came to you?

SK-0T:
Zep. Zep-zep-zut!

TEY:
Hmm. What is it, Skoot? (SPOTS WHO SK-0T HAS SEEN COMING) No. It *can't* be . . .

KRADON: (HOLO)
She is there, hmm? She has arrived?

TEY:
(CALLING OUT) Greyamina! Greyamina Tiss! Over here!

GREYAMINA TISS: (OFF MIC)
Tey!

SK-0T:
(EXCITED) Zep-zep-zep!

TEY:
Always takes my breath away. The image of her grandmother.

KRADON: (HOLO)
No one played electroharp like Madelina Song.

TEY:
This is brilliant. Brilliant. How can I ever repay you, Kradon?

KRADON: (HOLO)
You could pay your tab, for a start! Not to mention Matty's. And *Vildar's*!

TEY:
Sorry, my old mucker, you're breaking up.

KRADON: (HOLO)
Tey! Your husband owed me five hundred—

TEY:
Speak soon.

FX: Tey hurriedly switches off the holoprojector as Greyamina approaches.

TEY: (CONT)
Greyamina! Look at you!

FX: Greyamina grabs him in a crushing—but affectionate—bear hug.

GREYAMINA:
It's been so long!

TEY:
(STRANGLED) Yep, long time. And these bones aren't as solid as they used to be.

GREYAMINA:
Sorry.

She lets him go.

TEY:
(COUGHS) Thanks. Kradon said you had a ship.

GREYAMINA:
Kradon says a lot of things. But he's right. I have a ship with an . . . alternative to a Path drive.

TEY:
An alternative that will get us around the Occlusion Zone without blowing up?

GREYAMINA:
Probably.

TEY:
That's good enough for me.

SK-0T:
Zep-zep!

FX: Keeve and Lourna approach.

TEY:
But will it be good enough for my associates? Let's find out. Keeve! Lourna! This is Greyamina, a . . . a friend of the family.

KEEVE:
It's good to meet you, Greyamina.

LOURNA:
You have a ship for us?

GREYAMINA:
Direct and to the point. I like you.

TEY:
Careful she doesn't bite your fingers.

GREYAMINA:
A girl can dream. The ship's over here.

TEY:
That *yacht*?

GREYAMINA:
Behind the yacht. The planet hopper.

TEY:
(OBVIOUSLY DISAPPOINTED) Oh. But I like it. Yes. Compact and understated. Just like me!

KEEVE:
Does it have a name?

GREYAMINA:
The *Overtone*.

LOURNA:
Well, *that's* going to have to change.

KEEVE:
Don't even think about it.

GREYAMINA:
Do you need a crew?

LOURNA:
No.

TEY:
They have me and Skoot!

LOURNA:
(DISAPPOINTED) We do?

KEEVE:
Everyone else is occupied: OrbaLin, the twins. Which just leaves...

FX: Footsteps approach.

LOURNA:
Oh no! No way!

FX: The footsteps come to a halt in front of her.

AVAR:
Hello, Lourna.

LOURNA:
She's not setting foot on board my ship.

GREYAMINA:
Whose ship?

TEY:
Why don't we pop inside and run through the data, eh? Coming, Skoot?

SK-0T:
Zut-zut!

FX: Tey leads Greyamina away. Lourna turns to Keeve.

LOURNA:
Trennis...

KEEVE:
It's out of my hands. Really, it is. I told you the conditions. Your sponsor has to travel with you.

AVAR:
And I'm your sponsor.

LOURNA:
You? Kriff.

KEEVE:
It was Avar who persuaded Lina Soh to do this, not me.

LOURNA:
Why?

AVAR:
Because I stopped to breathe for a moment. Because I saw sense.

LOURNA:
Ha!

AVAR:
Whether I like it or not, you're our best chance to recover both Baron Boolan . . .

KEEVE:
And Sskeer.

AVAR:
I let him down before, and I won't do it again.

FX: Avar activates a bounty puck.

AVAR: (CONT)
This is the contract for Boolan.

LOURNA:
That's a *lot* of bounty.

AVAR:
But we have to bring him in alive. Do you hear me? Alive.

LOURNA:
(TO KEEVE) Is she going to be like this all the time?

KEEVE:
You have no idea.

LOURNA:
(SIGHS) Fine. Fine.

FX: She grabs the bounty puck, deactivating it, and walks toward the Overtone.

LOURNA: (CONT)
All aboard who's coming aboard. Time is money.

FX: Avar and Keeve hurry after her.

AVAR:
But wait. Where are we headed? Lourna!

LOURNA:
(CALLING BACK) Keep your hair on, Princess. We just need to follow the trail, that's all.

KEEVE:
What trail?

LOURNA:
A trail of slime!

CUT TO:

Part Five
PORT HUNAVON

SCENE 59. INT. THE *OVERTONE*.

FX: The thrum of the ship's engines. Beeps from the flight computers.

LOURNA:
And there you have it.

AVAR:
There we have *what*, precisely?

TEY:
Port Hunavon.

LOURNA:
You've been here before?

TEY:
A long time ago. And I still have the scars.

KEEVE:
That bad, huh?

LOURNA:
Worse, especially now.

AVAR:
Since Eiram, you mean.

LOURNA:
Since everything.

FX: Lourna presses buttons.

KEEVE:
Requesting permission to dock?

LOURNA:
Offering a bribe. I hope you girls have credits.

AVAR:
And if the bribe is accepted . . . ?

LOURNA:
We slip in under the sensors, which is the best place to be on Hunavon. It started life as a research station, believe it or not.

FX: Lourna continues to press controls.

LOURNA: (CONT)
Now it's the best place to get your throat cut.

KEEVE:
So why are we here?

LOURNA:
Looking for Straan Valgar. Wannabe crime boss and all-round slimeball. Quite literally, in his case. Straan's a Gloovan, and if anyone knows where Muglan is heading, it's him.

AVAR:
Partners in crime?

LOURNA:
And beneath the sheets, stars help us. They're married . . . or rather, they were. Not that it stops them from hooking up when desperation calls.

TEY:
Ah, romance . . .

LOURNA:
You wouldn't say that if you saw them slobber over each other.

FX: A beep from the comm.

TEY:
And we're in.

LOURNA:
Time to cough up. Oh, and keep the lightsabers tucked away . . .

FX: Lourna pulls a lever, and the engine noise swells as she takes them into the station.

LOURNA: (CONT)
This is the last place I want to be seen with a couple of Jays.

FX: More from the engine before—

CUT TO:

SCENE 60. INT. PORT HUNAVON. MAIN THOROUGHFARE.

Atmos: A busy, squalid space station. The general hubbub of a murderous crowd: shouts, fights, and even the odd blaster bolt going off in the distance. We can almost smell the grime as vents hiss and the station's superstructure creaks.

FX: A large, thickset alien shoulder barges into Keeve.

KEEVE:
Oof!

ALIEN:
(GRUFF) Rokaa Reena!

KEEVE:
Sorry!

FX: The alien trudges on. The heroes keep their voices down, huddled close together. SK-OT is hovering nearby.

TEY:
Don't apologize. Never apologize. In fact, don't engage. No eye contact. No anything.

AVAR:
Where's Lourna? You don't think she's—

TEY:
Done a runner? After dumping us in the murder capital of the sector. Perish the thought.

KEEVE:
She wouldn't. And besides, even if she did . . .

AVAR:
She's still wearing the tracker. I just wish I shared your trust, Keeve.

KEEVE:
She's trying, Avar. I know she is.

FX: Footsteps approach.

LOURNA:
Talking about me?

KEEVE:
Just the way you like it.

LOURNA: (GOING OFF MIC)
Ha! This way. And watch your valuables if you have any.

FX: Lourna marches off.

TEY:
She *really* likes being in control, doesn't she?

AVAR:
That's what worries me.

CUT TO:

SCENE 61. INT. PORT HUNAVON. FIGHT CHAMBER.

FX: A loud, claustrophobic fight arena with a large crowd crammed into the relatively small space. All eyes are on a laser cage in the middle of the room, where a large male Askajian is beating the living daylights out of a scrawny Kitonak. Our heroes are jostled as they push their way in.

Wild track: Lots of very loud cheering from a crowd loving every minute of the extreme violence on display.

KEEVE:
Well. This is . . .

TEY:
Cozy?

AVAR:
Malodorous.

TEY:
Sweat and bloodlust. It's a heady mix.

LOURNA:
The fight is organized by Straan. Organized and *rigged*, unless he's turned over a new leaf.

AVAR:
Which is unlikely, I presume.

LOURNA:
A Drengir never changes its spores. (SPOTS HIM) Over there. Beside the Sledfrid.

TEY:
That jellyfish thing?

LOURNA:
His bodyguard, Môr. Watch for the fronds. They pack a punch. Like being hit by an electroprod.

TEY:
Got it.

LOURNA:
We'll have to spread out. Straan won't like it if we descend on him all at once. Check your comm buds.

FX: A subtle beep.

KEEVE:
Working.

FX: Beep.

AVAR:
Mine, too.

TEY:
Yep, hearing you loud and clear.

LOURNA:
Let's go.

FX: They separate, pushing through the baying crowd. We stay with Lourna. There's a loud and painful-sounding crunch from the laser cage.

Wild track: A collective wince from the crowd.

TEY: (DISTORT/COMMS)
(SUCKS IN BREATH) Ouch! That's gotta hurt.

KEEVE: (DISTORT/COMMS)
Is this even legal?

LOURNA:
Do I *really* need to answer that?

AVAR: (DISTORT/COMMS)
Well, it's hardly... sporting. That Askajian is *twice* the size of the Kitonak.

LOURNA:
But the Kitonak is the favorite.

KEEVE: (DISTORT/COMMS)
How do you know?

LOURNA:
What did you think I was doing while you three were sticking out like sore thumbs on the promenade?

FX: Another punch.

Wild track: A bloodthirsty roar of approval.

LOURNA:
What did I tell you? That Kitonak is tough.

FX: A flurry of hits in the cage.

Wild track: Cheers, whoops, hollers, etc.

LOURNA: (CONT)
Okay. I'm going to make contact.

KEEVE: (DISTORT/COMMS)
We'll watch your back.

LOURNA:
If you can drag Tey's attention from the fight...

TEY: (DISTORT/COMMS)
Sorry. It's strangely compelling.

FX: Another hit.

TEY: (CONT, DISTORT/COMMS)
That's it! Go on! Hit him where it hurts!

LOURNA:
(TO HERSELF) What the hell am I doing?

AVAR: (DISTORT/COMMS)
Lourna, toward the back of the arena, behind Straan. Do you see?

LOURNA:
Figure in the helmet?

AVAR: (DISTORT/COMMS)
Black visor, leather jacket. They haven't taken their eyes off Straan since we arrived.

LOURNA:
If they have eyes . . .

KEEVE: (DISTORT/COMMS)
Another bodyguard?

AVAR: (DISTORT/COMMS)
I'm not sure. Something feels . . . off about them.

LOURNA:
That your gut or the Force?

KEEVE: (DISTORT/COMMS)
There's no difference.

FX: A flurry of violence from the cage. Rapid punches and kicks. The sound of a body being badly beaten.

Wild track: Gasps, jeers. "No!"

TEY: (DISTORT/COMMS)
(SUCKS IN BREATH) So much for being the favorite!

LOURNA:
(HISSES) Focus!

KEEVE: (DISTORT/COMMS)
Someone needs to do something. That Askajian is going to kill him!

AVAR: (DISTORT/COMMS)
It's barbaric.

LOURNA:
It's *sport*. And while everyone's watching the fight, no one's watching us!

FX: *Punch. Punch. Punch.*

TEY: (DISTORT/COMMS)
He's never going to get out of this.

KEEVE: (DISTORT/COMMS)
Unless . . .

LOURNA:
(REALIZING) Trennis, no! Don't!

FX: *A fwoosh of the Force. The Askajian is thrown into the laser field.*

Wild track: *Huge reaction from the crowd. They can't believe it!*

TEY: (DISTORT/COMMS)
Did you see that? Right into the laser field!

LOURNA:
(NOT HAPPY) Yes, I saw it all right. And so did everyone else!

TEY: (DISTORT/COMMS)
The Askajian's out cold!

KEEVE: (DISTORT/COMMS)
(FEIGNING INNOCENCE) However did *that* happen?

Wild track: *The crowd turns angry. Shouts! Jeers! Arguments break out!*

FX: *Fights break out as the people in the crowd turn on one another.*

TEY: (DISTORT/COMMS)
Um, I don't think the audience is too pleased.

FX: *A crash as someone is thrown onto (or rather through) a table.*

TEY: (CONT, DISTORT/COMMS)
Not one bit.

LOURNA:
Remember when I said the match was rigged? The Kitonak was *supposed* to take a beating!

AVAR: (DISTORT/COMMS)
Lourna! Straan. He's gone.

TEY: (DISTORT/COMMS)
Legged it?

LOURNA:
Can't say I blame him, all things considered.

AVAR: (DISTORT/COMMS)
But the character in the helmet. The one that was watching him ...

LOURNA:
They've gone, too. Kriff.

TEY: (DISTORT/COMMS)
Hey, watch who you're shoving.

KEEVE: (DISTORT/COMMS)
Tey?

FX: A punch as Tey joins a fight.

TEY: (DISTORT/COMMS)
(EFFORT)

KEEVE: (DISTORT/COMMS)
Tey! No!

FX: Blasters start firing.

AVAR: (DISTORT/COMMS)
This is getting out of control.

LOURNA:
You're the peacekeepers. I'm going after Straan. Lourna out.

FX: Lourna deactivates her comm.

CUT TO:

SCENE 62. INT. PORT HUNAVON. MAIN THOROUGHFARE—CONTINUOUS.

Atmos: As before, but now with a huge fight happening in the background, blasters firing.

LOURNA:
(TO HERSELF) Where have you gone, Straan?

MASKED FIGURE:
(DISTANT SCREAM IN THE DIRECTION OPPOSITE THE BACKGROUND FIGHT)

LOURNA:
Sounds promising.

CUT TO:

SCENE 63. INT. PORT HUNAVON. SIDE CORRIDOR—CONTINUOUS.

Atmos: The sounds of the station thoroughfare recede slightly.

FX: There's a brief, harsh electric buzz, the sound of the masked figure being zapped by a giant floating jellyfish's fronds.

When she speaks, Môr talks through a vocabulator.

MASKED FIGURE: (SLIGHTLY OFF MIC)
(CRIES OUT)

MÔR: (SLIGHTLY OFF MIC)
Do yourself a favor . . . Stay down!

FX: Lourna runs up and looks around the corner.

LOURNA:
(TO HERSELF) What did I say? Look out for the fronds.

STRAAN VALGAR: (SLIGHTLY OFF MIC)
No, I don't know what happened. Terno knew what he had to do: go down in the third round. I don't know what he was thinking.

FX: Another buzz of a frond.

MASKED FIGURE:
(CRIES OUT AGAIN)

STRAAN: (OFF MIC)
What? No, it's just Môr playing with her food. Some lowlife tried to jump me on the way out of the arena. (BEAT) Why do you think? Half the station is going to be after my blood!

FX: Buzz.

MASKED FIGURE: (OFF MIC)
(CRIES AGAIN)

STRAAN: (OFF MIC)
(TO MÔR) Oh, for pity's sake, just finish them off, will you?

MASKED FIGURE: (OFF MIC)
Gladly.

FX: A small device is thrown and sticks to Môr's body with a splot!

MÔR: (OFF MIC)
What was that? What did you throw at me?

MASKED FIGURE: (OFF MIC)
Not at you. *On* you and your sticky fronds.

FX: The device starts to beep as the giant jellyfish flails wildly.

MÔR: (OFF MIC)
Where is it? Get it off me! Get it off!

MASKED FIGURE: (OFF MIC)
You can flail all you like, Jellyhead. It isn't coming off.

MÔR: (OFF MIC)
(PANICKED) What is it? What is it?

FX: The device beeps rapidly as it builds toward detonation.

STRAAN: (OFF MIC)
What do you think? Get away from me. It's a crukking—

LOURNA:
(DISBELIEF) Grav charge!

FX: A gigantic boom—followed by the sound of wet jelly splatting against already grimy walls.

STRAAN: (OFF MIC)
Are you *nuts*? You could've killed us all.

FX: A blaster is cocked.

MASKED FIGURE: (OFF MIC)
Sorry about Môr. Still, your body won't need guarding much longer.

STRAAN: (OFF MIC)
W-what do you want?

MASKED FIGURE: (OFF MIC)
Muglan.

STRAAN: (OFF MIC)
Mug?

MASKED FIGURE: (OFF MIC)
Where is she?

STRAAN: (OFF MIC)
How am *I* supposed to know?

FX: Blaster shot. Straan hits the floor.

STRAAN: (CONT, OFF MIC)
(SCREAMS) My knee! You shot my kriffing knee!

FX: The masked figure walks a step nearer.

MASKED FIGURE: (OFF MIC)
Let's try again, shall we?

STRAAN: (OFF MIC)
I don't know where she is. I haven't seen her for ages.

FX: Another blaster shot. Another knee gone.

STRAAN: (CONT, OFF MIC)
(CRIES OUT)

BLOCKROLL: (DISTORT/COMMS, OFF MIC)
Boss? Boss, what's happening?

STRAAN: (OFF MIC)
Blockroll? Blockroll, is that you?

MASKED FIGURE: (OFF MIC)
Shut up!

FX: They kick the comlink away.

MASKED FIGURE: (CONT, OFF MIC)
No comlinks. No backup.

STRAAN: (OFF MIC)
But they're coming for me. And when they get here—

MASKED FIGURE: (OFF MIC)
They'll find themselves unemployed. This is your last chance, Straan. Tell me where to find Muglan.

STRAAN: (OFF MIC)
Never! I'll never betray her!

MASKED FIGURE: (OFF MIC)
(DESPERATE, SHOUTING) Tell me!

LOURNA:
Oh, for Storm's sake.

FX: Lourna fires, taking the masked figure down.

MASKED FIGURE: (OFF MIC)
Hhhk—

STRAAN: (OFF MIC)
Who's there? Who is it? Blockroll? Blockroll, is that you?

FX: Lourna steps out of her hiding place.

LOURNA:
Not Blockroll.

STRAAN: (OFF MIC)
Lourna? Lourna Dee?

FX: Lourna walks slowly toward him.

LOURNA:
Still making friends, Straan?

STRAAN:
I . . . I owe you, Lourna. My men are coming. They'll see you right.

LOURNA:
There's only one thing I want from you.

STRAAN:
Name it. (WINCES IN PAIN) Whatever you need.

LOURNA:
Muglan.

STRAAN:
Not you as well? What the hell has she done this time?

LOURNA:
Enough.

STRAAN:
I'm not going to betray her, Lourna. You know that, don't you? Not to you. Not to anyone.

LOURNA:
Yeah, thought that might be the case.

FX: She stands on one of his busted knees.

STRAAN:
Nnn—my knee.

LOURNA:
Where is she, Straan?

FX: Footsteps come up behind.

AVAR: (OFF MIC)
Lourna? (SEEING WHAT SHE'S DOING) Lourna, stop!

FX: The crunch of Lourna's boot.

STRAAN:
(SCREAMS)

AVAR:
That is enough!

FX: The deep thrum of the Force. Lourna is pulled back.

LOURNA:
Kriss! Let go of me!

AVAR:
We do not torture.

LOURNA:
And you don't touch me!

AVAR:
I didn't.

STRAAN:
(WHIMPERS) Never tell. I'll never tell.

LOURNA:
Well? How do you propose we get him to talk?

FX: Avar ignites her lightsaber.

STRAAN:
(GASPS)

LOURNA:
Such a hypocrite.

AVAR:
I'm merely encouraging our friend to make the right choice.

FX: Avar takes a step closer to Straan, who's suddenly very talkative.

STRAAN:
She's gone home! Our old base! Please, don't hurt me anymore.

FX: The lightsaber extinguishes.

AVAR:
I was never going to. (HER TONE SHIFTS AS SHE PERFORMS A MIND TRICK) Rest now. You feel no more pain.

STRAAN:
I . . . feel no more pain. (PASSES OUT)

AVAR:
That should keep him comfortable until help arrives.

LOURNA:
You're all heart.

FX: Avar turns the masked figure onto their back, then she stands.

AVAR:
We should go.

LOURNA:
Not until I find out who else is after Muglan.

FX: Lourna struggles with the helmet.

AVAR:
We haven't time.

LOURNA:
Then we'll *make* time. (FRUSTRATED) It's not coming off.

MASKED FIGURE:
(WEAK) Lourna?

LOURNA:
What?

FX: Lourna pulls the helmet off.

LOURNA: (CONT)
(SOFT) Quin?

AVAR:
You *know* her?

FX: Lourna tries to pick Quin up.

LOURNA:
We're taking her to the ship.

AVAR:
Who shot her?

LOURNA:
Me.

AVAR:
And now you want to save her?

LOURNA:
Are you going to help me or not?

CUT TO:

SCENE 64. INT. MUGLAN'S SHIP. CELLS.

Atmos: As before.

FX: The door slides open. Muglan, Renga, and Gabb enter. We hear the whine of the control unit and the snarling of the Nameless.

MUGLAN:
On your feet.

SSKEER:
What now?

RENGA:
You heard the captain.

BOOLAN:
We better do what they say.

FX: Sskeer and Boolan stand.

MUGLAN:
We're going to lower the pain fields. You try anything, anything at all, and we shoot. Got it? (BEAT) Well?

BOOLAN:
We understand, Muglan.

MUGLAN:
I hope so. For all our sakes.

FX: The energy cages deactivate.

MUGLAN: (CONT)
Bind 'em.

BOOLAN:
That won't be necessary.

MUGLAN:
Do it.

CUT TO:

SCENE 65. EXT. SPACE—CONTINUOUS.

FX: Muglan's ship comes alongside a larger vessel.

CUT TO:

SCENE 66. INT. MUGLAN'S SHIP. AIR LOCK—CONTINUOUS.

FX: The pirates march Boolan and Sskeer down the corridor.

MUGLAN:
Stop in front of the air lock.

BOOLAN:
(SPOTS SOMETHING THROUGH A VIEWPORT) That ship.

MUGLAN:
In front of the air lock!

FX: They halt.

SSKEER:
(WHISPERS) You recognize it?

BOOLAN:
(WHISPERS) Hm?

SSKEER:
(WHISPERS) The ssship.

BOOLAN:
(WHISPERS) You mean you don't?

MUGLAN:
That's enough. Keep it down.

FX: The air lock opens slowly.

MUGLAN: (CONT)
Go on, then. Into the boarding tube.

FX: They all walk into the tube.

BOOLAN:
You sound nervous, Captain.

MUGLAN:
I'm not telling you again.

SSKEER:
Why would they be nervous?

FX: The air lock ahead of them opens, a far more sophisticated mechanism.

MARCHION:
Captain Muglan. Welcome to the *Gaze Electric*.

SSKEER:
(GROWLS, FILLED WITH HATE) Marchion Ro.

CUT TO:

SCENE 67. INT. THE *OVERTONE*. CABIN.

Atmos: As before.

FX: Lourna is trying to bind Quin's wounds. We hear the sound of wet bandages being applied. The bunk squeaks as Quin struggles.

LOURNA:
Lie still!

QUIN:
(WEAK) Get off me.

LOURNA:
Quin, I need to dress the wound.

SK-0T:
Zet-zet?

LOURNA:
No, Skoot. I've got this.

SK-0T:
Zep?

LOURNA:
I know we *could* sedate her, but we're not going to, okay?

QUIN:
Don't even think about it!

LOURNA:
I just said we wouldn't, didn't I?

QUIN:
Like I . . . (GRUNTS IN PAIN) . . . believe a word you say.

LOURNA:
You don't have to believe me. You just need to let me help you.

QUIN:
(EXHAUSTED) Do what you want. You normally do.

Lourna continues dressing the wound.

LOURNA:
(TO HERSELF) Juvan strips. Would it have killed them to pack some bacta?

QUIN:
Who? The *Jedi*? (LAUGHS WEAKLY) What game are you playing now, Lourna? What have you promised them?

The last bandage is applied.

LOURNA:
You need to rest.

QUIN:
You finished?

LOURNA:
It'll do for now. As long as you lie still.

FX: The bunk squeaks as Quin sits up.

QUIN:
Not going to happen.

LOURNA:
What are you doing?

QUIN:
Getting the hell out of here. Thanks for the juvan. Would say I owe you, but— (WINCES)

LOURNA:
You're not going anywhere. You're coming with us.

QUIN:
Like void I am. I have a job I intend to finish.

LOURNA:
Job? What job? (REALIZES) You're a bounty hunter.

QUIN:
I'm leaving. (CRIES OUT IN PAIN)

LOURNA:
Careful. The wound needs to heal.

QUIN:
(ALMOST DOUBLES OVER IN PAIN)

LOURNA:
Quin!

QUIN:
(THROUGH GRITTED TEETH) I need. To get. To my ship.

LOURNA:
What's wrong?

QUIN:
(SHOUTING) Just let me go, will you? You did it before, why not now?

LOURNA:
(GETTING SUSPICIOUS) This is more than just a blaster shot.

QUIN:
I don't need you, Lourna! I need . . . I need . . .

LOURNA:
What?

TEY:
Are you going to tell her, or shall I?

Lourna turns around, surprised by Tey's appearance. He's standing, having been watching them for quite a while.

LOURNA:
Sirrek! This . . . has nothing to do with you.

TEY:
Yeah. But it has everything to do with Quin.

FX: Footsteps as Tey walks into the room.

TEY: (CONT)
What is it, Quin? Not ryll? Gy'lan? Filaxian?

FX: The only response is Quin shivering.

TEY: (CONT)
Come on. You can't kid an addict. We know all the signs.

A beat, and then . . .

QUIN:
(QUIET) Reed.

LOURNA:
Reed? You're on reedug? Quin!

QUIN:
Please. Your entire Tempest was on stims. As per your orders.

LOURNA:
But not you. Never you.

QUIN:
Because you care so much.

Tey holds out a bottle.

TEY:
Here.

QUIN:
What's that?

TEY:
Something that will help with the withdrawal.

QUIN:
I'm not staying.

TEY:
That's your choice, of course.

LOURNA:
What did I say, Sirrek?

TEY:
You said it had nothing to do with me, and you're right, it doesn't. But if you are intent on leaving, Quin, you should know that your ship has already been impounded by Straan's mob.

QUIN:
(GROANING) No.

LOURNA:
How do you know?

TEY:
Avar sliced into their comms. She's pretty resourceful for a Jedi. I had a friend back on Jedha who would've loved her ... in just about every way possible. The thing is, we need to leave before they find us, too.

QUIN:
Then I better get out of your hair.

FX: She stands, taking the bottle.

QUIN: (CONT)
Thanks for this. I owe you one.

TEY:
You're very welcome.

LOURNA:
Quin. No.

FX: Quin lurches out of the cabin, stopping to look back at Tey.

QUIN:
Just watch out for that one, eh? She won't wait for your back to be turned before sticking in the knife.

TEY:
Noted.

FX: Quin exits.

LOURNA:
Quin. (BEAT) Quin!

CUT TO:

SCENE 68. INT. THE *GAZE ELECTRIC.*

Atmos: Everything about the Gaze Electric *is vast. Its echoing chambers, the rumble of its engines underpinning every scene.*

FX: Heavy footsteps as a huge, spiderlike Harch enters. This is Vulax, a member of the She'ar, Marchion Ro's elite guard. He places a chest on a metal table and opens the lid.

MUGLAN:
(WHISTLES) That is a lot of ingots.

VULAX:
Five thousand aurei, as agreed with the Eye. *Tk-tk-tk-tk.*

MUGLAN:
Five thousand? I thought we agreed on four thousand.

MARCHION:
Consider it a bonus. For recovering the baron's control unit along with the baron. (HOLDS OUT HIS HAND) If I may.

MUGLAN:
Of course. Silly of me. Here.

Muglan passes the control unit to him. Marchion turns it over and over in his hand.

MARCHION:
Fascinating. Absolutely fascinating. As ingenious as ever, Boolan.

FX: Muglan closes the lid of the chest.

MUGLAN:
Whatever you say. It was a pleasure doing business with you, Eye.

MARCHION:
The beginning of a long and mutually beneficial partnership, I hope, Captain Muglan. You may no longer consider yourself a member of the Nihil, but you can still serve the Storm.

MUGLAN:
For the right price.

MARCHION:
Of course. My She'ar will help you carry the payment to your ship.

MUGLAN:
I can manage.

FX: A scrape as she picks up the chest.

MUGLAN: (CONT)
Thanks.

MARCHION:
Safe travels, my friend.

FX: Muglan leaves, her mechanical legs stomping. A door whooshes open, then closes as she exits.

MARCHION: (CONT)
And there she goes, a most valuable resource. Vulax, follow Muglan to whatever miserable rock she calls home and . . .

VULAX:
Blow her out of the sky? *Tk-tk-tk-tk.*

MARCHION:
A waste to be sure, but our part in all this must be kept—

VULAX:
Secret?

MARCHION:
Safe. (BEAT) Away from prying eyes, yes.

FX: Marchion strides away.

MARCHION: (CONT)
Meet the *Gaze* at the rendezvous once the deed is done. Understood? For the Storm, Vulax.

VULAX:
For *you,* my lord. *Tk-tk-tk-tk.*

CUT TO:

SCENE 69. INT. THE *OVERTONE*. HATCH.

Atmos: As before.

AVAR:
(CALLING OUT) Tey. Lourna. We need to go.

FX: Quin lurches in.

QUIN:
Don't let me stop you.

KEEVE:
Whoa! Should you be on your feet?

QUIN:
Should you even care?

FX: Lourna enters.

LOURNA:
Quin! Get back to that cabin!

QUIN:
Lower the ramp.

LOURNA:
(TO AVAR) Don't you dare!

QUIN:
Lower the ramp . . . please.

AVAR:
We can't keep her here against her will, Lourna.

FX: Avar hits a button. The ramp starts to lower.

QUIN:
Thanks, Blondie.

LOURNA:
No!

FX: Avar puts herself in front of Lourna.

AVAR:
Lourna, what are you doing?

LOURNA:
Trying to stop her from making a mistake. She's not well. We can't leave her behind.

AVAR:
And we can't force her to stay.

LOURNA:
Yeah. And what are you doing with me?

QUIN:
See you around, Lourna. Good to see you've landed on your feet. As usual.

FX: The clang of boots on the ramp as Quin exits.

KEEVE:
Avar? Are you sure about this? That woman... she can barely walk.

AVAR:
She's made her choice, Keeve. And we have a mission. There have been enough distractions.

KEEVE:
Distractions?

LOURNA:
Let me pass, Kriss.

AVAR:
We're leaving.

LOURNA:
Let. Me. Pass.

FX: Avar's lightsaber activates.

KEEVE:
(SOTTO) Great.

FX: The sound of a comm opening.

AVAR:
Tey, are you in the cockpit?

TEY: (DISTORT/COMMS)
Getting there.

AVAR:
We need to get under way.

TEY: (DISTORT/COMMS)
Roger that.

KEEVE:
We're supposed to be a team. We're supposed to be working together.

AVAR:
We are. Aren't we, Lourna?

LOURNA:
(ANTAGONISTIC) Whatever the marshal says.

FX: Blaster shots from outside. They continue beneath the following action, a firefight raging outside, the odd blast even striking the ship's hull.

KEEVE:
Sounds like we've been discovered.

TEY: (DISTORT/COMMS)
We have company!

AVAR:
We hear. Go!

LOURNA:
Oh, to hell with this!

FX: Lourna draws her sword, the energy crackling on. She swings, and Avar's lightsaber meets Lourna's blade.

LOURNA: (CONT)
(GRUNTS)

AVAR:
Don't do this, Lourna. You can't win.

KEEVE:
Neither of you should be doing this!

FX: Lourna and Avar fight, lightsaber against energized sword. All the time the Overtone's *engine swells, ready for takeoff.*

LOURNA:
(EFFORT) Protectors. Of light. And life. What a *joke.*

FX: On "joke," Lourna manages to get in a punch, her hilt striking Avar.

AVAR:
(REACTS)

FX: Avar stumbles back.

KEEVE:
Avar!

TEY: (DISTORT/COMMS)
What's going on back there? Should I take off?

FX: Lourna runs for the ramp.

LOURNA:
One minute, Sirrek. That's all I need.

TEY: (DISTORT/COMMS)
For what?

CUT TO:

SCENE 70. EXT. THE *OVERTONE*. RAMP—CONTINUOUS.

FX: The blasterfire is loud and fast, as the engines reach a peak.

FX: Lourna hurtles down the ramp.

QUIN:
(SHOUTING OVER THE BLASTERFIRE, SCARED) Lourna!

LOURNA:
What did I tell you?

FX: Lourna stops and returns fire with her DeathHammer.

LOURNA: (CONT)
You're in no condition for a firefight.

FX: A shot glances off her armored lekku.

LOURNA: (CONT)
Aah!

QUIN:
Lourna!

LOURNA:
It's nothing.

FX: Lourna shoots back.

QUIN:
There's too many of them!

LOURNA:
(STILL FIRING) So I see.

FX: A lightsaber snaps on at the top of the ramp. Keeve runs down, deflecting bolts.

KEEVE:
Back on board. Both of you.

LOURNA:
Chosen a side finally?

KEEVE:
(EFFORT) There are no sides here. Move it!

LOURNA:
(TO QUIN) You coming?

QUIN:
Do I have a choice?

FX: Lourna squeezes off another shot.

LOURNA:
Put your arm around me.

FX: More blasts blocked by Keeve as Lourna and Quin run up the ramp.

CUT TO:

SCENE 71. INT. THE *OVERTONE*. HATCH—CONTINUOUS.

Atmos: As before. The sound of the fight outside, lightsaber versus blaster bolts. Lourna and Quin run in.

AVAR:
They're back in! Let's go, Tey.

QUIN:
What about the other one?

AVAR:
Keeve knows what she's doing.

FX: Avar slams the ramp control.

CUT TO:

SCENE 72. EXT. THE *OVERTONE*. RAMP—CONTINUOUS.

FX: Battle as before.

KEEVE:
(TO HERSELF AS SHE BLOCKS BOLTS) What the *kriff* am I doing?

FX: The ship starts to take off behind her, the ramp rising.

LOURNA: (OFF MIC, FROM ABOVE)
Trennis! We're leaving!

KEEVE:
Not getting rid of me that easy.

FX: Keeve turns, runs, and jumps.

KEEVE: (CONT)
(EFFORT)

FX: Keeve lands on the ramp, her lightsaber still blazing.

LOURNA:
That was some jump.

KEEVE:
All in a day's work.

FX: Her lightsaber snaps off.

FX: *The ramp clangs shut. Blasterfire continues to hit the outside of the ship.*

TEY: (DISTORT/COMMS)
Hope you're all present and correct. We're out of here!

CUT TO:

SCENE 73. EXT. SPACE—CONTINUOUS.

FX: The Overtone *blasts away from the port.*

CUT TO:

SCENE 74. INT. THE *OVERTONE*—CONTINUOUS.

Atmos: The ship in flight.

AVAR:
That was close.

LOURNA:
No thanks to you.

Quin's legs buckle.

QUIN:
(GROANS)

FX: Keeve goes to catch her, but Lourna gets there first.

KEEVE:
Careful.

LOURNA:
I've got her. (TAKES STRAIN) Come on, Quin. Let's get you back to the bunk.

FX: They exit, leaving the two Jedi standing awkwardly until…

KEEVE:
Well. That was—

AVAR:
(QUIET) Don't, Keeve.

KEEVE:
We need to be better, Avar.

AVAR:
Than them?

KEEVE:
No. Than this.

CUT TO:

SCENE 75. EXT. HEIKLET. UPPER ATMOSPHERE.

FX: A monumental, planetwide storm. Rain is lashing and thunder rolling.

FX: The Gaze Electric *descends through the clouds.*

CUT TO:

SCENE 76. INT. THE *GAZE ELECTRIC*. FLIGHT DECK—CONTINUOUS.

Atmos: As before, the Gaze's *engines underpinning everything.*

FX: The rain lashes the hull, and we hear thunder rolling.

FX: The Leveler growls.

MARCHION:
Yes, my pet. Exhilarating, isn't it? Almost like home.

FX: Doors open. Sskeer and the baron are marched in by She'ar.

MARCHION: (CONT)
And here are our guests.

FX: Marchion rises from his chair.

MARCHION: (CONT)
Baron. Master Sskeer. I trust you have been made comfortable.

BOOLAN:
I would be a lot more comfortable without these restraints.

MARCHION:
Of course. Of course. My She'ar can be . . . overcautious at times. Keskar, release the baron.

KESKAR:
As you wish, my lord.

FX: *The sound of binders being released.*

BOOLAN:
Thank you.

FX: *Marchion takes a few steps toward Sskeer.*

MARCHION:
You'll forgive me if we keep *you* in binders, Sskeer. For the moment, at least.

SSKEER:
I get the feeling you'll do whatever you want.

MARCHION:
(SMILES) I see the rumors about you are true.

SSKEER:
Rumorsss?

MARCHION:
That you are . . . unperturbed in the presence of a Nameless.

FX: *The Leveler growls.*

MARCHION: (CONT)
A Jedi who has lost his connection to the Force. Fascinating, wouldn't you say, Baron?

BOOLAN:
A unique specimen.

FX: *Marchion takes another step toward Sskeer, standing almost nose to nose.*

MARCHION:
And I wonder what else you have lost along the way, Sskeer. And what you may yet gain.

SSKEER:
The Force is ssstrong.

MARCHION:
Indeed it is.

FX: *He walks away, turning to the viewport.*

MARCHION: (CONT)
As is the Storm, as you can see for yourself.

SSKEER:
What isss this place?

MARCHION:
Heiklet. A body in the Gosling [*GO-sling*] system. The entire planet has been beset by storms for millennia, a tempest that rages from pole to pole.

SSKEER:
Like Everon.

MARCHION:
You know of my homeworld. I am honored. Most are unaware of its existence, let alone the vortex storm that scattered my people across the galaxy. No one came to our aid—did you know that, Sskeer? Not a single Republic relief vessel. Not even the Jedi. We were left to fend for ourselves, despised by all we encountered.

But that is the past. Ancient past. This is about the future!

SHE'AR PILOT:
We are approaching the fortress, my lord.

MARCHION:
Excellent. Excellent.

BOOLAN:
Fortress?

MARCHION:
I daresay you are wondering why I've brought you here, Baron. Why I had Muglan steal you away from our enemies. And here it is.

FX: A swell of music as a huge castle appears beneath them.

SSKEER:
Sssurik's Blade!

MARCHION:
Impressive, is it not? Heiklet once supported life, long before the storms. This castle, perched atop its barren peak, is all that

remains of the Heikletians. Like the Evereni, no one came to their rescue. They were killed, an entire civilization washed away.

BOOLAN:
But the fortress survived.

MARCHION:
A fortress with a full laboratory.

BOOLAN:
I have laboratories. On Hetzal. On the asteroid.

MARCHION:
And there we have the problem, Baron. *Your* laboratories, for *your* work. I find myself growing tired of your distractions. Your delays. The Children of the Storm. Your ... experiments on the Nameless. You have a job to do, and here you will do it. Without interruption. Here, you will complete your cure for the blight.

BOOLAN:
The blight?

MARCHION:
I gave my word, Baron. To the galaxy. That we ... not the Republic ... not Chancellor Soh ... the *Nihil* will deliver them from the blight. It is all that matters.

SSKEER:
(CHUCKLES TO HIMSELF)

MARCHION:
You find something amusing, Master Sskeer?

SSKEER:
They are all ssso ssscared of you. The Eye of the Ssstorm. And yet you know nothing. Nothing at all.

MARCHION:
Then why don't you enlighten me?

SSKEER:
The cure for the blight already exists.

MARCHION:
Is this true?

BOOLAN:
Marchion...

SSKEER:
And it liesss in the hands of the Republic.

MARCHION:
(QUIET, DANGEROUS) What?

SSKEER:
You have already lossst.

FX: Marchion's lightsaber snaps on.

MARCHION:
Tell me this isn't so, Baron. Tell me you haven't betrayed me.

BOOLAN:
No. Of course I haven't. The data the Jedi stole from my records is incomplete. It won't work. *Can't* work. They think they have the victory, but they have nothing. Nothing. I would never betray you. I have always been faithful to you. For the Path. For the Storm!

MARCHION:
(CONTROLLING HIS TEMPER) For the Storm. (BEAT) Then you must begin again, here on Heiklet, under the watch of my droids and my She'ar. I meant what I said, Boolan. No more distractions. Do you understand?

BOOLAN:
Yes, Marchion. The work shall be completed.

MARCHION:
And as for you, Sskeer.

FX: Marchion walks toward him slowly, lightsaber thrumming.

MARCHION: (CONT)
On your knees.

BOOLAN:
Marchion.

MARCHION:
The Leveler has its place. All those bodies. All those husks. But I miss the satisfaction of ending a Jedi's life with my own hands.

FX: The lightsaber buzzes.

MARCHION: (CONT)
On your knees!

BOOLAN:
Marchion, no! Please!

FX: Boolan steps in front of Marchion.

MARCHION:
Stand aside, Boolan.

BOOLAN:
If I am to perfect my solution to the blight, I'll need test subjects. Sskeer is healthy. Strong. He will be useful. Unless you are willing to sacrifice one of the She'ar. Keskar, maybe?

SSKEER:
I'll never help you.

BOOLAN:
You won't have a choice, *Jedi.*

SSKEER:
There is alwaysss a choice! The Force is ssstrong!

FX: Sskeer breaks his binders.

SSKEER: (CONT)
(ROARS IN FURY)

FX: Marchion's lightsaber flashes.

SSKEER: (CONT)
(CRIES OUT IN PAIN)

BOOLAN:
Marchion! What did I say? I need him in one piece! One piece!

FX: Sskeer goes down on his knees, breathing hard.

MARCHION:
He is Trandoshan. He will regenerate.

FX: Marchion brings the lightsaber around to the baron.

MARCHION: (CONT)
This is your final warning, Baron. I need results.

BOOLAN:
And you will have them, my lord.

FX: Marchion glares at him for a minute before snapping off the blade.

He turns to his pilot.

MARCHION:
Take us down.

FX: The engines rumble as they descend.

CUT TO:

SCENE 77. EXT. LANJER. JUNGLE—DAY.

Atmos: A tropical planet. Frogs are chirping, birds squawking, insects buzzing.

FX: Keeve slaps a bug on her neck.

KEEVE:
(SUCKS IN BREATH)

LOURNA:
And I thought all life was sacred to a Jedi. Even the mosquitoes.

KEEVE:
There's enough of them.

LOURNA:
So one less doesn't matter?

KEEVE:
You *know* that's not what I mean.

TEY:
And we're sure this is where Muglan should be?

LOURNA:
Straan said she would be heading home.

AVAR:
So he could have meant Gloon, their homeworld.

LOURNA:
He said their "base," not "Gloon." Neither of them has set foot on that gloopfest for years.

QUIN:
Like you'd know.

LOURNA:
(SIGHS) You should be on the ship.

QUIN:
I'm still on the clock.

TEY:
Can see why they picked Lanjer, though. Hot and humid. Thick jungle.

FX: The buzz of another mosquito followed by a tiny bite.

KEEVE:
(THROUGH GRITTED TEETH) Plenty of bugs.

TEY:
Home away from home for a Gloovan.

AVAR:
And yet they're not here.

LOURNA:
We don't know that.

AVAR:
Then where's their ship? Where's this fabled camp?

LOURNA:
You could light your pretty sword, if you like? Start hacking down trees for a better look?

KEEVE:
That's enough!

TEY:
Skoot, how's about you make a few sweeps? See if you can spot anything from the air.

SK-0T:
Zep-zep.

FX: SK-0T flies up into the trees.

KEEVE:
I suppose we should at least consider the possibility that this is a dead end. No matter what Lourna's . . . informant told her.

LOURNA:
He had no reason to lie.

AVAR:
You were torturing him.

LOURNA:
And you threatened to chop him into little pieces.

KEEVE:
You did what?

AVAR:
There's nothing here.

QUIN:
Blondie does have a point.

FX: Tey's comm starts beeping.

TEY:
Maybe not.

FX: Tey answers the call.

TEY: (CONT)
What you got for us, buddy?

SK-0T: (COMMS)
Zet-zet!

TEY:
A ship?

LOURNA:
A ship? Where?

FX: A sudden roar of engines in the sky, followed by laserfire.

KEEVE:
Up there.

QUIN:
It doesn't sound alone.

TEY:
Show us, Skoot.

FX: A holo activates.

KEEVE:
That's Muglan's ship.

TEY:
And it's under attack.

AVAR:
By Nihil!

CUT TO:

SCENE 78. INT. MUGLAN'S SHIP. COCKPIT—CONTINUOUS.

Atmos: The ship is in flight and under fire.

FX: An explosion shakes the craft.

MUGLAN:
(REACTS) I thought you said we could lose them.

RENGA:
I thought we could. But, Captain, that's one of Ro's elite.

MUGLAN:
So were we!

RENGA:
Yeah. And then we went with Lourna.

FX: Another hit.

MUGLAN:
For Storm's sake.

FX: Muglan opens a comm.

MUGLAN: (CONT)
Gabb, what are you playing at? You're in the turret. Shoot back.

RENGA:
Yeah. Don't think that's gonna happen.

MUGLAN:
What do you mean?

RENGA:
That last explosion? That *was* the turret.

FX: Another hit.

MUGLAN:
We had a deal. We had a deal and he sent one of his freaks to kill us. Nothing ever changes. Always the same.

FX: Muglan gets up and runs from the cockpit.

RENGA:
Where are you going?

MUGLAN:
(CALLING BACK) Rear guns. Try to put space between us.

RENGA:
How?

CUT TO:

SCENE 79. INT. MUGLAN'S SHIP. REAR GUNS—CONTINUOUS.

Atmos: As before.

FX: Muglan comes clattering down the passage to the cannon.

FX: There's another explosion. Muglan is thrown against a wall.

MUGLAN:
(REACTS)

RENGA: (DISTORT/COMMS)
We've lost the starboard thruster. Captain? Muglan? Can you hear me?

MUGLAN:
I hear you.

FX: Muglan drops into the cannon seat and brings the gimbal around.

FX: Lasers zip by outside.

MUGLAN: (CONT)
I'm at the cannon. Hold her steady.

RENGA: (DISTORT/COMMS)
If I do that, we're dead.

MUGLAN:
We're dead anyway.

FX: A targeting computer tries to lock on. Muglan fires a series of bolts.

MUGLAN: (CONT)
(NYAHH!)

The bolts miss.

MUGLAN: (CONT)
Damn it! Missed!

FX: She shoots again.

MUGLAN: (CONT)
Targeting computer's shot. Keep us level, Renga.

FX: Another explosion. The ship shakes.

MUGLAN: (CONT)
Renga!

RENGA: (DISTORT/COMMS)
The stabilizers have gone. The ship's not respon—

FX: Lasers hit. A deadly hit.

RENGA: (CONT, DISTORT/COMMS)
(SCREAMS, ABRUPTLY CUT OFF AS THE COMM FAILS)

MUGLAN:
Renga? *Anyone?*

FX: Another explosion, and then the ship starts to fall.

CUT TO:

SCENE 80. EXT. LANJER. JUNGLE—CONTINUOUS.

Atmos: As before.

FX: A ship is coming down from above, out of control.

QUIN:
They're coming down.

LOURNA:
Can you two stop them?

KEEVE:
Stop them from what? *Crashing?*

FX: Lourna is running in the direction of the inevitable crash.

LOURNA:
This way! Hurry!

FX: The others follow.

KEEVE:
(RUNNING) I'm not sure what you think we're going to do.

QUIN:
(RUNNING) Save lives? Isn't that your thing?

FX: Tey runs in the other direction, opening his comlink.

TEY:
Skoot! Meet me at the *Overtone*.

AVAR:
Tey?

TEY:
(CALLING BACK) You help Muglan. I'm going to try to stop that Nihil.

AVAR:
(TO HERSELF) Light preserve us.

CUT TO:

SCENE 81. INT. SHE'AR FIGHTER—CONTINUOUS.

Atmos: The closed canopy of the She'ar fighter. We hear the distinctive sound of the She'ar fighter from within. Outside, we catch the tail of Muglan's ship going down.

FX: Vulax brings their ship around.

VULAX:
Vulax to Ro. Target eliminated. *Tk-tk-tk-tk.* Am returning to the *Gaze*.

FX: Lasers blast toward the She'ar fighter. Vulax only just manages to avoid them.

VULAX: (CONT)
What in the Eye's name?

FX: The Overtone *is coming in fast from below.*

TEY: (DISTORT/COMMS)
Aw. You're not leaving already? Hoped you'd hang around for a bit. Maybe grab a drink? Have a natter? What do you say?

VULAX:
I'd say you've picked the wrong fight. *Tk-tk-tk-tk.*

FX: The She'ar fighter comes about and fires on the Overtone.

CUT TO:

SCENE 82. INT. THE *OVERTONE.* COCKPIT—CONTINUOUS.

Atmos: The battle continues from Tey's point of view. The Overtone *is in flight.*

FX: An explosion as the She'ar's lasers glance off the hull.

SK-OT:
Zep-zep-*zep*!

TEY:
I *know* they're firing at us, Skoot. What did you think they were going to do? Well, go on. Fire back!

SK-OT:
Zet?

TEY:
Yes, you! Come on. We've been in worse scrapes than this!

FX: We hear the scream of the She'ar fighter and more laserfire.

TEY: (CONT)
Probably!

FX: We stay with the battle for a couple of beats before:

CUT TO:

SCENE 83. EXT. LANJER. JUNGLE—CONTINUOUS.

FX: Muglan's ship is still in its dive.

FX: Lourna, Avar, and Keeve come running. Quin trails behind.

QUIN: (OFF MIC)
(OUT OF BREATH) Lourna. It's no good. We won't be able to stop it.

LOURNA:
(RUNNING) Is she right? Is there nothing you can do?

KEEVE:
No. I mean . . . (TO AVAR) Is there?

LOURNA:
At least *try*.

AVAR:
There is no try. Keeve, those trees.

KEEVE:
You're kidding.

AVAR:
With me.

FX: The Jedi stop and raise their hands.

AVAR: (CONT)
The Force is with us.

AVAR & KEEVE TOGETHER:
The Force is with us!

FX: We hear the thrum of the Force, and the ship's trajectory changes slightly. It plows into the trees, which cushion its descent somewhat but not enough.

QUIN:
(OUT OF BREATH) You changed its direction.

LOURNA:
Giving it a soft landing. Well, soft*er*. Not bad.

QUIN:
Not bad? By the stars, it's . . . it's incredible!

FX: The ship crashes through the trees, splintering wood and tearing metal.

AVAR:
Not by the stars, Quin. By the Force.

CUT TO:

**SCENE 84. INT. THE *OVERTONE*. COCKPIT—
CONTINUOUS.**

Atmos: As before. We hear the scream of the She'ar fighter coming in fast. The two ships pass, lasers blasting past with them.

SK-0T:
Zep-zep-zet!

TEY:
No, I don't know how much longer we can last, either. Whoever they are, they're better than your average gashead.

VULAX: (DISTORT/COMMS)
You say the nicest things. *Tk-tk-tk-tk.*

TEY:
Oh, shut your face.

FX: The Overtone *fires.*

SK-0T:
Zet-*zet*!

TEY:
I know I said you were in charge of weapons, but he's really starting to get on my wick.

FX: More lasers from the Overtone, *followed by an explosion somewhere in the back.*

TEY: (CONT)
What the hell? Were we hit?

SK-0T:
Zep-zep-zep?

TEY:
The *what* has overloaded? Static charge compensators? Now that's just embarrassing. Just you wait until I see Greyamina. Fobbing us with this piece of s—

FX: Another explosion covers Tey's expletive.

FX: The She'ar fighter streaks away.

SK-0T:
Zep-zut!

TEY:
I can see he's getting away ... but there's ... gah! There's not a lot I can do!

VULAX: (COMMS)
For the Eye!

TEY:
Aw, stick it up your exhaust port.

CUT TO:

SCENE 85. INT. MUGLAN'S SHIP—SOON AFTER.

Atmos: The ship is on the ground, wrecked, fires raging, sparks falling. The engines are silent.

FX: A lightsaber slices into the hull and cuts a new door. Then we hear the thrum of the Force and the metal is thrown aside.

LOURNA:
(COUGHING ON SMOKE) What a mess.

AVAR:
It would've been worse.

LOURNA:
Finished patting yourself on the back? Swing that saber over here. Let me see.

KEEVE:
Let me.

FX: Keeve ignites her lightsaber.

LOURNA:
(HISSES)

QUIN:
Are they—

AVAR:
Dead.

MUGLAN: (OFF MIC)
(COUGHS WETLY)

LOURNA:
Not everyone. Trennis, over here. That bulkhead.

KEEVE:
(EFFORT)

FX: The thrum of the Force and the creak of the heavy metal being shifted.

QUIN:
Muglan.

KEEVE:
(BREATHES OUT)

FX: The metal crashes to the side.

FX: Quin drops down beside Muglan.

MUGLAN:
(WEAK, DYING) Quin?

QUIN:
Surprise.

MUGLAN:
What . . . what are you . . . (COUGHS)

QUIN:
Would you believe I'm here to collect your bounty?

MUGLAN:
Atta girl. Is the reward much?

QUIN:
I've seen bigger.

MUGLAN:
Figures. (WINCES IN PAIN)

AVAR:
Let me see her.

QUIN:
Can you help?

AVAR:
We're not miracle workers.

KEEVE:
Avar.

AVAR:
Her injuries are too severe. Even for a Gloovan.

QUIN:
Take more than a juvan wrap, huh?

MUGLAN:
(TO KEEVE) You. You're the Jedi. You were with . . .

FX: Lourna steps forward.

LOURNA:
Where did you take Boolan, Muglan?

MUGLAN:
(SIGHS) Lourna crikking Dee.

LOURNA:
The *baron,* Muglan. And the Trandoshan, too.

MUGLAN:
(COUGHS) Client confidentiality. Integrity's a wonderful thing . . . You should . . . (WHEEZES) try it sometime.

LOURNA:
And you need to stop being so damned stubborn. You're done, Muglan. Dead and buried.

QUIN:
Lourna!

LOURNA:
It's true, isn't it? Even if we could get her to a surgeon, there's not enough cybernetics in the galaxy to stitch all that together.

KEEVE:
Never become a nurse, Lourna. Not with a bedside manner like that.

Lourna gets down beside Muglan.

LOURNA:
Just tell me, Mug. Tell me where you took them. One of Ro's enemies? Is that why the Nihil shot you down? Revenge? Who was it, Muglan? Where did you take them?

MUGLAN:
(WEAKER THAN EVER) Closer. Can't... You need... to get closer.

LOURNA:
I'm here, Muglan. Tell me.

MUGLAN:
(A RATTLING BREATH) Go... go to hell... (DIES)

LOURNA:
(QUIET) Damn you.

FX: Lourna slams her metal hand down onto the floor.

LOURNA: (CONT)
Damn you!

AVAR:
She's gone.

LOURNA:
You think?

KEEVE:
That can't be it. There must be a way to find out.

QUIN:
There is.

FX: Quin gets up and heads deeper into the ship.

AVAR:
Where are you going?

LOURNA:
(REALIZING) The computer core.

CUT TO:

SCENE 86. INT. MUGLAN'S SHIP. COMPUTER CORE.

Atmos: As before, although there's not so much on fire here.

FX: Computer keys are pressed. Weak beeps and bloops. Quin keeps working beneath the following, typing and flicking switches.

QUIN:
(COUGHS)

LOURNA: (COMING UP ON MIC)
Quin?

QUIN:
Hard to work with all this smoke.

KEEVE:
And that's what's left of the computer?

LOURNA:
Looks that way.

AVAR:
You'll never get anything out of it.

LOURNA:
Don't underestimate her.

QUIN:
Junkie or not, I'm still a slicer.

LOURNA:
The best I ever had.

FX: The bulkhead creaks behind them, and both Jedi turn with their lightsabers.

TEY:
Whoa, whoa, whoa. Easy with those things. It's me. It's me.

KEEVE:
Tey, what happened with the Nihil?

TEY:
Got away. Skoot's fixing the damage.

AVAR:
How much damage?

FX: More tapping from Quin in the background.

TEY:
Nothing the little guy can't handle. Although he'll be sorry he missed this. That's some pretty nimble finger work right there, Quin old girl.

QUIN:
There's something here. Just need to—

FX: The computer boops, and a screen fizzes on.

QUIN: (CONT)
And there you have it.

LOURNA:
Let me see.

A beat as she scans the screen.

LOURNA: (CONT)
(UNDER HER BREATH) No.

KEEVE:
What is it?

QUIN:
The last instruction received from Muglan's "employer."

AVAR:
Rendezvous with the *Gaze Electric*!

LOURNA:
Ro!

KEEVE:
Marchion Ro. But that makes zero sense. Boolan was ... *is* Ro's minister of advancement. Why engage pirates to take him from us? Why not send in a swarm of Cloudships? Why not do it himself?

QUIN:
Dirty his hands? Not the Eye's style.

LOURNA:
He didn't want anyone to know he was behind this. Not the Republic.

AVAR:
Not even his own people.

KEEVE:
But why not?

QUIN:
Only the Eye knows.

LOURNA:
Same as always.

KEEVE:
But if Muglan was working for Ro—

AVAR:
Why did the Nihil shoot her down?

TEY:
And not just any Nihil. I caught a glimpse of the pilot, a Harch by the look of things, and unless my old eyes were deceiving me, one that was dressed head to toe in the getup of the She'ar.

QUIN:
Ro's elite guard.

KEEVE:
So Muglan, what . . . ? Double-crossed Ro?

LOURNA:
Somehow I doubt it.

AVAR:
Ro double-crossed her?

LOURNA:
Covering his tracks. Sacrificing his pawns. Same as always.

FX: Lourna slams the wall.

LOURNA: (CONT)
Nothing changes. No matter what we do.

FX: She storms out.

LOURNA: (CONT, GOING OFF MIC)
Nothing ever changes.

QUIN:
Lourna.

CUT TO:

SCENE 87. INT. HEIKLET. CASTLE LAB.

Atmos: Rain lashes against tall windows, the gale raging as lightning flashes and thunder cracks. A cold wind rushes through the castle's corridors, the storm ever present.

FX: Restraints creak. Sskeer is on an operating slab, bound tight but continually trying to break free.

BOOLAN:
Hold still.

SSKEER:
Why would I make it easssier for you?

KESKAR: (OFF MIC)
Do you require assistance?

BOOLAN:
I require peace and quiet. I require uninterrupted work. Wait outside.

KESKAR: (OFF MIC)
Marchion told me—

BOOLAN:
Marchion told you to watch my every move, but you have cams for that. Not to mention that accursed droid you've posted at the door. Your presence is . . . distracting.

KESKAR: (OFF MIC)
I have my orders.

BOOLAN:
Which you must obey, of course. (TO HIMSELF) Which we must *all* obey.

FX: The hiss of an injector gun.

SSKEER:
(REACTS)

BOOLAN:
It will be easier on you if you don't struggle.

FX: He puts the injector down on a medical table.

BOOLAN: (CONT)
(TO THE SHE'AR) Keskar, I apologize for my outburst. The work is... taxing. I need to concentrate, that is all. For the good of the Storm.

FX: Thunder crashes outside.

KESKAR:
I will... give you room. But the cams will be watching.

BOOLAN:
Of course. Thank you.

KESKAR:
For the Storm.

FX: The creak of a wooden door opening and then closing as he leaves.

BOOLAN:
Good. Better.

FX: His implements whir.

BOOLAN: (CONT)
(TO SSKEER) How are you feeling?

SSKEER:
Does it matter? I am a mere test sssubject, after all.

FX: Bleeps as Boolan checks Sskeer's monitors.

BOOLAN:
The regenerative process is already under way. Your stats are good. Heart rate slightly elevated.

SSKEER:
Is that any sssurprise?

FX: Another clap of thunder. Boolan's Nameless react with a hiss.

BOOLAN:
Tell me, does the presence of my Nameless disturb you?

SSKEER:
One is missing a head.

BOOLAN:
But can you feel their presence? Their effect on the Force?

SSKEER:
It will be fine as long as you keep them in their cage.

BOOLAN:
Hm. (BEAT) Another injection, then.

SSKEER:
Why?

FX: Boolan picks up the device and delivers the shot.

SSKEER: (CONT)
(REACTS) How is this helping with your work on the blight?

FX: More bleeps as Boolan monitors Sskeer's condition.

BOOLAN:
I've always been fascinated with the life of a Jedi. Taken at such a young age from your families. Your people.

SSKEER:
The Jedi are my people.

BOOLAN:
And yet you are Trandoshan. And afflicted by a disease unique to your species. A disease that reduces your ability to manipulate the Force. Do you remember much about your childhood? On Dosh, I mean, before the Jedi came for you.

SSKEER:
(SHOWS SIGNS OF DISCOMFORT) Very little.

BOOLAN:
My own childhood was traumatic. My father was . . . a troubled individual. Brilliant, a scientist like myself, but one who never found a place to call home, to belong. I loved him, of course, loved him dearly. I was his only child. We went everywhere together.

FX: A clank of equipment.

BOOLAN: (CONT)
Do you remember your parents, Sskeer?

SSKEER:
No.

BOOLAN:
I went with him gladly, of course, my father. Would have followed him to the ends of the cosmos. But instead, we went to Dalna. To the Path of the Open Hand. Some called them a cult. Terrorists even. But they were more than that. They were home. They gave us purpose, a crusade. A crusade that killed him.

SSKEER:
(GASPS, HIS BREATH BECOMING RAGGED)

BOOLAN:
They called it the Night of Sorrow. There was a flood. The Jedi were there. The Nameless, too. So many people died. Washed away.

SSKEER:
(SHAKY) Boolan . . .

BOOLAN:
I stayed, after the evacuation, after the Jedi cleaned up their mess. What choice did I have? I was little more than a child and my father was long gone, killed on a mission to find more Force Eaters.

FX: One of the Nameless trills.

BOOLAN: (CONT)
Our secret weapon. (BEAT) They died, too. All except one. The Leveler. I hid in the caverns beneath the compound, in my father's laboratory. Hid and studied. Long nights in the darkness, scavenging for what food I could. There was so much to do. So much to understand. The Mother, our leader, she left artifacts, you see, treasures gathered by her followers. I pored over them, desperate to learn their secrets, venturing back up to the surface only when my curiosity was exhausted. My work was too important, you see, to hide away in the shadows. I needed to step into the light, to free the Force of its chains.

SSKEER:
Boolan, please.

BOOLAN:
You're feeling it now, aren't you?

FX: He places a hand over Sskeer's heart.

BOOLAN: (CONT)
Here, in your chest. The panic. The fear.

SSKEER:
What was in that injection? What did you give me?

FX: Boolan walks away, heading for the Nameless. The cybernetic Nameless whines.

BOOLAN:
What was that you said about keeping them in their cages?

FX: He opens the cages.

SSKEER:
No. Don't.

BOOLAN:
Out you come.

FX: The Nameless pad out.

SSKEER:
Boolan, pleassse.

BOOLAN:
Approach the Jedi.

FX: The Nameless obey.

SSKEER:
(ACTUALLY SOUNDING SCARED) Keep them away. Keep them away.

BOOLAN:
Stop.

FX: The Nameless stop.

FX: Boolan walks back to Sskeer.

BOOLAN: (CONT)
When Marchion found me, rotting in a Republic cell, he recognized my anger. Saw how he could manipulate me. He told me that the Jedi were responsible for my father's death, for the destruction on Dalna. Persuaded me to experiment on his creatures, to twist them into weapons. Look what I did to them, Sskeer. How I abused them.

SSKEER:
(FRIGHTENED BREATHING)

BOOLAN:
I've wandered so far from the Path. Creating monsters, monsters who abuse the Force in ways unimaginable to that child hiding in his father's laboratory. Ways far worse than the Jedi. (TO THE NAMELESS) Come closer.

FX: The Nameless growl and approach.

SSKEER:
(SCARED) No.

BOOLAN:
What's the matter, Sskeer? They can't hurt you. Not really. Not like they hurt the others, feeding on the Force. You have lost your connection.

SSKEER:
(GASPS, REALIZATION DAWNING) I feel them. I feel their effect.

BOOLAN:
Their effect on a *Jedi*. (TO THE NAMELESS) Back in your cage.

FX: The Nameless complain.

BOOLAN: (CONT)
(STERNER) In your cage!

FX: They lope back and curl up in their cages.

BOOLAN: (CONT)
(TO SSKEER) Better?

SSKEER:
(STILL SHAKEN) Yes. But . . . I don't underssstand.

BOOLAN:
I promised to cure your condition. Marchion called it a distraction. But we have a long way to go.

SSKEER:
But why? Why help me? After all you said . . .

BOOLAN:
About the Jedi? (BEAT) I had such plans, Sskeer. Plans forged in the tunnels of Dalna. I was going to do what none of them could—Marda Ro, the Herald, even the Mother herself. I was going to free the Force once and for all. And look at what I've become, where I've ended up. My laboratory, a prison. My assistants, guards.

FX: He draws close to Sskeer.

BOOLAN: (CONT)
What if I have been wrong all these years? What if the *Path* was wrong? I wish I could go back. To see him again.

SSKEER:
Your father.

BOOLAN:
To talk to him. Father always knew what to do, for all his faults. (BEAT, AND THEN, LOUDER, MAKES HIMSELF BUSY) But the work must continue. The blight must be stopped. And we will stop it together, Sskeer. Our childhoods were stolen from us, you and me, but our future will be secured. A future when we change everything!

MUSICAL SEGUE:

SCENE 88. EXT. LANJER. JUNGLE. OUTSIDE THE OVERTONE—NIGHT.

Atmos: Night has fallen on the jungle. Crickets chirp. Simians howl in the distance. A grave is being filled.

QUIN: (OFF MIC)
Lourna?

FX: More soil is patted down.

QUIN: (CONT, COMING UP ON MIC)
Lourna, what are you—oh.

LOURNA:
(SNIFFS) Gloovans prefer to be buried. I don't know about the rest of her crew. Not enough left to identify the species.

QUIN:
You didn't have to.

LOURNA:
No one else was going to do it.

FX: Lourna throws the shovel down.

QUIN:
Should we . . . should we say something?

LOURNA:
Muglan said it all. (QUIET) Go to hell.

FX: A moment of silence between them. The sounds of the jungle fill the void.

QUIN:
She took it badly. When you . . .

LOURNA:
When I abandoned you.

QUIN:
When you left us behind. She would've followed you into a supernova—you know that, don't you? After the *Restitution*? After Hest. You gave her something to believe in. (QUIETER) And she wasn't the only one.

LOURNA:
I . . . did what I thought was best. For all of us.

QUIN:
Don't do that. Don't lie. It wasn't about us. It never was.

LOURNA:
That's not true.

QUIN:
They warned me, you know, the other members of the Tempest. Said I was being a fool, that I shouldn't trust you. *Couldn't* trust you. Not like that. Not how we were. Even Muglan told me to be careful. She worshipped the ground you walked on, but she knew in her heart of hearts what you would do when the poodoo hit the fan. And she was right. She was right, and I was wrong. I just thought . . . I just thought that it was different. That *we* were different. That it wasn't just Lourna Dee anymore. That it was the two of us.

LOURNA:
It was.

QUIN:
And there you go again. You can't help yourself.

LOURNA:
What do you want me to say? What do you want me to do? I can't change who I am. Who I've always been.

QUIN:
But that's just it, isn't it, Lourna? There was one night, after the raid on Ferrix—you were so happy, so energized. We lay in our bunk, and you talked for hours about all these adventures you'd had, long before the Nihil. About being a mercenary, a cadet. Even a princess.

LOURNA:
I was *never* a princess.

QUIN:
But you were all those things. All those things and more. Some you chose for yourself, some were thrust upon you, but I could tell, lying there in the dark, that you owned them all, those different parts of you—the woman you had become, the woman I held on to, the woman I loved. I thought it was always going to be that way. Not the Tempest or even the Nihil. But us. You and me. That the Lourna you were then, in that moment, was the Lourna you wanted to be. The Lourna that would hold me every night of my life. The Lourna who loved me back.

LOURNA:
(SOFTLY) Quin.

FX: Quin takes a step closer.

QUIN:
She's still in there, you know. Beneath the masks and the scowl. (SMILES) Even the teeth. I can see her in your eyes.

FX: And another.

QUIN: (CONT)
And I should run. I should get off this planet and never look back again. Because I'm not sure I could cope with being proved wrong again. It could break me like it broke me before. Worse, even. I don't know if there would be any coming back. But something in me, deep in my chest, thinks it's worth the risk. Here.

FX: She grabs Lourna's hand and puts it to her chest.

QUIN: (CONT)
Can you feel it, Lourna? In my heart. Maybe in yours, too.

LOURNA:
(QUIET, INTIMATE) Quin. I'm . . . sorry.

Their heads are close together, their lips close.

QUIN:
(BARELY A WHISPER) It's okay. It's all okay, Lourna.

Quin moves in for the kiss . . . but Lourna jerks away.

LOURNA:
No! Quin, don't.

QUIN:
Don't? Why not?

LOURNA:
Because . . . because I can hear him. In my head. I can hear his voice.

QUIN:
What? (REALIZING) Are you talking about *Ro*?

LOURNA:
I can hear him lying to her, to Muglan, like he lied to me. To all of us, over and over again. This is his doing, Quin. This grave. You and me. It's on him. And whatever you think of me . . . whatever Muglan thought at the end . . . I did do it for us. We had to get away from him. From his games. His crusade. I knew that the moment I saw Starlight fall. If we didn't, if we stayed, we would've ended up like all the others. You know that, don't you? We would've ended up like Kassav. Like Pan.

QUIN:
You killed Pan.

LOURNA:
Yes. For him. For Ro. *Because* of Ro. I thought we could get away from him, but we can't. Not while he's alive. Not while he still has breath in his body.

FX: Quin takes a step back.

QUIN:
I don't believe you. I really don't believe you.

LOURNA:
It's been him every step of the way. This is what he's done to me. To us. What he's made us. And it stops here.

FX: Sudden footsteps behind them.

TEY:
Funny you should say that.

FX: Lourna spins around.

LOURNA:
What the—Sirrek, you *have* to stop doing that! (SEEING WHO ELSE IS THERE) And you're not alone. Of course. The gang's all here.

KEEVE:
Sorry. We didn't mean to eavesdrop.

QUIN:
(ICY) It's fine. We were done anyway.

AVAR:
Skoot's found something on the Nihil comm network.

TEY:
Found some*one*.

LOURNA:
Ro?

KEEVE:
The planet Waskiro is holding a gala.

TEY:
In honor of their Nihil overlords.

AVAR:
In particular, the Eye of the Storm.

QUIN:
And he's going? Marchion Ro is going to a ball?

LOURNA:
Of course he is. It will all be about him.

TEY:
The question is, what do we do about it?

LOURNA:
I assumed that would be obvious. Tell me, Marshal, how do you look in a ball gown? Ravishing, I'd suspect.

KEEVE:
A ball gown? (THE PENNY DROPS) Oh no. No, no, no, no, no. We are *not* going to the ball. Avar, we discussed this. We track his movements from Waskiro, keeping our distance. Find out where he's taken Boolan. Where he's taken Sskeer. Avar . . . tell her. Tell her we are not going to face Marchion Ro. (WHEN THERE'S NO RESPONSE) Avar!

LOURNA:
What's the matter, Trennis? Don't know how to dance?

CUT TO:

Part Six
DANCE OF DEATH

SCENE 89. INT. STAR CRUISER—NOW.

Atmos: As before.

RHIL:
You must have thought all your birthdays had come at once.

LOURNA:
Why's that, Rhil?

RHIL:
Your chance to get near Marchion Ro.

LOURNA:
I would've been happy if I never saw him again.

FX: Rhil leaves a beat of silence. The only sound is the buzz of the cam droid.

LOURNA: (CONT)
I know what you want me to say. That this was my opportunity to face the man who had ruined my life, who had used me when it suited him, only to throw me aside when I had played my part in his "dastardly plan."

RHIL:
The thought had crossed my mind, as I'm sure it had crossed yours.

LOURNA:
To strike at the Eye of the Storm in the middle of his territory? To wipe that smug, overconfident smile from his face once and for all. (BEAT) Never occurred to me in the slightest. Besides... I had Trennis watching my every move.

RHIL:
Surely you would've been a hero. To strike down the Republic's ogre in his time of triumph?

LOURNA:
Or make a martyr of him. That was the Jedi's fear, and the Republic's, too. Ro had positioned himself as the savior of the galaxy, and there was a chance, however minuscule, that he would be as good as his word.

RHIL:
Providing a solution to the blight.

LOURNA:
Ro, the great redeemer. No one was allowed to touch him. Not Kriss, not Trennis...

RHIL:
Not you?

LOURNA:
Not while I wore my tracker.

RHIL:
Or while you wanted a pardon. You had to play by the rules. Maybe for the first time.

LOURNA:
(LAUGHS WRYLY) When you put it like that, maybe I can see why Trennis was so anxious.

CUT TO:

SCENE 90. INT. WASKIRO. PALACE OF JADALLA—THEN.

Atmos: A grand ball. Refined. Elegant. Sophisticated. Music plays in the background. People are milling around, talking and laughing.

WAITER DROID:
A drink, madam?

LOURNA:
Don't mind if I do.

FX: A glass is removed from a silver tray.

LOURNA: (CONT)
Thank you.

WAITER DROID:
Of course. The Royal House of Jadalla welcomes you to Waskiro. Enjoy the festivities.

FX: The droid whirs off.

LOURNA:
I intend to. (TAKES SIP) Not bad. Not bad at all.

KEEVE: (DISTORT/COMMS)
Just take it easy on the wine, Lourna. We're supposed to blend in, not get blended ourselves.

LOURNA:
Relax, Keeve. I know what I'm doing. (TO HERSELF) More than you, I bet.

KEEVE: (DISTORT/COMMS)
What was that?

LOURNA:
Just saying hello to the Ramsirian ambassador.

FX: Quin approaches.

QUIN:
Is that right?

LOURNA:
Quin, I . . . You look . . .

QUIN:
Emaciated?

LOURNA:
(GENUINE) Stunning. Absolutely stunning.

QUIN:
Thanks. Don't scrub up bad, eh?

TEY: (DISTORT/COMMS)
None of us do, even if I do say so myself.

AVAR: (DISTORT/COMMS)
I don't even want to know where you rustled up these gowns.

KEEVE: (DISTORT/COMMS)
These very *tight* gowns.

AVAR: (DISTORT/COMMS)
But you did good, Tey.

LOURNA:
I'd say.

QUIN:
Lourna.

KEEVE: (DISTORT/COMMS)
If we could keep the flirting to a bare minimum, please.

TEY: (DISTORT/COMMS)
Spoilsport.

LOURNA:
We weren't flirting.

KEEVE: (DISTORT/COMMS)
Good, because we're here to find someone close to the Eye who can tell us what happened to Sskeer and Boolan. And that's all.

LOURNA:
Yes, yes, we get it. No direct contact with Ro himself. We keep ourselves out of sight. Blend in.

WAITER DROID: (OFF MIC)
A drink, madam.

AVAR: (OFF MIC)
No, thank you.

QUIN:
(AWESTRUCK) That's going to be easier for some more than others.

LOURNA:
(REALIZES WHERE QUIN IS LOOKING AND SIGHS) Don't mind Quin. She just got a little distracted, that's all.

KEEVE: (DISTORT/COMMS)
We cannot afford to get distracted.

LOURNA:
(ICY) Then maybe Sirrek should have provided Marshal Kriss with a different dress.

AVAR: (DISTORT/COMMS)
(GENUINE) Is there something wrong with it?

QUIN:
Not in the slightest. (REALIZING LOURNA IS GLARING AT HER) I mean, you look . . . er . . . you look . . .

LOURNA:
(TO QUIN, POINTED) No direct contact. Remember?

TEY: (DISTORT/COMMS)
Oh, tonight is going to be *fun*!

KEEVE: (DISTORT/COMMS)
And it's just getting started. Heads up.

FX: There is a fanfare from the musicians. The crowd hushes.

MASTER OF CEREMONIES: (OFF MIC)
Friends, delegates, and esteemed representatives. Please welcome the Royal House of Jadalla's guest of honor: Marchion Ro, Eye of the Storm and supreme commander of the Nihil Union.

FX: Another fanfare as doors open and Marchion enters, accompanied by the Leveler on a chain. The crowd applauds.

LOURNA:
(SCATHING) "Nihil Union"...

TEY: (DISTORT/COMMS)
You have to give it to him—he knows how to make an entrance.

QUIN:
And he's brought company...

FX: The Leveler trills with its trademark "Riiiiiiii."

FX: Avar takes a sudden sharp breath. The proximity to the Leveler is uncomfortable for her and Keeve. The effect is there in the background throughout the scene—an uncomfortable, unsettled feeling for them.

Performance note for actors: Again, the Jedi and Tey would find this an uncomfortable experience throughout. Think of it as feeling groggy and strained in the Nameless's presence.

AVAR: (DISTORT/COMMS)
(GROGGY) The Leveler.

KEEVE: (DISTORT/COMMS)
(GROGGY) That's a complication we didn't account for.

LOURNA:
Then you deserve everything you get. Of *course* he would bring a Nameless. Lina Soh has her targons. He has the Leveler.

FX: The Leveler growls as the applause fades away.

MARCHION: (OFF MIC)
Please, please. On behalf of the Nihil and myself, I thank you for such a warm and lavish welcome. You honor us, one and all.

MASTER OF CEREMONIES: (OFF MIC)
May I introduce His Majesty, King Sokidharan of the Royal House of Jadalla.

KING SOKIDHARAN: (OFF MIC)
It is the Waskirons who are honored, great Eye, both by your presence and your protection.

KEEVE: (DISTORT/COMMS)
(GROGGY) Protection? Seriously? They can't believe that, surely?

LOURNA:
They know what would happen if they resisted. All this—the pomp, the ceremony—it's all just a protection racket. The king gets to pretend he made a choice, but it's intimidation on a galactic scale. Ro really has outdone himself this time.

KING SOKIDHARAN: (OFF MIC)
Waskiro is yours, sir. Yours and the Union's. For tonight and evermore.

MARCHION: (OFF MIC)
Yes, and the . . . the Union is . . . grateful for your hospitality, our loyal and faithful subjects.

LOURNA:
Well, well, well. That *is* interesting.

TEY: (DISTORT/COMMS)
(GROGGY) What is? What have you seen?

KING SOKIDHARAN: (OFF MIC)
Let the celebrations begin. Music, food, and dance. Music, food, and dance!

FX: The orchestra picks up again.

FX: The burble of conversation returns, excited but nervous.

QUIN:
Not exactly a night at the Great Hall, is it?

TEY: (DISTORT/COMMS)
(GROGGY) Now *that* sounds like a party!

LOURNA:
You wouldn't have lasted an hour.

KEEVE: (DISTORT/COMMS)
(GROGGY) And neither will we if the Leveler catches our scent.

AVAR: (DISTORT/COMMS)
(GROGGY) We have the plan, and we stick to it. Keep to the edges of the room. As far from that thing as we can.

LOURNA:
Bet you wish you'd brought your lightsabers, eh?

QUIN:
In those frocks? Where would they have put them?

LOURNA:
Put your tongue back in, Quin. (TO WAITER) Droid, I need a refill.

WAITER DROID:
Of course, madam.

FX: Clinks of glasses being swapped.

KEEVE: (DISTORT/COMMS)
(GROGGY) What did we say about the wine?

LOURNA:
I'm not the one unsteady on my feet. Behind you!

KEEVE: (DISTORT/COMMS)
(GROGGY) What?

QUIN:
A member of the She'ar. Next to the statue.

KEEVE: (DISTORT/COMMS)
(GROGGY) I . . . I didn't notice.

LOURNA:
That'll be the Leveler. Messing with your minds.

AVAR: (DISTORT/COMMS)
(GROGGY) It's okay, Keeve. They haven't spotted you.

LOURNA:
Yet.

AVAR: (DISTORT/COMMS)
(GROGGY) Keep moving. Stay out of their way.

TEY: (DISTORT/COMMS)
(GROGGY) There's one up here, too. The Harch who brought down Muglan.

LOURNA:
(FLASH OF ANGER) Where?

KEEVE: (DISTORT/COMMS)
(GROGGY) The mission, Lourna. Remember the mission.

LOURNA:
As if I could forget.

AVAR: (DISTORT/COMMS)
(GROGGY) Identify a member of the retinue we can—

LOURNA:
Mind trick?

AVAR: (DISTORT/COMMS)
(GROGGY) *Persuade* to reveal the location of Boolan and Sskeer. No dramatics.

KEEVE: (DISTORT/COMMS)
(GROGGY) No noise.

AVAR: (DISTORT/COMMS)
(GROGGY) And for light's sake, don't let Ro see you.

LOURNA:
Perish the thought . . .

MUSICAL SEGUE:

SCENE 91. INT. WASKIRO. PALACE OF JADALLA.

Atmos: As before. Keeve is still fighting grogginess.

KEEVE: (DISTORT/COMMS)
Anything, Tey?

TEY:
Not a sniff. Ro's team is locked down tighter than a miser's credit box.

SK-0T:
Zut!

TEY:
Hm? (SARCASTIC) Oh, *wizard*.

KEEVE: (DISTORT/COMMS)
What's wrong?

TEY:
The She'ar from Lanjer. I approached a pretty little Morganian, and now the pretty little Morganian's approached everyone's least favorite Harch. The Harch who is now looking this way.

AVAR: (DISTORT/COMMS)
You were *supposed* to be subtle.

TEY:
I was. I *am*!

SK-0T:
Zut-zut-zep!

TEY:
I see him, Skoot. And he sees me.

AVAR: (DISTORT/COMMS)
Get out of there.

TEY:
I'm trying. Lots of people. Lots and lots of people. (TO GUEST) Excuse me. Excuse me.

KEEVE: (DISTORT/COMMS)
Where are you?

TEY:
Second level. There's a balcony straight ahead.

AVAR: (DISTORT/COMMS)
We'll meet you there.

TEY:
Great. I just need a drink.

KEEVE: (DISTORT/COMMS)
What?

TEY:
Trust me. I know what I'm doing.

CUT TO:

SCENE 92. EXT. WASKIRO. PALACE OF JADALLA. BALCONY.

Atmos: The sounds of the ball are muffled. A slight wind is blowing. Insects chirp.

FX: The doors are suddenly pushed open, and Vulax storms onto the balcony. The music and hustle of the ball are loud and then muffled as the doors shut again.

VULAX:
Hmm.

FX: Bleep of a comlink.

VULAX: (CONT)
He's not out here.

CATKIT: (DISTORT/COMMS)
Vulax, are you sure it was the pilot?

VULAX:
No. Of course not. *Tk-tk-tk-tk.* I . . . I caught only a glimpse, but I'm convinced it was a Sephi in that crate.

CATKIT: (DISTORT/COMMS)
A Sephi who's now asking about the Eye?

VULAX:
Everybody's asking about the Eye. It's probably nothing. But I'll check. *Tk-tk-tk-tk.* Just in case. Vulax out.

FX: Comlink beeps off.

FX: Vulax takes a couple of slow, heavy steps.

VULAX: (CONT)
Where are you, little fly? *Tk-tk-tk-tk.*

TEY: (OFF MIC)
HIC!

VULAX:
Who's there? Show yourself. *Tk-tk-tk-tk.* (BEAT) I can see you, trying to hide.

TEY: (OFF MIC)
(SLURRING) Hiding? Who's hiding? Not me.

FX: Tey stumbles out of the shadows, acting drunk.

TEY: (CONT)
I just needed ... a fresh of breath air.

SK-0T:
Zep-zep-zep!

TEY:
How dare you! I am *not* intok ... not intoxsy ... I've just had a couple of drinks. Spot of the old splishy-splashy. (GIGGLES, AND THEN TO VULAX) Would you like a drink? You're a big fella, aren't you? I like your robes. Do ... do you think they'd suit me?

VULAX:
Whose party are you with?

TEY:
Party? I'm a party of one. But you could make it two. Don't mind the droid. He doesn't know how to have fun. Party pooper! (GIGGLES AGAIN)

FX: Vulax slams Tey against the wall.

VULAX:
Why were you asking about the Eye?

TEY:
Who?

VULAX:
Marchion Ro. *Tk-tk-tk-tk.*

TEY:
I . . . I don't know who that is.

VULAX:
You were asking questions. *Tk-tk-tk-tk.* And she never said you were drunk.

TEY:
That's because I'm not! I told you! But we *could* get a little tiddly, if you like, you big hairy beast . . .

VULAX:
(BELLOWS)

FX: Vulax throws Tey across the balcony. He hits the floor and slides, whacking into the wall.

TEY:
Ow! Enough of the rough stuff!

SK-OT:
Zep-zep-*zut*!

VULAX:
(BELLOWS)

FX: Vulax strikes SK-OT with a vibrosword he pulls from his robes.

SK-OT:
(SQUEALS)

FX: SK-OT clatters to the floor. The vibrosword is still buzzing.

TEY:
Hey! I know he's a bit of a killjoy, but there's no need for that. I just had his bodywork buffed up. (FLIRTY) Could do the same for you?

VULAX:
Drop the act. It was you, wasn't it? *Tk-tk-tk-tk.* At the controls of that rust bucket on Lanjer.

TEY:
(SIGHS) We could've had so much fun, you and me.

VULAX:
What do you want with the Eye?

FX: A rustle of silk and satin as Keeve and Avar enter through the door.

AVAR:
(SWALLOWS, TRYING TO KEEP HERSELF TOGETHER) That is none of your concern.

FX: Vulax spins around to face them.

VULAX:
Huh?

KEEVE:
You've never seen this drunkard before.

TEY:
Hey!

VULAX: (MIND-TRICKED)
I've . . . *Tk-tk-tk-tk.* I've never seen this drunkard before.

TEY:
Now you've got *him* saying it.

FX: Avar takes a step closer.

AVAR:
You will drop the weapon.

VULAX:
I will . . . *Tk-tk-tk-tk.* Will . . . (SHAKES HEAD TO CLEAR IT) No.

AVAR:
You will drop the vibrosword!

VULAX:
You're . . . you're Jedi!

TEY:
Well, that's out of the bag! Don't be too hard on yourself. I'm surprised you can even walk with Nameless around.

VULAX:
Stinking Jays! *Tk-tk-tk-tk.*

KEEVE:
Now I *really* wish we had our lightsabers.

VULAX:
Protect the Eye!

FX: He lunges at them with the vibrosword.

TEY:
Avar!

FX: Avar dodges the sword.

AVAR:
(EFFORT)

FX: Clang. The vibrosword hits the wall.

VULAX:
Avar? Avar Kriss?

TEY:
Whoops. Sorry. My fault!

FX: Avar blocks another attack using martial arts.

AVAR:
(EFFORT) We don't want to hurt you.

FX: Comlink chimes.

CATKIT: (DISTORT/COMMS)
Vulax? Well? Who was it?

FX: Avar blocks another couple of blows.

AVAR:
Keeve, the comlink.

KEEVE:
Can do better than that!

FX: The fwoosh of the Force. Vulax crashes into the wall, the vibrosword clattering to the floor along with the comlink.

AVAR:
Really? We were supposed to *not* be attracting attention.

KEEVE:
As Tey said, it's a miracle we're still on our feet.

VULAX:
Not for long!

FX: Vulax bellows as he charges at them, grabbing both of them with his powerful arms.

KEEVE:
(EFFORT) Why do Harch need to have so many damned arms?

VULAX:
All the better—*tk-tk-tk-tk*—for crushing you to death, Jedi!

CATKIT: (DISTORT/COMMS)
Vulax? Respond now. Vulax!

AVAR:
(EFFORT) Tey, cut that off.

FX: Tey scrabbles for the comlink.

TEY:
On it.

FX: Impacts. Punches.

AVAR:
Aah!

KEEVE:
Avar, I can't. He's . . . too strong.

FX: Vulax knocks Keeve, sending her flying. She hits her head on the wall.

KEEVE: (CONT)
(THROUGH GRITTED TEETH) My head!

CATKIT: (DISTORT/COMMS)
Last chance, Vulax. Do you require assistance?

TEY:
Where's the damned off switch? Off switch. Off switch. Oh—kriff it.

FX: Tey smashes the comlink against the wall with two solid strikes. One. Two.

TEY: (CONT)
That'll do it.

FX: The doors fly open again. Another She'ar enters.

CATKIT:
Vulax!

TEY:
And that'll do us. This party's getting overcrowded.

FX: He throws himself at the newcomer before the She'ar can pull his weapon.

CATKIT:
Damned Jedi!

TEY:
Not quite, but I'll take it!

FX: The scuffle. Meanwhile, Avar kicks at Vulax.

VULAX:
(GRUNTS) Takes more than that to keep me down.

FX: He smacks her aside violently.

AVAR:
(SHARP CRY OF PAIN) Keeve!

KEEVE:
(SLIGHTLY SLURRED) I'm here. I'm here.

TEY:
Jedi or not, that's a nasty lump you've got there. Stay down, Keeve.

FX: Catkit gets a punch in, connecting with Tey's chin.

TEY: (CONT)
Aah!

SK-0T:
Zep-zep?

TEY:
Skoot! You're still with us, buddy. And just in time. Flash-bang, as localized as you can manage. Now!

SK-0T:
Zep-zep!

FX: The whumph of a bright light flashing.

CATKIT:
(CRIES OUT) My eyes.

TEY:
That's the least of your worries, handsome! Watch out for the balcony!

CATKIT:
What? Where?

TEY:
Behind you. Here, let me point you in the right direction.

FX: Tey whirls around with a kick, catching the She'ar in the chest. He goes over the edge of the balcony.

CATKIT: (FALLING OFF MIC)
(SHARP CRY)

TEY:
(CALLING AFTER HIM) Or knock you over it. Watch out for the rocks!

FX: Crunch down below.

TEY: (CONT)
Oops! Ah, well—

He turns back to the fight.

TEY: (CONT)
One down . . .

AVAR:
(STRUGGLES TO BREATHE AS SHE'S THROTTLED) Keeve.

TEY:
One to—

KEEVE:
(EFFORT)

FX: A whoosh of the Force. The sound of the abandoned vibrosword flying through the air and then—thud—embedding itself in Vulax's back.

VULAX:
(GASPS IN PAIN)

FX: Vulax collapses. Seemingly dead.

AVAR:
(COUGHS NOW THAT SHE'S BEEN RELEASED)

TEY:
That one's not on me. Although I'm impressed. Vibrosword right between the shoulder blades. Nasty.

AVAR:
Keeve.

KEEVE:
(SHAKEN) I . . . I didn't mean to kill him.

TEY:
You did what was necessary. Let me take a look at your head.

KEEVE:
I just reached out with the Force.

AVAR:
Is she—?

TEY:
It's a bad cut. And her pupils are the size of small moons. The flash-bang couldn't have helped. Sorry. I needed a distraction.

AVAR:
Do you think anyone heard?

TEY:
The fight? No one's come yet. But we need to get her out of here.

KEEVE:
I . . . I didn't mean . . .

AVAR:
Keeve, listen to me. We need to think of the mission. None of us are thinking straight this near the Leveler. With that, and your head injury...

TEY:
I'm going to get her back to the ship.

KEEVE:
No. I need to stay.

TEY:
Avar's here, Keeve. She'll be able to handle it. Besides, the only way out of here is over the edge, unless you want to leave a trail of blood through the ballroom. I'm going to need you to jump with me. Think you can manage that?

AVAR:
Jump off the balcony? In *her* condition?

TEY:
She's still a Jedi, concussed or not. Besides, we should check that the other She'ar is...you know. (MAKES FINGER-ACROSS-THE-THROAT NOISE)

AVAR:
We should never have listened to Lourna.

TEY:
But we did, and here we are. Check in with the others. If word got out, we'll scarper. Find another way to follow Ro. Yes?

AVAR:
Agreed.

TEY:
Good. That's settled, then. Skoot, you stay with Avar.

SK-0T:
Zet-zet?

TEY:
What? Oh. No, you look fine. Hardly a dent at all.

SK-0T:
(SAD) Zeeeeep.

AVAR:
Okay. Go.

KEEVE:
Avar?

AVAR:
Both of you. The Force will be with us, Keeve. Each and every one.

CUT TO:

SCENE 93. INT. WASKIRO. PALACE OF JADALLA. BALLROOM.

Atmos: As before.

LOURNA:
(KEEPING VOICE LOW) What is going on up there?

QUIN: (DISTORT/COMMS)
I can't hear a thing. Interference from the walls?

LOURNA:
Who knows with this Jedi junk. Trennis? Kriss? Come. In.

QUIN: (DISTORT/COMMS)
Lourna! Lourna, Ro's coming this way. Heading right for me.

LOURNA:
If it's not one thing, it's another. Don't let him see you.

QUIN:
(SARCASTIC) Really? You think?

CUT TO:

SCENE 94. INT. WASKIRO. PALACE OF JADALLA. BALLROOM.

Atmos: As before.

MARCHION:
Yes. Thank you. It has been . . . fascinating meeting you.

FX: A She'ar approaches, a bulky Ereesi called Argaz.

ARGAZ:
Marchion.

MARCHION:
(TO THE OTHER GUESTS) If you would excuse me for a moment.

FX: Marchion turns and steps away. The Leveler growls.

MARCHION: (CONT)
(TO HIMSELF) Path preserve me from fools and simpletons. (TO ARGAZ) What is it, Argaz?

ARGAZ:
We have lost contact with Vulax and Catkit.

MARCHION:
Both of them? When?

ARGAZ:
Just now.

MARCHION:
And you haven't thought to *look* for them?

ARGAZ:
My lord.

FX: The Leveler growls.

MARCHION:
You sense something, don't you? What is it? Jedi?

FX: Another growl. Almost... hungry.

ARGAZ:
My lord, if there are Jedi here—

MARCHION:
They'd be every match for you, my so-called elite. Here. Take its chain.

ARGAZ:
(NERVOUS) The Leveler.

MARCHION:
I can hardly let it run wild in a ballroom, can I? (TO THE LEVELER) You know what to do.

FX: The Leveler trills its understanding. Marchion hands over the chain.

FX: The master of ceremonies approaches.

MASTER OF CEREMONIES:
Lord Ro? Supreme Commander?

MARCHION:
(HOLDING IN HIS DISPLEASURE) Master of ceremonies.

MASTER OF CEREMONIES:
The dance is about to begin. His Majesty, the king, was wondering if it would please you to dance with Her Highness, Princess Shikara?

FX: Marchion is distracted by someone in the crowd.

MARCHION:
Wait...

MASTER OF CEREMONIES:
Your Excellency?

MARCHION:
Now there's a face I haven't seen in a while.

MASTER OF CEREMONIES:
The princess?

MARCHION:
Will have to wait. Excuse me.

FX: Marchion strides across the ballroom.

MASTER OF CEREMONIES:
Well, of course. I... er... I... Oh dear.

CUT TO:

SCENE 95. INT. WASKIRO. PALACE OF JADALLA. BALLROOM—CONTINUOUS.

Atmos: As before.

LOURNA: (DISTORT/COMMS)
Quin, look out.

QUIN:
Look out for what?

LOURNA: (DISTORT/COMMS)
Ro. He's heading straight for you!

QUIN:
Ro is? *Kriff. Kriff!*

LOURNA: (DISTORT/COMMS)
Get out of there.

FX: Quin tries to press through the crowd.

QUIN:
Er. Excuse me. Excuse me. I need to... Need to... (SNAPS) Oh, get out of my way!

MARCHION:
Quin?

Quin turns to face the Eye.

QUIN:
Marchion! Marchion Ro! Fancy, er . . . fancy running into you here. What are the odds?

MARCHION:
Yes. What *are* the odds of you being here, with me? (STEPS CLOSER, VOICE LOWERING, ALWAYS A DANGEROUS THING) Who are you with?

QUIN:
I—I don't know what you mean.

MARCHION:
Don't make me repeat myself, Quin. The Leveler senses Jedi, and I look up to see a familiar face in the crowd. A familiar face with track marks on her arms.

FX: He grabs her arm.

QUIN:
(WHIMPERS IN FRIGHT)

MASTER OF CEREMONIES: (OFF MIC)
Friends, delegates, if you would please take your partners. The evening's entertainment is about to begin.

MARCHION:
(QUIET, DANGEROUS) Well. What do you say, Quin? Shall we dance?

LOURNA:
I was hoping that honor would be mine.

Marchion turns, surprised.

MARCHION:
Lourna?

LOURNA:
Marchion.

MARCHION:
(LAUGHS) Oh, this is too delicious.

Music: The first bars of a waltz.

LOURNA:
(EXTENDS A HAND) Shall we?

He lets Quin go.

MARCHION:
Of course.

QUIN:
(BREATHLESS) Lourna . . .

LOURNA:
(HISSING) Get. Out.

CUT TO:

SCENE 96. EXT. WASKIRO. PALACE OF JADALLA. COURTYARD.

Atmos: Night as before. The sound of aircars ferrying guests back and forth.

Wild track: Gasps—and alarm—from the guests as they see the Leveler.

FX: The Leveler snarls and scrabbles as it pulls on its chain, desperate to hunt.

ARGAZ:
(HISSING) Not yet. Not yet!

Wild track: Consternation from the guests. "Is that Ro's creature?" "I hear it eats Jedi," etc.

FX: The Leveler growls.

ARGAZ: (CONT)
Oh, what do I care.

FX: The She'ar removes the chain, and the Leveler bursts forward.

ARGAZ: (CONT)
That's it. Off you go. Happy hunting.

CUT TO:

SCENE 97. EXT. WASKIRO. PALACE OF JADALLA. BALCONY.

Atmos: As before.

SK-OT:
Zep-zet!

AVAR:
Yes. I'll be right with you, Skoot. Someone has to hide the body.

FX: A squeal of feedback in Avar's comlink.

AVAR: (CONT)
(WINCES)

QUIN: (DISTORT/COMMS)
(PANICKED) Avar? Keeve? Anyone! Our cover is blown. Repeat: Our cover is blown.

AVAR:
Quin, it's Avar. What happened?

QUIN: (HEAVY DISTORT/COMMS)
Ro spotted me.

AVAR:
Quin, I can't . . . Quin, you're breaking up.

QUIN: (HEAVY DISTORT/COMMS)
He knows you're here, Avar. He knows there's Jedi.

AVAR:
(SIGHS IN FRUSTRATION) Skoot, go to her.

SK-OT:
Zep-zep!

AVAR:
I know what Tey told you, but Quin needs your help.

SK-OT:
Zet-zet-zet!

FX: SK-OT opens the door and leaves. The sound of the waltz swells and then falls again as the doors close.

AVAR:
At last. Quin, where's Lourna? What's she doing? [STATIC] (SIGHS AGAIN) Maybe it's best I don't know. Whatever she's up to, it can't be any worse than what I have to do.

VULAX:
(MOANS WEAKLY) *Tk-tk-tk-tk.*

FX: Avar crouches down beside Vulax.

AVAR:
Still alive. Good. Vulax, wasn't it? I can help you, I promise. But I also need you to help me.

CUT TO:

SCENE 98. INT. WASKIRO. PALACE OF JADALLA. BALLROOM.

Atmos: As before. The waltz is in full swing.

FX: Marchion and Lourna glide across the dance floor, their voices becoming more intimate as the scene goes on.

MARCHION:
Everyone's watching.

LOURNA:
As well they might. But they were watching before, Marchion, as you knew they would, the moment you strode through those doors.

MARCHION:
You flatter me.

LOURNA:
I tell it how it is. You finally got what you wanted, Marchion. The eyes of the galaxy upon you.

MARCHION:
While everyone knows your name.

LOURNA:
Hardly.

MARCHION:
The great Lourna Dee.

LOURNA:
Dancing with you.

MARCHION:
Hasn't that always been the way? First my father, and now me.

LOURNA:
Ah, Asgar. Now there was a man. A legend.

MARCHION:
A man you killed?

LOURNA:
I thought you'd never work it out.

MARCHION:
(LAUGHS) Look at you in that dress. So vibrant, so sure of yourself. I've missed you, Lourna Dee. More than I thought possible.

LOURNA:
Missed your scapegoat, you mean.

MARCHION:
If you could've taken the Eye from me, you would have. Out of all of them, you were the one who showed the most . . . promise. The most threat.

LOURNA:
You didn't need me, not in the end. I was there, Marchion. I was there, over Eiram, when Starlight fell, fire blossoming along its hull, the spire cracking.

MARCHION:
Oh, how marvelous. To see it how you did.

LOURNA:
Your finest hour.

MARCHION:
Ours, Lourna. You played your part, and I will always thank you for that.

LOURNA:
As you slip a knife between my shoulder blades.

MARCHION:
Or tear out your throat.

LOURNA:
(ALMOST SEDUCTIVE) Then why don't you? We've never been so close. No armor, no defenses. All it would take is one bite.

CUT TO:

SCENE 99. EXT. WASKIRO. PALACE OF JADALLA. BALCONY.

Atmos: As before. The waltz continues at the exact same spot in the music, only now muffled behind the doors.

FX: Avar turns over Vulax's body, laying him on his back.

VULAX:
(GROANS)

AVAR:
(SPEAKS SOFTLY) There. Is that comfortable?

VULAX:
(WEAK) If ... *Tk-tk-tk-tk* ... you're going to kill me ...

AVAR:
I'm not going to kill you. But I can't save you, either. I thought I could, but the wound is too deep. The loss of blood ... I'm sorry.

VULAX:
(CHOKING ON HIS OWN BLOOD) Death ... to the Jedi. *Tk-tk-tk-tk.* To the Republic.

AVAR:
I can't save you, Vulax, but I *can* make the pain stop, if you let me. If you ... tell me what I need to know. Where is Baron Boolan? Where is the Jedi who was with him?

VULAX:
(PAINED, A LITTLE PANICKED) No... *Tk-tk-tk-tk*. I will not betray the Eye.

AVAR:
You *want* to tell me. You *want* me to stop the pain.

VULAX:
I... It *hurts*. *Tk-tk-tk-tk*.

AVAR:
Where is Baron Boolan? Where is the Jedi?

VULAX:
Heiklet. We... we took them to Heiklet. (WINCES IN PAIN)

AVAR:
(SOFTER, LIKE SOOTHING A CHILD) There. There it is. No more pain. No more hurt. Sleep now. Sleep.

VULAX:
(FINAL WHISPER) Sleep.

AVAR:
(STIFLES A SOB) I'm sorry. I'm so, so sorry.

FX: The Nameless growls nearby.

AVAR: (CONT)
No.

FX: The Nameless leaps up onto the balcony from below and growls like a cat that has spotted a mouse.

FX: We hear the Nameless effect heartbeat again, building the tension, the fear.

FX: Avar reactivates her comlink.

AVAR: (CONT)
(FRIGHTENED) Skoot? Lourna? I'm in trouble. The Nameless. It's found me.

FX: The Nameless snarls, and immediately:

CUT TO:

SCENE 100. INT. WASKIRO. PALACE OF JADALLA. BALLROOM.

Atmos: The waltz doesn't miss a beat. Marchion and Lourna continue to dance.

MARCHION:
Why would I want to kill you, Lourna?

LOURNA:
Why wouldn't you? You could snap me in two. Wring the life from me in an instant. Although, you can't, can you? Not in front of all these people. Your people, Marchion. Hanging on your every word. Fearing for their lives. A great predator in their midst...

So weak.

So powerless.

Because that's what you are. That's the man I'm dancing with. A man who has reached the top and discovered that there's nowhere else to go. No, worse than that. A man who has trapped himself on his own throne. Power isn't what you expected. How can it be? You thrive in the shadows, the puppet master controlling everything from a distance. Safe. Secure. But you can't hide anymore, not with everyone watching.

I saw you with them as they fawned and belittled themselves, so desperate for your approval. Like children hanging on your every word. And all the time, all you wanted to do was grind them beneath your feet. Like you want to kill me now. But what would the galaxy say, oh mighty Eye of the Storm? What would *Ghirra Starros* say?

MARCHION:
You have no idea what you're talking about.

LOURNA:
No. But I know you, and I can see how much this burns you. Burns at your soul. You're scared . . . scared of what you've become. Poor little Marchion. He made a wish, and it was granted. And now all he wants is to escape.

CUT TO:

SCENE 101. EXT. WASKIRO. PALACE OF JADALLA. BALCONY.

Atmos: As before.

FX: The Nameless growls, padding toward Avar, who backs away. The Nameless effect intensifies.

AVAR:
(TRYING TO SOUND STRONG EVEN THOUGH SHE'S TERRIFIED) It was you, wasn't it? You're the one who killed Loden. The one they call the Leveler.

PRA-TRE VETER: (GHOSTLY)
A Nameless with a name. Imagine that.

AVAR:
(GASPS) Master Pra-Tre? Pra-Tre, is that you?

PRA-TRE: (GHOSTLY)
Doesn't it look like me, Avar? Like your old friend. The master who made you who you are. Marshal of Starlight Beacon. Protector of the Jedi. Not that you protected me...

AVAR:
(SOBBING) I didn't... I couldn't...

PRA-TRE: (GHOSTLY)
Couldn't do your duty? You failed me, Avar, like you failed Loden. And Orla and Nooranbakarakana. (BEAT) Like you failed Stellan.

AVAR:
(SOBBING) No... Don't...

PRA-TRE: (GHOSTLY)
Don't what, Avar Kriss? Force you to face the truth? How many more will die before you realize that it should be *you* beneath the Shrii Ka Rai's jaws? Turned to stone. Turned to dust.

KEEVE: (GHOSTLY)
Will it be your protégé?

AVAR:
(SOBBING) Keeve.

ELZAR: (GHOSTLY)
Or your lover?

AVAR:
(SOBBING) No, Elzar. It's not real. It's not real.

ELZAR: (GHOSTLY)
But now you can save us all, Avar.

KEEVE: (GHOSTLY)
You can give your life for ours.

PRA-TRE: (GHOSTLY)
Marshal of Starlight.

YODA: (GHOSTLY)
Savior of the Jedi, hmm?

AVAR:
Master Yoda?

LOURNA: (GHOSTLY)
Failure of the Jedi, more like.

AVAR:
No! Lourna... All of you...

PRA-TRE: (GHOSTLY)
It is inevitable, Avar.

KEEVE: (GHOSTLY)
You *shall* die.

ELZAR: (GHOSTLY)
And we will never be together, Avar.

AVAR:
Stay back. Stay—

FX: She stumbles and falls back, landing hard on the floor.

AVAR: (CONT)
(REACTS)

FX: The Nameless stalks closer, trilling. The Nameless effect is at its height.

AVAR: (CONT)
(HYSTERICAL) You're not here. None of you. The Force will protect me. The Force will protect me. The Force will... (SCREAMS)

CUT TO:

SCENE 102. INT. WASKIRO. PALACE OF JADALLA. BALLROOM.

Atmos: As before. The waltz continues.

MARCHION:
Little Marchion. (BEAT) What must you think of me, Lourna?

LOURNA:
I believe I just told you.

MARCHION:
Speaking your mind was rarely an issue, as I recall.

LOURNA:
I learned from the best.

MARCHION:
And did precisely what they required of you, always so obliging, so predictable. Lourna Dee: Tempest Runner, fugitive, pirate . . . *slave.*

You *were* the greatest of them—Pan, Kassav, Zeetar. Lourna, *my* Lourna, always mine. You still are to this day. You just don't realize it.

LOURNA:
I've *never* been yours!

MARCHION:
Then who *do* you belong to, Lourna Dee, daughter of Yudiah, sister of Haleena? Of Inun? Whose pawn are you now? Lina Soh's? The Jedi's? Because that's who you're with, is it not? The enemy. Everything we fought so hard to destroy. *My* fight, not yours, because to fight, dear Lourna, you require a cause, something to believe in, and you... you have nothing. *Are* nothing. A series of masks worn and discarded, of loyalties pledged and forgotten as soon as the wind turns. Clinging to power wherever you find it, because it is you who are scared, Lourna. You who are desperate. For respect. For acceptance. To hear your name echoed over and over. Lourna Dee. Lourna Dee. Lourna Dee.

(LAUGHS) You even think you killed my father. My father, who used you like everyone else has from the moment you were born. Who would've tossed you aside without a second thought. If he had lived. (WHISPERS IN HER EAR) It was me, Lourna. *I* killed him. I who heard his skull crack, heard his breath rattle in his throat as he whispered my name. *My* name. Not yours. You couldn't even do that.

Lourna.

Dee.

FX: They continue to dance for a couple more beats, the waltz coming to an end... but not quite.

MARCHION: (CONT)
You're so quiet, so very quiet. They really have broken you, haven't they? Your new playmates. Or are you waiting for me to accept your offer? To sink my teeth into your neck, rip out your throat as the orchestra reaches its crescendo.

LOURNA:
No, Marchion. I told you. You can't do that, not here, not now, no matter how much you want to.

But I... can.

FX: Lourna sinks her teeth into Marchion's neck with the sound of someone biting into an apple.

MARCHION:
(CRIES OUT)

Wild track: General alarm and shock.

MASTER OF CEREMONIES: (OFF MIC)
What? What? No. No! Guards. Guards!

FX: Marchion pushes Lourna away.

MARCHION:
Witch.

LOURNA:
(SPITS, THEN GRINS) Oh. Is the dance over? (SHOUTS OUT, ENJOYING THE SPECTACLE) Let the band play on!

Wild track: General chaos. Screams. Shouts. Panic.

FX: Lourna slips away in the mayhem as the She'ar come running.

ARGAZ:
My lord! Marchion.

MARCHION:
Where is she?

ARGAZ:
You're bleeding.

MARCHION:
Where has she gone?

ARGAZ:
The Twi'lek?

MARCHION:
Dee. Where is Lourna Dee?

FX: The master of ceremonies runs up.

MASTER OF CEREMONIES: (COMING UP ON MIC)
My lord Eye. I . . . I cannot apologize enough. We will get you help. Medical attention. I—

FX: A lightsaber ignites, straight through the master of ceremonies.

MASTER OF CEREMONIES: (CONT)
(STRANGLED GASP)

MARCHION:
The only fool who needs medical attention is you, "master" of ceremonies.

FX: The master of ceremonies slides dead from the blade, his body hitting the floor.

Wild track: Screams. The guests now fear for their lives.

MARCHION: (CONT)
Kill them. Kill them all.

ARGAZ:
Eye?

MARCHION:
Anyone who saw me bleed. (YELLING) Do it!

FX: Blasters start firing.

CUT TO:

SCENE 103. EXT. WASKIRO. PALACE OF JADALLA. BALCONY.

FX: The sound of blasters muffled behind the doors. The Nameless turns, distracted for a moment by the sound.

AVAR:
(QUIET AT FIRST) Help. Won't someone help me? (LOUDER) Out here! Out here!

FX: The doors crash open. We can hear the chaos and murder louder now.

Wild track: Off-mic muffled screams.

GUEST:
My gods, that's ... that's the thing that came in with Ro. Hey! Get away from her. Get away!

FX: The Nameless snarls. More guests pile out.

GUEST: (CONT)
They can't do this! They promised they'd protect us. Stop it! Throw it over the balcony! They need to be stopped!

Wild track: Ballroom guests surge forward, empowered by their fear and anger, shouting. Throwing things.

FX: The Nameless snarls as the crowd turns on it.

GUEST: (CONT)
Get away! We'll hold it back!

AVAR:
(SINCERE, BUT STILL WEAK) Thank you. We are all the Republic. The Force is with us.

GUEST:
Wait. I didn't mean over the balcony!

AVAR:
I need . . . need to get away.

GUEST:
Don't jump!

FX: Avar jumps over the side of the balcony.

FX: The Nameless howls.

CUT TO:

SCENE 104. EXT. WASKIRO. PALACE OF JADALLA. MAIN EXIT.

FX: The massacre continues as Lourna runs from the building, blasterfire filling the air.

Wild track: Screams.

LOURNA:
(RUNNING) Best party I've been to in a long time.

ARGAZ: (OFF MIC)
There she is!

FX: Blasters fire in her direction, a shot going wide, disintegrating a marble statue next to her.

LOURNA:
(REACTS) That was too close for comfort.

FX: More blasterfire in the opposite direction.

ARGAZ: (OFF MIC)
(SCREAMS)

QUIN:
Lourna! Lourna, over here!

LOURNA:
Quin? I told you to leave.

QUIN:
I did.

FX: Quin fires twice.

QUIN: (CONT)
And then I came back, with blasters. Catch.

FX: Lourna catches it.

LOURNA:
(TO QUIN) Oh, I love you.

FX: Lourna fires.

QUIN:
I'll pretend I didn't hear that.

LOURNA:
Maybe you don't have to. Where are the others?

QUIN:
Tey and the Jedi are back at the ship.

LOURNA:
Jedi? Which one?

FX: Avar lurches up.

AVAR: (COMING UP ON MIC)
(GASPING) Lourna!

LOURNA:
Never mind. You've looked better, Marshal.

AVAR:
The Leveler.

LOURNA:
I guessed.

FX: Avar stumbles, and Lourna catches her.

AVAR:
(GASPS)

LOURNA:
I've got you.

AVAR:
I know where they are, Lourna—Boolan and Sskeer. I know where he took them.

LOURNA:
A mission that's a success. Who would've thought it?

FX: A shuttle blasts off noisily.

QUIN:
Ro?

LOURNA:
Who else would it be?

AVAR:
Lourna, your mouth. Is that . . . is that blood?

LOURNA:
Later, Princess. We have incoming.

QUIN:
Where?

LOURNA:
Straight up.

FX: Missiles drop from above, hitting the palace. A shock wave rolls out, knocking them from their feet.

QUIN:
Lourna.

LOURNA:
I'm all right. I'm all right. But we won't be for long. Those missiles have to be coming from the *Gaze Electric*. Ro's carpet-bombing the palace!

FX: More missiles rain down. More explosions.

LOURNA: (CONT)
The entire city! Can you run, Marshal?

AVAR:
(BESIDE HERSELF WITH GRIEF) Those people. All those people.

LOURNA:
I'll take that as a no. Hope you don't mind being carried.

FX: Lourna hauls Avar over her shoulder.

LOURNA: (CONT)
(EFFORT) Better than being left behind. Quin, *run!*

FX: More laser bolts and more explosions—more destruction.

CUT TO:

SCENE 105. INT. HEIKLET. CASTLE LAB.

Atmos: As before.

FX: The whine of medical equipment. An energy field.

SSKEER:
Boolan. (NO RESPONSE) Boolan!

BOOLAN:
You must remain calm, Sskeer.

SSKEER:
I feel asss though I am on *fire*.

BOOLAN:
It is the treatment. It is working, Sskeer. It is working.

SSKEER:
I cannot bear it.

BOOLAN:
But you must, for both our sakes. (GETS CLOSER TO SSKEER) They are watching. All the time. If they suspect, even for a moment, that I am trying to help you ...

SSKEER:
(MOANS IN PAIN THROUGH GRITTED TEETH)

BOOLAN:
I'm not sure how long I can keep stalling. I don't want him to have it, Sskeer. The cure for the blight. It shouldn't be him. But he will kill me.

SSKEER:
So you *can* ssstop it? You can ssstop the blight? (CRIES OUT IN PAIN) Boolan.

BOOLAN:
Stop it? Yes. I can stop it. The question is, should I? Have you considered, Sskeer, that the blight could be balance returning to the galaxy? Restoration even.

SSKEER:
I . . . I don't understand.

BOOLAN:
(GETTING MORE AGITATED) How could you? How could any of us? The Jedi, the Nihil. Think of all the damage that has been done to the Force by all of us, even me! What if it was meant to be, the blight? What if it is the galaxy's way of putting things right? Who am I to stop it? The Force must be free, Sskeer! The Force must be free.

SSKEER:
(TALKING THROUGH HIS PAIN) Boolan, lisssten to me. That's not how the Force works, not how the galaxy works.

BOOLAN:
But the Path . . . my father . . .

SSKEER:
All that was a long time ago, and by the ssstars, I can sssee how you've sssuffered. How those events have ssscarred you, deep within. (PAIN INCREASES FOR A MOMENT) But you said it yourself . . . the people who taught you . . . when you were a child . . . your father . . . thisss "Mother" . . . they were *wrong*. You follow a different path now . . . a path of light. Look what you're doing for me. You're not the person you were.

FX: Sskeer gives in to the pain, unable to stop himself from crying out.

FX: The door opens, and Keskar hurries in.

KESKAR:
Baron.

BOOLAN:
Not now, Keskar.

KESKAR:
We've had word from the Eye. He wants to know how long.

BOOLAN:
How long?

KESKAR:
For the blight.

BOOLAN:
The experiment is at a critical juncture...

KESKAR:
He needs results, Boolan. He needs them *now*.

FX: Keskar throws a lever on "now," shutting down the energy field.

SSKEER:
(GASPS FOR AIR)

BOOLAN:
What have you done? You fool! You could ruin everything!

KESKAR:
You've had long enough.

FX: Keskar grabs Boolan, shoving him back into his equipment.

BOOLAN:
(CRIES OUT)

KESKAR:
I've given you space, Baron. Let you play with your experiments. But it's over. The deadline is now.

BOOLAN:
Unhand me.

KESKAR:
Not until you've told me what I need to know, what the Eye wants to hear.

BOOLAN:
That I am victorious? That I have held back the blight?

FX: Boolan pushes back, shoving the She'ar away.

KESKAR:
(REACTS)

BOOLAN:
You want results? Then here they are.

FX: Bleeps as Boolan hits controls. Data starts scrolling down the screen.

BOOLAN: (CONT)
Do you see?

KESKAR:
I . . . I don't know what I'm looking at.

BOOLAN:
Of course not. Because you're an ignoramus! A blunt instrument! This is it, you gibbering ape, the cure for the blight. Not just to hold it back, but to eradicate it completely.

SSKEER:
(WEAK) Boolan, no. Don't give it to the Nihil.

BOOLAN:
What do I care? Let Ro have his triumph, his victory. I'm done with him, with all of you.

KESKAR:
You have done well, Boolan. The Eye will be pleased.

BOOLAN:
Like I care. (BEAT) What are you waiting for? Run back to your master. Tell him the good news.

KESKAR:
Oh, I will. But not quite yet. Not until I've had a little fun. Not until payback.

FX: Keskar produces Boolan's control device.

BOOLAN:
What? My control device?

KESKAR:
That's what you get for pushing me about. Been picking pockets since I was knee-high to a Jawa.

BOOLAN:
Give it back to me!

FX: Keskar slaps him down.

BOOLAN: (CONT)
(CRIES OUT)

FX: He hits the floor.

KESKAR:
Stay there. You'll want to see this.

FX: The Nameless control device activates. The Nameless bay in their cages.

KESKAR: (CONT)
I've been looking forward to this from the moment you arrived, Jedi. (TO THE NAMELESS) Out! Come to me!

FX: The cage doors clang open. The Nameless stalk out, growling.

KESKAR: (CONT)
No need for experiments now.

SSKEER:
(FEELING THE NAMELESS EFFECT) Please. No. Keep them away. Keep them away from me!

BOOLAN:
He can feel them. He can really feel them.

KESKAR:
I never get sick of this. The pleading, the screams.

FX: The Nameless bay.

BOOLAN:
And they can smell the Force in *him*. It worked. It really worked.

KESKAR:
Well, Jedi . . . any final words? Last requests?

SSKEER:
(SPEAKING THROUGH HIS TERROR) I want nothing from you. The Force is ssstrong! The Force is ssstrong!

KESKAR:
(LAUGHS) Have at him! Feed!

FX: The Nameless pounce on Sskeer. Feeding on him. Turning him into a husk.

SSKEER:
(SCREAMS)

KESKAR:
Yeah, that's it. Turn him to stone.

SSKEER:
(SCREAMS AGAIN)

FX: The Nameless feed.

CUT TO:

SCENE 106. EXT. SPACE.

FX: The Overtone *blasts its way through space.*

CUT TO:

SCENE 107. INT. THE *OVERTONE*. COCKPIT—CONTINUOUS.

Atmos: The ship in flight.

FX: A strip of adhesive medical tape is pulled from a reel.

TEY:
Steady. Steady now.

FX: He attaches the tape to Keeve's wound.

KEEVE:
(WINCES)

TEY:
There you go. Almost good as new.

KEEVE:
Thanks.

TEY:
It would be better if you took some stims.

KEEVE:
No! (LESS FORCEFUL) No. I . . . I need to keep my wits about me. We have no idea what we're facing.

AVAR:
The Force will provide.

KEEVE:
(SUSPICIOUS) As it provided the name of the planet?

AVAR:
The She'ar—

KEEVE:
Confessed?

AVAR:
Saw the light.

TEY:
I'm just glad you got out of there. When I saw the missiles...

LOURNA:
Just be glad you weren't in the middle of it. Any news on the *Gaze,* Skoot?

SK-0T:
Zep-zep!

TEY:
Nothing at all?

QUIN:
It jumped to hyperspace and then vanished from the comm channels. No chatter at all.

LOURNA:
That'll change. Ro will want everyone to know what he did.

AVAR:
Because of you. We had a plan, Lourna. We had—

LOURNA:
Mission parameters? Spoken like a true general. Yes, Marshal. No, Marshal.

AVAR:
I am *not* a general. I am not a *marshal.* I am a *Jedi,* and that loss of life was unacceptable!

LOURNA:
Then talk to Ro, not me. He was going for Quin. I *had* to step in.

AVAR:
Did you have to humiliate him?

LOURNA:
Jealous it wasn't you?

AVAR:
People *died,* Lourna. Thousands of people.

TEY:
And thousands more will die if we don't find the key to the blight.

LOURNA:
More like billions.

TEY:
Precisely. So we can sit here blaming one another or we can work out what the hell we're going to do when we reach Heiklet.

KEEVE:
Does it really matter?

AVAR:
You need to rest, Keeve. We all need to rest.

KEEVE:
Yeah, you're right. Because I'm tired. I'm so, so tired of the setbacks and the defeats and the *death*!

AVAR:
Keeve.

KEEVE:
I *killed* that Harch. I plunged a sword into his back.

LOURNA:
Isn't that what you Jedi do?

FX: Keeve stands.

KEEVE:
No. No, it is not. And it shouldn't be. I remember Master Malli telling us in the crèche that a lightsaber was a Jedi's last resort, never the first. That even drawing the hilt from our belts would

be enough to defuse any situation. Any. But not anymore. She wouldn't recognize us if she were here. I don't recognize us.

AVAR:
You've suffered a head injury.

KEEVE:
We've *changed*, Avar. You know that, don't you? We've become something else, something we were never supposed to be.

AVAR:
The Guardian Protocols—

KEEVE:
To *hell* with the Guardian Protocols! To hell with us!

AVAR:
(GENUINELY SHOCKED) Keeve.

KEEVE:
Everywhere I've gone since Starlight, everything I've seen, I've been looking for the light. And it's out there. Thank the stars, it's out there, in the people we meet, that we help and in the people that help *us*. But I'm struggling to see it here, struggling to see it in you or me. You said I was the "Light of the Jedi," Avar. You said I could make sense of it all. But I can't. I thought I could, but I don't know who we are! Do *you*, Avar? Would Loden? Would *Stellan*?

AVAR:
(SHAKEN BUT TRYING TO HOLD IT TOGETHER) Keeve, we should meditate on this. We should—

KEEVE:
I'm through with meditating. I'm through with the—

SSKEER: (DISTORTED)
(SCREAMS IN PAIN)

KEEVE:
(GASPS)

TEY:
Keeve?

KEEVE:
Did you feel that? Did you hear it? Avar, tell me you heard it!

AVAR:
(QUIET) Sskeer.

KEEVE:
In the Force.

AVAR:
Through the Force.

KEEVE:
Does that mean... (TO LOURNA) We need to make the jump.

LOURNA:
Course is already set in.

KEEVE:
Then go. Go! Before it's too late.

CUT TO:

Part Seven
FOLLOW THE PATH

SCENE 108. INT. HEIKLET. CASTLE LAB.

Atmos: As before. The Nameless feed. Sskeer screams. Boolan continues to work at the console.

KESKAR:
Incredible. It happens so fast. The Eye will want to see this—another Jedi to add to his tally.

BOOLAN:
And he will, he will. You are recording everything, aren't you?

KESKAR:
Yes, the Eye commanded... Wait. Are those cams on? They should be on!

BOOLAN:
They should be, yes, but it would've been slightly inconvenient, would it not? After all, they would see me do *this*!

FX: A defiant bleep from the computer.

FX: The Nameless stop feeding.

SSKEER:
(WHEEZES)

KESKAR:
What are you doing? Finish him off.

FX: *The Nameless growl at the She'ar. Keskar slaps the control device.*

KESKAR: (CONT)
Boolan, your control matrix, it's stopped working.

BOOLAN:
Oh, it's working all right. You're just not in charge of it anymore.

FX: *The Nameless jump down from Sskeer, focusing on Keskar instead.*

KESKAR:
W-what are they doing?

BOOLAN:
Whatever I tell them. Did you really think I wouldn't be able to slice into my own device? Or the systems beyond this room? The cams? The *doors*?

FX: *The doors lock—clunk!*

BOOLAN: (CONT)
You should've contacted the Eye when you had the chance.

FX: *The Nameless move toward Keskar, growling.*

KESKAR:
Tell them to stay back!

FX: *Keskar throws aside the control device, pulling out his blaster.*

KESKAR: (CONT)
I'll kill them, and then I'll kill you!

BOOLAN:
One of them is already dead, Keskar. Do you really think a blaster will stop them?

KESKAR:
(CRIES OUT AS HE FIRES)

FX: *Blaster bolts blast. Nameless pounce.*

KESKAR: (CONT)
(SCREAMS)

FX: *Another couple of blaster bolts going wild, hitting equipment, before the blaster is knocked from the struggling She'ar's hand to skitter over the floor. And all the time the She'ar screams as the Nameless maul him.*

FX: *Boolan rushes to Sskeer's side, speaking over the messy, prolonged death.*

BOOLAN:
Sskeer. Sskeer, are you still with me?

SSKEER:
(WEAK) I . . . I am . . .

FX: *Boolan starts undoing the leather straps.*

BOOLAN:
I acted as swiftly as I could. There has been some tissue damage, but nothing that won't heal. You are luckier than most of your compatriots. That Trandoshan DNA of yours works in your favor.

FX: *The She'ar falls silent. The Nameless snuffle at his corpse, but there is banging at the locked doors.*

BOOLAN: (CONT)
That will be Ro's enforcer droids. I deactivated the cam but couldn't access their systems remotely. Can you stand?

SSKEER:
(STILL GROGGY) I felt the Force being ripped from me, Boolan. I felt the Force.

BOOLAN:
And I am happy for you, my friend, but we need to leave!

FX: *The doors shake as they're pounded by blaster bolts.*

SSKEER:
There's no way out.

BOOLAN:
Yes, there is.

FX: *The doors are blasted from their hinges.*

ENFORCER DROID:
Halt. Halt.

BOOLAN:
One last command, my creations. Attack. Attack the droids!

FX: The Nameless roar and spring forward into the enforcer droids' line of fire. Blaster bolts zing as the creatures attack the droids.

ENFORCER DROID:
Desist. Desist. (ELECTRONIC SCREAM)

FX: The Nameless roar.

CUT TO:

SCENE 109. INT. HEIKLET. CASTLE CORRIDOR.

Atmos: Wind rages outside the castle walls. Rain lashes the windows.

FX: Boolan helps Sskeer along the corridor.

BOOLAN:
We're almost there, Sskeer. Keskar's fighter is straight ahead.

SSKEER:
(STILL WEAK) My Padawan's lightsssaber. I must find it.

BOOLAN:
There's no time. Ro could be here at any moment.

FX: The clank, clank, clank of enforcer droids ahead.

BOOLAN: (CONT)
No.

SSKEER:
More droids.

BOOLAN:
And this time I don't think the Nameless are in any state to help us.

FX: The enforcer droids raise their blasters.

ENFORCER DROID:
Halt.

SSKEER:
You will let us past.

BOOLAN:
I appreciate the enthusiasm, Sskeer, but your mind powers won't work on droids.

SSKEER:
Who sssaid they would? (GIVES A BELLOW OF EFFORT)

FX: The whoosh of the Force slamming the droids into the wall, smashing them beyond repair.

BOOLAN:
It's fair to say your abilities have returned.

SSKEER:
Or I've returned to my abilitiesss.

FX: A small component from the droids falls to the floor—tink—and rolls to a stop.

SSKEER: (CONT)
We must hurry. There may be more.

FX: They make their way to the fighter and open the hatch.

CUT TO:

SCENE 110. INT. HEIKLET. SHE'AR FIGHTER—CONTINUOUS.

FX: They clamber in. Boolan drops into the pilot's seat.

BOOLAN:
Quite a squeeze.

SSKEER:
I will pilot.

BOOLAN:
I mean no disrespect, Sskeer, but you are recovering from surgery and much worse.

FX: Boolan starts the fighter's systems.

BOOLAN: (CONT)
Closing the hatch.

FX: He flicks a control, and the hatch seals tight.

SSKEER:
Where are you taking us?

BOOLAN:
To my father. To the answers we seek.

FX: The engine swells and engages.

CUT TO:

SCENE 111. INT. HEIKLET. CASTLE HANGAR—CONTINUOUS.

FX: The She'ar fighter launches, zooming out of the castle and into the storm. Thunder crashes, and rain lashes down.

CUT TO:

SCENE 112. INT. HEIKLET. SHE'AR FIGHTER—CONTINUOUS.

FX: The fighter is buffeted in the gale. Rain hammers against the fuselage.

SSKEER:
(REACTS)

BOOLAN:
Maybe I should've let you fly after all. I can barely see in all this rain.

FX: Lightning strobes.

BOOLAN: (CONT)
And that doesn't help!

FX: There is a small explosion from the back of the craft.

BOOLAN: (CONT)
(REACTS) Were we hit?

SSKEER:
That wasn't lightning!

FX: Sskeer looks back as the fighter is buffeted.

SSKEER: (CONT)
It's one of the droids!

BOOLAN:
What?

SSKEER:
Hanging on to the foils.

BOOLAN:
Not as damaged as we hoped, it appears.

SSKEER:
Although the sssame can't be sssaid of this ssstarfighter.

FX: Another explosion.

SSKEER: (CONT)
It's attempting to bring us down.

BOOLAN:
With some considerable success.

SSKEER:
Hold us sssteady. I will deal with the droid.

FX: The hatch opens, and wind and rain rush into the cramped space. Sskeer and Boolan have to pitch up to be heard.

BOOLAN:
By going out on the wing? You're in no condition—

SSKEER:
I am a *Jedi*!

CUT TO:

SCENE 113. EXT. HEIKLET. SHE'AR FIGHTER—CONTINUOUS.

Atmos: The fighter is in flight in the middle of the storm. Sskeer climbs out onto the wing.

ENFORCER DROID:
Halt. Halt.

SSKEER:
(TALKING OVER THE STORM) If we go down, you go down with usss, droid!

ENFORCER DROID:
Halt. Halt.

FX: The droid pulls out a handful of wires. The fighter lurches.

BOOLAN: (OFF MIC, FROM INSIDE)
Sskeer! I can't pull up!

SSKEER:
(CALLING BACK) It has disabled the stabilizers. Pulled out the cables.

ENFORCER DROID:
Die. Die.

SSKEER:
No, droid. You!

FX: Sskeer throws himself at the droid, and they scuffle on the wing.

BOOLAN: (OFF MIC, FROM INSIDE)
Sskeer! Sskeer, what's happening?

SSKEER:
(FIGHTING) The Force is with me. The Force is—

FX: A lightning bolt hits the fighter, knocking both droid and Jedi from the wing.

SSKEER AND DROID:
(CRYING OUT, FALLING AWAY)

BOOLAN: (OFF MIC, FROM INSIDE)
Sskeer! Sskeer!

CUT TO:

SCENE 114. INT. HEIKLET. SHE'AR FIGHTER—CONTINUOUS.

BOOLAN:
Gone. Both gone. All that work wasted!

FX: Lightning strikes again, hitting the fighter.

BOOLAN: (CONT)
Well, I'm not going the same way. Struck down by lightning. (LAUGHS IN HIS NERVOUSNESS) So much for riding the storm!

FX: He hits a switch, and the hatch closes, cutting off the sound of the wind.

BOOLAN: (CONT)
(TO HIMSELF) Close hatch. Prime systems.

FX: Beeps as Boolan presses buttons and hits switches.

BOOLAN: (CONT)
I'm just sorry you won't see the fruits of our labor, Sskeer. But it will be worth it, I promise. Because the Force is precious. The Force is life. The Force is precious. The Force is *life*.

FX: On "life," he guns the engines, escaping to the stars.

CUT TO:

SCENE 115. EXT. SPACE. ABOVE HEIKLET—CONTINUOUS.

FX: Boom—the Overtone *drops out of hyperspace into realspace, a stark contrast to the sound of the storm in the previous scenes.*

CUT TO:

SCENE 116. INT. THE *OVERTONE*. COCKPIT—CONTINUOUS.

Atmos: As before.

LOURNA:
There it is. Heiklet, in all its glory.

QUIN:
Look at that storm.

LOURNA:
No wonder Marchion likes it. Ready?

AVAR:
Take us down.

CUT TO:

SCENE 117. EXT. THE SKIES OF HEIKLET—CONTINUOUS.

Atmos: As before.

FX: The Overtone *is buffeted by the storm, its engines straining.*

CUT TO:

SCENE 118. INT. THE *OVERTONE*. COCKPIT—CONTINUOUS.

Atmos: The ship is barely coping with flying through the turbulence. The hull is pelted with rain.

TEY:
When we said we were ready . . .

FX: The ship hits an air pocket.

ALL BUT LOURNA:
(REACT)

QUIN:
Sensors are down.

SK-0T:
Zet-zet-zep!

LOURNA:
It'll be fine if we don't hit anything.

QUIN:
Or get hit by lightning.

TEY:
Are you *trying* to tempt fate?

FX: More buffeting.

AVAR:
Keeve, we should meditate.

LOURNA:
That's your solution to our imminent destruction?

KEEVE:
I'm not sure I can, Avar.

AVAR:
You want us to be Jedi, Keeve. *This* is the moment. This is when it *matters*. Trust in the Force. Trust in *us*.

TEY:
May I join you?

AVAR:
You?

TEY:
It's been a while, but once a Guardian, always a Guardian, I guess.

AVAR:
Of course. *Please.*

FX: The ship is struck by lightning. Sparks rain down.

QUIN:
Yep, definitely shouldn't have mentioned the lightning!

AVAR:
(TENDER) Keeve?

KEEVE:
(SIGHS, THEN QUIETLY) The Force surrounds us. The Force dwells in us.

AVAR:
The Force flows through us. The Force protects us.

TEY:
The Force is light. For the Force is strong.

SSKEER: (DISTORTED, TELEPATHIC)
For the Force isss ssstrong.

KEEVE:
Sskeer! Avar, I heard him. Tell me you heard him, too.

AVAR:
Go to him, Keeve. For the Force is strong.

TEY:
You bet it is.

FX: Keeve gets up and moves to the copilot position.

LOURNA:
Keeeeve? What are you doing in the copilot's seat?

KEEVE:
(CALM) Give me the controls.

LOURNA:
The controls. Of the ship.

TEY:
Just do it, Lourna.

LOURNA:
She has her eyes shut!

FX: Keeve takes hold of the yoke.

KEEVE:
Trust me.

LOURNA:
Trust you? (SIGHS) Sure. Why not?

FX: A beep as control is passed to Keeve.

LOURNA: (CONT)
You have the controls.

AVAR:
Follow his song, Keeve.

TEY:
Follow his light.

LOURNA:
We're all going to die.

FX: A minor explosion.

QUIN:
Damn. (CALLING TO THE DROID FOR HELP) Skoot?

SK-OT:
Zep-zet!

FX: SK-OT goes to work fixing the damage.

LOURNA:
You need to get us down, Trennis. We can't take much more than this.

FX: More buffetting. More reaction from Quin and now Lourna.

AVAR:
A fortress—

TEY:
In the mist.

KEEVE:
I see it.

LOURNA:
Where?

FX: Suddenly it's in front of them. A proximity alarm sounds.

QUIN:
(PANICKED) There! Pull up! Pull up!

FX: Keeve yanks hard on the yoke. The Overtone *narrowly misses the castle.*

LOURNA:
That was too damned close.

KEEVE:
He's not in the castle.

LOURNA:
Whereas *we* were nearly smeared all over it.

AVAR:
He is nearby.

QUIN:
Ground. There's ground! Lots and lots of ground.

LOURNA:
Coming in hot, Trennis!

KEEVE:
Take the yoke!

LOURNA:
Now you need me to fly?

FX: Keeve gets up and runs to the hatch.

KEEVE: (GOING OFF MIC)
Just bring us down safely.

LOURNA:
(EFFORT) Because it's that easy. Right.

CUT TO:

SCENE 119. EXT. THE SURFACE OF HEIKLET—CONTINUOUS.

FX: The Overtone's *engines roar as the ship tries to land. Rain lashes down. All characters have to shout to be heard.*

FX: A hatch opens.

LOURNA: (OFF MIC, INSIDE)
If we land, we might never take off again!

KEEVE: (AT THE HATCH)
Then hold her steady! Avar?

AVAR:
I'm with you!

FX: They jump to the surface, battling to stay on their feet.

KEEVE:
He's nearby! I know he is! Sskeer! *Sskeer!*

SSKEER: (OFF MIC)
(EFFORT)

FX: Sound of fighting nearby. The whir of servos. Metal being struck.

AVAR:
Keeve! There!

CUT TO:

SCENE 120. EXT. THE SURFACE OF HEIKLET—CONTINUOUS.

FX: Sskeer fights the remains of the enforcer droid that stubbornly refuses to die.

ENFORCER DROID:
Desist! Desist!

SSKEER:
You first! (ROARS)

FX: Sskeer pulls the droid apart.

ENFORCER DROID:
(ELECTRONIC CRY)

SSKEER:
(BREATHES HEAVILY)

FX: There is movement behind him in the rain. Sskeer spins around.

SSKEER: (CONT)
(REACTS)

KEEVE: (COMING UP ON MIC)
Sskeer! Be careful! You're on a ledge!

SSKEER:
(OVERJOYED) Keeve!

FX: She runs straight into his arms, her tears lost in the rain.

KEEVE:
(CRYING) You need to stop running off, do you hear me?

SSKEER:
Or being kidnapped.

KEEVE:
Just . . . stay with me, all right?

SSKEER:
Keeve, I can hear the Force! I can feel its presence!

KEEVE:
I know. I heard you!

She pulls herself from the hug.

KEEVE: (CONT)
But how . . .

SSKEER:
My Magrak sssyndrome. The baron, he . . . he found a way.

KEEVE:
The baron did this?

FX: More movement near them. Avar approaches, having given them a moment.

AVAR: (COMING UP ON MIC)
And where is the baron now?

Sskeer stands a little taller, almost standing to attention.

SSKEER:
Marshal Kriss!

AVAR:
It is good to see you, Sskeer. But I'm afraid I must press you for an answer.

SSKEER:
I do not know. We escaped the fortress only to be attacked by one of Ro's enforcers. I dealt with the droid but got . . . sssseparated from Boolan's fighter.

KEEVE:
You fell all the way to the ground, didn't you?

SSKEER:
Quite sssome way. It . . . er . . . it sssmarts.

AVAR:
Then we are no closer to unlocking the data.

SSKEER:
No, but Boolan admitted that the sssolution we found in his records was complete. It will work.

KEEVE:
So we just have to find him. Again!

SSKEER:
I think I know where he has gone.

FX: A sudden rush of engines as the Overtone *sweeps nearby.*

SSKEER: (CONT)
That is *not* a Jedi ship.

KEEVE:
You have no idea.

TEY:
(CALLING DOWN) We need to leave. Pronto.

AVAR:
What's wrong? Is it the engines?

TEY:
No, it's the company!

CUT TO:

SCENE 121. INT. THE *GAZE ELECTRIC*. FLIGHT DECK—CONTINUOUS.

Atmos: As before, the Gaze *barely buffeted by the storm outside.*

SHE'AR PILOT:
Lord Eye, there is no response from Keskar or any of the droids.

MARCHION:
Something is wrong.

FX: A sensor bleeps urgently.

SHE'AR PILOT:
Incoming craft.

MARCHION:
A ship?

SHE'AR PILOT:
To port.

MARCHION:
I see it. Could it be? (BEAT) Don't let them escape! Blow it to pieces!

CUT TO:

SCENE 122. INT. THE *OVERTONE*. COCKPIT—CONTINUOUS.

Atmos: As before. Turbolasers scream by.

KEEVE:
Yep, that's the *Gaze Electric*.

FX: The Overtone *fires back.*

QUIN:
And they're not happy.

AVAR:
We can't engage. We're no match for their guns.

FX: More turbolasers blast past.

LOURNA:
I don't think they're giving us a choice!

SSKEER:
If we fight, we die. Essscape, and we can recover Boolan. We can recover hisss key.

TEY:
If he's where you *say* he is.

SSKEER:
He will be. I know it in my heart and sssoul.

LOURNA:
Sounds like you boys got real cozy together.

FX: Explosion.

AVAR:
Sskeer's right. Get us out of here, Lourna.

LOURNA:
We can take them.

QUIN:
We can't. And you know that, don't you?

LOURNA:
The man bleeds, Quin. I've *proved* it. And if he bleeds...

QUIN:
This is bigger than the two of you, Lourna. Bigger than all of us.

LOURNA:
(SNARLS) Strap yourselves down.

CUT TO:

SCENE 123. INT. THE *GAZE ELECTRIC.* FLIGHT DECK—CONTINUOUS.

Atmos: As before.

MARCHION:
What is she *doing*?

FX: A sudden volley of shots from the Overtone *as the smaller ship spins, zooming dangerously near as it screams past the* Gaze Electric*'s viewport.*

MARCHION: (CONT)
(GROWLS IN HIS THROAT)

SHE'AR PILOT:
The ship is on an escape vector, my lord.

MARCHION:
Only Lourna. It has to be her. Take out their engines, you fool. Don't let her get away.

FX: The Gaze *fires, but:*

SHE'AR PILOT:
They are out of range, sir. Should we pursue?

MARCHION:
(DESPERATELY TRYING TO CONTROL HIS BREATHING) We need to see what she has done. Take us to the fortress. The fortress!

CUT TO:

SCENE 124. EXT. SPACE—CONTINUOUS.

FX: The Overtone *roars up from the planet.*

CUT TO:

SCENE 125. INT. THE *OVERTONE*. COCKPIT—CONTINUOUS.

Atmos: Calmer. Relief now that the battle's done.

TEY:
Everyone still in one piece?

SK-0T:
Zup-zup-zet.

TEY:
Skoot! Don't talk like that. Too old for this? You've got years in you, just like me!

KEEVE:
Speak for yourself.

LOURNA:
(SOTTO) He usually does.

AVAR:
And you're sure about this location, Sskeer?

SSKEER:
I am.

AVAR:
Then that's where we're heading.

FX: The navicomp bleeps.

QUIN:
Course plotted in.

LOURNA:
And off we go.

FX: Lourna pulls back the levers, plunging the ship into hyperspace.

CUT TO:

SCENE 126. INT. HEIKLET. CASTLE LAB—SOON AFTER.

Atmos: As before, the storm rages outside, with the added sound of still-steaming droid parts in the laboratory.

FX: Marchion's boots echo as he walks slowly into the devastation. The She'ar stalk close behind. The Leveler prowls alongside.

FX: Marchion's steps slow and come to a halt.

MARCHION:
(BREATHES OUT, RAGING INSIDE) And there is no sign of the baron?

SHE'AR PILOT:
No, my lord. Keskar's fighter is not in its dock.

MARCHION:
Jumped to hyperspace?

SHE'AR PILOT:
Gone.

MARCHION:
And yet Keskar is here, butchered, along with the equipment.

SHE'AR PILOT:
And the Nameless.

MARCHION:
Killed by the enforcer droids. A fight to the death.

A beat and then:

MARCHION: (CONT)
(ROARS SUDDENLY IN FURY)

FX: Marchion brings his fist down on an already wrecked console.

MARCHION: (CONT)
(VOICE DANGEROUSLY QUIET AGAIN) His Nameless dead, records smashed, the droids... wrecked beyond repair. What was he thinking? How did she get to him?

SHE'AR PILOT:
She?

MARCHION:
Check every memory cell of his computer. Salvage whatever information you can. We will uncover his work, V'eax. We will claim victory over the blight. We will not let her win.

A MUSICAL STING, LEADING TO:

SCENE 127. EXT. DALNA. PLANET SURFACE—DAY.

Atmos: A barren wasteland, wind blowing dust over volcanic plains. We hold on the eerie sound for a moment, and then hear footsteps in the grit.

TEY:
I . . . I can't believe it. The last time I was here . . . well, it was bad enough, but nothing like this. The devastation. On such a scale.

SSKEER:
Welcome to Dalna.

AVAR:
Welcome to the handiwork of Lourna Dee.

FX: Dirt crunches beneath her feet.

AVAR: (CONT)
You *are* awfully quiet.

LOURNA:
What do you want me to say?

AVAR:
What can you? The planet was once a paradise, and then you came with your Tempest, with the Nihil. It was alive, Lourna, with a thriving population.

LOURNA:
Who will be returned to its surface once the relief effort is completed.

KEEVE:
But when will that be? When you consider everything the Republic has endured over the last year... when will the people get home?

AVAR:
And what will they find when they get here?

Lourna does not want to hear this or accept her part in Dalna's destruction.

LOURNA:
We should find the baron, if he's even here at all.

SSKEER:
He will be. At his father's ssside.

CUT TO:

SCENE 128. INT. DALNA. THE PATH OF THE OPEN HAND CAVERNS—LATER.

Atmos: A small cavern, deep underground. The drip, drip, drip of water. Candlelight flickering.

Note: Boolan no longer has his whirring implements. He has changed into the simple robes of the Path of the Open Hand, robes that once belonged to his father.

BOOLAN:
(UNDER HIS BREATH, OVER AND OVER) The Force will be free. The Force will be free. The Force will be free. The Force will be free. (REPEAT)

FX: He continues as we hear movement in the tunnels beyond along with the buzz of lightsabers used to light the way.

TEY: (OFF MIC)
Getting down here was a lot easier when the entrance wasn't covered in lava.

KEEVE: (OFF MIC)
And people lived in these caverns?

TEY: (OFF MIC)
Lived and died.

AVAR: (OFF MIC)
Sskeer?

SSKEER: (OFF MIC)
(SNIFFS ONCE, TWICE) This way.

BOOLAN:
The Force will be free. The Force will be—

FX: A curtain is pulled aside by Sskeer.

BOOLAN: (CONT)
You have found me, my friend.

SSKEER:
There was only one place you could be.

BOOLAN:
I . . . I am sorry that I ran. When the lightning hit the fighter, I feared the worst, feared you had died.

SSKEER:
The Force was with me. Thanks to you.

BOOLAN:
The Force. Yes.

FX: Boolan rises and turns to them.

BOOLAN: (CONT)
We meet again, Jedi Master Trennis. And you have brought friends.

FX: Avar enters the small chamber.

AVAR:
Baron Boolan, I am Jedi Master Avar Kriss.

BOOLAN:
I am aware of who you are, Master Kriss. And this is who I am. Truly.

AVAR:
The robes you wear.

BOOLAN:
The robes of my people. My . . . religion. The Path of the Open Hand.

TEY:
Not the Closed Fist?

BOOLAN:
(AMAZED) You were there? On the Night of Sorrow?

TEY:
I was kinda late to the party, but yeah.

BOOLAN:
Then you know what we went through. The price that we paid. (TO THE JEDI) I am ready, Master Jedi.

KEEVE:
For what, Boolan?

BOOLAN:
To return with you, to the Republic, to unlock the secrets of my research.

TEY:
Just like that.

BOOLAN:
A gift freely given.

TEY:
But that's the thing, Baron. I do remember the Path of the Open Hand, and they weren't too hot on working with the Jedi. With anyone who—how did you put it—"abused" the Force.

BOOLAN:
These lines I have painted on my forehead, they were the symbols of our faith, of the living Force. Freedom, harmony, and clarity. For the first time in my life, I feel I see things clearly. When I was small, when I first walked these tunnels, I obeyed without question, trusted those who claimed to know the way. But the Path was flawed. It had been for a long time, long before my father first put on these robes I now wear. His robes.

He wanted to believe in the Path, wanted it to show him the way, but it was poisoned, corrupted by those who thought only of revenge and power.

The Nihil are no different, and yet I allowed myself to follow their path willingly. And willingly I say, no more.

Everything I was taught... everything I believed... it was wrong. You showed me that, Sskeer. All of you did. Through all this, you never gave up. You put others first for the sake of the Force. And now, now it is my turn.

I realize you will be wary, and for good reason. I am not a person who engenders trust. I hope to change that, too, if you will let me. For the sake of the Force.

CUT TO:

SCENE 129. EXT. DALNA. PLANET SURFACE—DAY.

Atmos: As before. Lourna stands alone on the windswept plain.

LOURNA:
Quin? How are the repairs going back there? Will we be able to get—

QUIN: (DISTORT/COMMS)
Home?

LOURNA:
To get the Jedi where they need to be.

QUIN: (DISTORT/COMMS)
The Path drive is hanging together by a thread, but I think so. Skoot's a good little worker. We could do with him on our crew.

LOURNA:
Do we have a crew?

QUIN: (DISTORT/COMMS)
We could. You're a bounty hunter. I'm a bounty hunter . . .

LOURNA:
I honestly don't know what I am these days. If you could see it out here, Quin . . .

QUIN: (DISTORT/COMMS)
I can. It's—

LOURNA:
A lot.

QUIN: (DISTORT/COMMS)
You can say that again.

LOURNA:
Kriss was right. This planet was beautiful, and then we came here with our war against everything, with our bombs and scheming. We did this. *I* did this.

QUIN: (DISTORT/COMMS)
You were obeying orders.

LOURNA:
And isn't that what I always say? It wasn't me. It was Ro. It was Fry. (BEAT, THEN QUIETER, ALMOST WISTFUL) It was Bala.

QUIN: (DISTORT/COMMS)
Who?

LOURNA:
I never took you to my home, did I? My real home, I mean. Aaloth.

QUIN: (DISTORT/COMMS)
(TEASING) Where you were a princess?

LOURNA:
You're not going to let me forget that, are you?

QUIN: (DISTORT/COMMS)
No.

LOURNA:
(ALMOST WISTFUL) Perhaps we should pay a visit. See what's happened to the old place.

FX: An electric burst on the other side of the comm.

QUIN: (DISTORT/COMMS)
Ow!

LOURNA:
You okay?

QUIN: (DISTORT/COMMS)
Burnt fingers. Nothing a glass of revnog won't cure. What were you saying?

FX: There is movement. The party is returning, snapping Lourna out of her reflective mood, at least on the surface.

LOURNA:
Nothing that matters.

FX: A beep as Lourna closes comms.

LOURNA: (CONT)
(PITCHING UP, TO THE GROUP) You found him, then. Nice threads. Not my color, but it's a strong look.

KEEVE: (COMING UP ON MIC)
How's the *Overtone*?

LOURNA:
Ready for takeoff, more or less. Where are we heading? Back to Coruscant?

AVAR:
No, the Yarvellian Institute on Protobranch, center of blight research, where Boolan can do the most good.

LOURNA:
You're the boss.

TEY:
Careful. You almost sound like you mean it.

LOURNA:
I just want to get off this . . .

KEEVE:
Rock?

LOURNA:
Bad choice of word.

SSKEER:
Maybe. Maybe not. Look there, at your feet, where you're ssstanding.

KEEVE:
A flower.

LOURNA:
Could be a weed.

AVAR:
Whatever it is . . . it's life.

KEEVE:
It's hope.

TEY:
A gift freely given.

LOURNA:
You are all *so* sentimental.

SSKEER:
(SMILING) It's the Jedi way.

LOURNA:
Whatever.

FX: The crunch of dirt beneath her boots as Lourna leads the way. A beep as she opens comms again.

LOURNA: (CONT)
(INTO COMLINK) Quin, we're coming back in. Have Skoot prime the engines.

CUT TO:

SCENE 130. INT. HEIKLET. CASTLE CHAMBER— LATER.

Atmos: As before, the storm raging outside.

FX: The Nameless growls quietly as Marchion broods. Heavy footsteps rush up.

SHE'AR PILOT: (COMING UP ON MIC)
Lord Eye, we've found something in the databanks. A backup of the baron's findings that the traitor didn't destroy.

MARCHION:
Show me.

FX: Marchion snatches the datapad.

SHE'AR PILOT:
We think it is an earlier version of his work, but the basis should be there.

FX: We hear data scrolling as Marchion runs a finger down the screen.

MARCHION:
Yes. This is it. This is—

FX: The scrolling stops abruptly. Marchion has noticed something.

MARCHION: (CONT)
(QUIET) No.

SHE'AR PILOT:
My lord? Marchion?

MARCHION:
(ROARS IN FRUSTRATION)

FX: Marchion throws the datapad across the room. It smashes against the wall.

FX: The Leveler reacts to Marchion's anger, growling more fiercely.

SHE'AR PILOT:
What is it? What did you find?

FX: Marchion is already marching from the chamber, cloak billowing, the Nameless at his heels.

MARCHION: (GOING OFF MIC)
Ready the *Gaze*.

SHE'AR PILOT:
We're leaving?

MARCHION: (OFF MIC)
Now!

CUT TO:

Part Eight
THE FORCE WILL BE FREE

SCENE 131. EXT. PROTOBRANCH SPACEPORT—DAY.

Atmos: A busy spaceport. People moving from ship to ship. Aircars and speeders coming and going.

FX: The Overtone *comes in, its landing gear deploying. It lands, and the main ramp descends.*

FX: The heroes march down the ramp.

KEEVE:
They're expecting us at the medcenter.

LOURNA:
How far is it?

AVAR:
A couple of klicks. The other side of Protobranch City.

TEY:
I'll hire a speeder.

LOURNA:
No, I will. The baron is our bounty, mine and Quin's.

QUIN:
Ours?

LOURNA:
We're responsible for taking him in.

SSKEER:
He came here freely.

LOURNA:
And we need our pardons. No offense, Baron.

BOOLAN:
We must all do what we think is right.

CUT TO:

SCENE 132. EXT. PROTOBRANCH MEDCENTER—DAY.

Atmos: The middle of a busy town.

FX: A speeder whizzes up and stops.

QUIN:
This is it.

LOURNA:
The first of many paydays, Quin. (BEAT) Baron, if you wouldn't mind...

BOOLAN:
Of course.

FX: They exit the vehicle and approach the medcenter.

FX: Doors open, and a familiar figure meets them, accompanied by a snakelike Anacondan clattering along on cybernetic limbs.

AVAR:
Elzar? You're on Protobranch?

ELZAR:
I came as soon as I received your message. (SPOTTING WHO ELSE IS IN THE PARTY) Sskeer! Thank the Force.

SSKEER:
Master Mann.

ELZAR:
You remember Dr. Gino'le?

SSKEER:
Of course.

TEY:
(SOTTO) An Anacondan doctor! Just when you think you've seen it all...

SSKEER:
It is gratifying to sssee you again, Doctor.

DR. GINO'LE:
I wish only that the reasons for our reunion were more pleasant, Master Sskeer. Most of those affected by the blight have been moved to secure wards. Nothing like Starlight's facilities, of course, but needs must...

FX: Boolan taps his wide head.

BOOLAN:
I have the key to my research here, Doctor.

DR. GINO'LE:
In your head. I was hoping for something a little more... tangible.

BOOLAN:
Trust me. Your troubles will soon be behind you.

DR. GINO'LE:
Hmm. After testing, at least. You'll forgive me if I don't take you at your word, Baron.

BOOLAN:
I would expect nothing less. But time *is* of the essence.

LOURNA:
Okay, let's get him inside. There's quite a crowd forming.

ELZAR:
We'll take him from here, Lourna.

LOURNA:
No, you won't. He's our responsibility.

ELZAR:
Which you have delivered as promised. The Republic is grateful and will honor its side of the deal.

LOURNA:
With all due respect, *Master* Jedi, I want to see this through to the end.

ELZAR:
And that is what this is for you. The end.

KEEVE:
Elzar, Lourna has proved herself. We couldn't have done this without her.

ELZAR:
Which is gratifying to hear, but you also heard the doctor. This is a *secure* facility. Essential personnel only. (TO TEY) If you could accompany the baron . . .

FX: Elzar turns and leaves. Gino'le scuttles alongside him.

LOURNA:
Wait. Sirrek gets to go in but not us?

TEY:
Skoot, stay with them, will you? We won't be long, I promise.

FX: They all head inside, except for Lourna and Quin. The doors shut.

LOURNA:
I don't think so.

FX: She takes a step forward. The doors remain stubbornly shut, represented by an electronic error beep.

LOURNA: (CONT)
Well? Open up. (NO RESPONSE) Open up!

QUIN:
Lourna, it's no good. They don't want us in there.

LOURNA:
They can't do this. (SHOUTING THROUGH THE GLASS) You can't do this! Can't shut me out! Don't you know who I am?

QUIN:
I think that's the problem.

LOURNA:
I'm Lourna Dee!

FX: Lourna slaps her hand against the glass.

LOURNA: (CONT)
Do you hear me? Lourna Dee!

MUSICAL SEGUE:

SCENE 133. INT. PROTOBRANCH MEDCENTER. LAB—LATER.

Atmos: A sterile lab. The slight burble of computer equipment.

ELZAR:
Well?

DR. GINO'LE:
We have accessed the baron's data and added the new findings that he has provided.

ELZAR:
And?

DR. GINO'LE:
See for yourself.

KEEVE:
What are they doing?

DR. GINO'LE:
That is a wasaka plant infected with the blight.

SSKEER:
So I can sssee. I had no idea it was ssso virulent.

AVAR:
As if the galaxy hasn't suffered enough.

ELZAR:
You can actually see it spreading along the stems.

KEEVE:
And the droids will be safe?

DR. GINO'LE:
To a degree. We still don't understand how the blight spreads.

AVAR:
But the baron's research will help.

BOOLAN:
The doctor has already tested my cure on inanimate objects affected by the . . . condition.

DR. GINO'LE:
Minerals and the like.

ELZAR:
And the results?

DR. GINO'LE:
Early days, although the solution does seem to keep the blight at bay.

KEEVE:
But not cure it.

BOOLAN:
It will, with the appropriate modification.

DR. GINO'LE:
One step at a time.

FX: Dr. Gino'le presses a button with a mechanical arm.

DR. GINO'LE: (CONT)
You may proceed.

FX: The whine of an energy field.

DR. GINO'LE: (CONT)
Good. Good. (BEAT) This is excellent.

SSKEER:
It's working?

DR. GINO'LE:
The spread has halted. (GASPS IN EXCITEMENT) And there are even signs of regeneration! This is incredible!

BOOLAN:
What did I tell you? My work with Master Sskeer was key.

ELZAR:
I will report back to the Senate. The chancellor will want to know immediately.

DR. GINO'LE:
Early days, Master Mann. Remember that when you speak to them.

Elzar turns to the doors.

ELZAR:
Of course. But any progress is good news—

FX: The doors open, revealing Tey hurrying in.

TEY:
Good news. That's exactly what I hoped to hear.

KEEVE:
Tey?

TEY:
I've just been visiting the patients. Our young Yacombe friend, to be precise.

DR. GINO'LE:
Behind an energy field, I trust.

SSKEER:
Tey, what's happened?

TEY:
She's deteriorated, Sskeer. I . . . I don't think she has long.

SSKEER:
What?

KEEVE:
Doctor?

DR. GINO'LE:
Yes, yes. I'll go and check.

FX: He scuttles off, activating a comlink.

DR. GINO'LE: (CONT)
Nurse Okana, meet me at the primary ward immediately.

CUT TO:

SCENE 134. EXT. PROTOBRANCH SPACEPORT—DAY.

Atmos: As before.

FX: The speeder approaches and screeches to a halt.

QUIN:
Lourna—careful! You nearly hit that Bonbrak.

LOURNA:
Then they should've gotten out of the way.

FX: Lourna jumps from the speeder.

QUIN:
They did. Just.

BONBRAK:
(ANGRY) *Mata-ta karaley!*

FX: Lourna stalks past the diminutive alien.

LOURNA:
Don't make me try again.

BONBRAK:
Mara-charalene!

FX: Quin jumps out and chases after Lourna.

QUIN:
Lourna, wait. Wait up!

LOURNA:
For what? To be put back in my place? Again.

FX: SK-0T whizzes up.

SK-0T: (COMING UP ON MIC)
Zut-zut-zep!

QUIN:
Don't blame me, Skoot. I told her to wait for you.

SK-0T:
Zet-zup!

LOURNA:
(CAN'T BELIEVE WHAT SHE'S JUST HEARD) The others will be wondering where we've gone? You mean, our "friends"? Our "teammates"? I've been such a *fool*! "It's life. It's hope. It's the Jedi way." Damn right, it is.

FX: Quin grabs her arm.

QUIN:
Where are you going?

FX: Lourna reacts badly, slapping her away. Hard.

LOURNA:
Don't touch me! I don't want you near me!

QUIN:
(HURT) What happened to "us"?

LOURNA:
Us? (SNORTS) There is no us. There's never been an us. Go on. You're in a spaceport. A dealer on every corner. Choose your poison. Knock yourself out. You know you want to.

QUIN:
(QUIET, HURT) You haven't changed. You'll never change.

LOURNA:
Nothing changes, Quin. Not me, not them. And if you believe you can, you're a bigger fool than I am. Go on, get.

FX: She pushes Quin back viciously.

LOURNA: (CONT)
Get away from me!

FX: Quin lands on the ground. SK-OT buzzes down to her.

SK-OT:
Zeb-zeb.

QUIN:
Don't worry, I'm going.

FX: Quin gets up, while SK-OT tries to help.

QUIN: (CONT)
And you'll do the same if you have any sense, Skoot.

FX: Quin leaves, shouting back angrily.

QUIN: (CONT)
Lourna Dee can go rot!

LOURNA:
(QUIET, SEETHING) Maybe I will.

FX: SK-OT bobs near Lourna.

SK-OT:
Zet-zet.

LOURNA:
(SIGHING) Just . . . don't, Skoot. I don't want to hear it. Why are you even here anyway?

SK-OT:
Zet-zub.

LOURNA:
To prep the *Overtone*. For return to its owner. (LAUGHS QUIETLY) Good luck with that.

FX: She marches toward the Overtone *with purpose. SK-OT whirs after her.*

SK-OT:
Zub-zep?

LOURNA:
You think I'm hanging around? I need a ship, and the *Overtone* is as good as any other.

FX: A bleep of a control, and the ramp lowers.

LOURNA: (CONT)
Until I find something that's a bit more "me," of course. Something with more teeth.

FX: Lourna marches up the ramp.

LOURNA: (CONT)
Bye, Skoot. Stay lucky.

FX: The ramp rises. SK-OT bobs around, agitated.

SK-OT:
Zub-zub-zub-zub!

FX: The engine fires up.

SK-OT: (CONT)
Zeb-zep!

CUT TO:

SCENE 135. INT. PROTOBRANCH MEDCENTER. WARD.

Atmos: Similar to lab.

KEEVE:
And you're *sure* this is a good idea?

DR. GINO'LE:
No.

TEY:
But you're trying anyway?

DR. GINO'LE:
Please. There is a risk, yes, but I have run numerous tests. The treatment seems stable.

KEEVE:
Seems?

SSKEER:
Keeve.

KEEVE:
I can't believe that you're happy with this, Sskeer. You found this girl, looked after her when... when you weren't even in your right mind!

TEY:
Harsh.

SSKEER:
But fair.

DR. GINO'LE:
And with all respect, Jedi Trennis, we are *not*—

KEEVE:
Experimenting.

DR. GINO'LE:
Testing the procedure on your young friend. This Lasat has given his consent.

KEEVE:
This *man* is desperate.

DR. GINO'LE:
We *all* are.

FX: Elzar enters.

ELZAR:
Is there a problem?

KEEVE:
No, we're just playing games with people's lives, nothing out of the ordinary.

DR. GINO'LE:
I do not play games, young lady. I don't care if you're a master or a member of the Jedi Council, you do not speak to me like that in my own department. Is there a risk? Yes, but like it or not, that Ithorian out there is a genius. Need I remind you that Magrak syndrome is incurable, hmm? And yet here is Sskeer. I examined your former teacher earlier—the same examination I carried out on Starlight the day I diagnosed his condition. I could find no indication that he had ever suffered from the syndrome at any point in his life. None whatsoever. Baron Boolan did that. He did the impossible.

KEEVE:
Yes, but . . .

DR. GINO'LE:
But nothing. These are desperate times, Master Trennis . . .

KEEVE:
So we take desperate measures.

DR. GINO'LE:
So we take a leap of faith.

KEEVE:
And if it doesn't work?

DR. GINO'LE:
Nothing changes. These poor unfortunates will still have the same prognosis. I take full responsibility for what we are doing. Let me try to save these people. Let me try to save your friend.

ELZAR:
Keeve?

KEEVE:
It's your call. But if it goes wrong . . .

DR. GINO'LE:
We still have options.

SSKEER:
At the very least, you could place the patients in ssstasis fields, yesss?

DR. GINO'LE:
If we thought it would do any good, yes, Sskeer. That is something we could indeed do.

ELZAR:
We will let you get on with your work, Doctor. May the Force be with you.

DR. GINO'LE:
May it be with us all.

CUT TO:

SCENE 136. EXT. SPACE—SAME TIME.

FX: The Overtone *blasts up from the planet.*

CUT TO:

SCENE 137. INT. THE *OVERTONE*. COCKPIT—CONTINUOUS.

Atmos: As before.

FX: Lourna hits controls as she pilots.

LOURNA:
And we're away. The question is . . . heading where?

FX: More beeps.

LOURNA: (CONT)
(TRYING TO SOUND DECISIVE) Who cares? As long as I'm on my own. That's all that matters.

FX: SK-OT buzzes out from a hiding place.

SK-OT:
Zup-zep!

LOURNA:
What the—what are *you* doing here? How did you even get back on board?

SK-OT:
Zep-zeb-zub!

FX: Lourna pulls her blaster on him.

LOURNA:
Then you can head back *out* the exhaust filter or get shot right between the processors. Your choice, wise guy.

FX: An alarm sounds.

SK-0T:
(SQUEALS IN PANIC)

LOURNA:
Wha—?

FX: Outside, the sound of a huge ship suddenly dropping out of hyperspace.

LOURNA: (CONT)
No. The *Gaze Electric*? Here? What's going on?

FX: She hits controls, tuning in to space traffic control's communication. We hear "radio" tuning.

LOURNA: (CONT)
Come on. Come on.

FX: The interference solidifies into:

SPACE TRAFFIC CONTROL: (COMMS)
Unidentified craft, please transmit ID markers.

LOURNA:
Seriously? Can't you *see* what ship that is?

SPACE TRAFFIC CONTROL: (COMMS)
Transmit identification markers immediately, or we will be forced to intervene.

LOURNA:
Like to see them do that. Time to leave.

FX: Beeps as she prepares to depart.

SPACE TRAFFIC CONTROL: (COMMS)
We repeat—

SHE'AR PILOT: (DISTORT/COMMS)
Space traffic control, this is She'ar V'eax of the *Gaze Electric*. You will not "intervene," and you will make no more demands. Is that understood?

FX: Three beeps on Lourna's systems.

SPACE TRAFFIC CONTROL: (COMMS)
RDC forces have been dispatched. You will lower your defenses and retreat from Protobranch space.

SK-0T:
Zep-zep-zet.

LOURNA:
Yes, of course, I'm still leaving. It's just . . .

FX: Outside, RDC fighters whiz past. Lasers start firing as battle commences.

LOURNA: (CONT)
Ro would *never* let anyone speak on behalf of the *Gaze*. It has to be a decoy. But for what?

FX: The battle continues outside.

SPACE TRAFFIC CONTROL: (COMMS)
All ships not engaged in the conflict, please vacate Protobranch space for your own safety.

LOURNA:
Our own safety. Ha.

FX: She flicks more switches and pushes forward before turning back to the planet.

SK-0T:
Zeb-zeb?

LOURNA:
You wanted me to go back, didn't you? Your wish is granted!

FX: The Overtone *descends back into the planet's atmosphere.*

CUT TO:

SCENE 138. EXT. PROTOBRANCH SPACEPORT. ALLEY BESIDE HANGAR—DAY.

Atmos: As before.

QUIN:
Hey, handsome. Know where a girl can score some reed?

GAMORREAN:
(SQUEALS)

QUIN:
I was only asking.

GAMORREAN:
(GRUNTS IN ANGER)

FX: The Gamorrean slopes off.

QUIN:
(CALLING AFTER HIM) Yeah, well, you should look in a mirror sometime! Stupid mort-licker! (BEAT) Yeah, because *he's* the stupid one. What are you doing, Quin? Lurking beneath a grav-crane, propositioning *Gamorreans* for a fix? I mean, it's one step up from the gutter, but . . . (SIGHS) Maybe I should take a leaf out of Lourna's book. Look after number one. Steal a planet hopper . . .

FX: *Nearby, a shuttle descends with a throaty rumble of engines.*

DROID: (OFF MIC)
(ANGRY BURBLE OF BEEPS AND BLOOPS)

QUIN:
(GENUINELY IMPRESSED) Or a shuttle! That's ...

FX: *The hatch lowers, and a speeder roars out.*

QUIN: (CONT)
That's *Ro*!

FX: *He's heading in her direction.*

QUIN: (CONT)
Hey.

FX: *She throws herself in front of him.*

QUIN: (CONT)
Ro! Stop!

FX: *Quin fires a shot at the ground in front of Marchion. The speeder screeches to a halt.*

MARCHION: (HELMETED)
Quin? You have some nerve.

QUIN:
If I wanted you dead, you'd be on your back.

MARCHION: (HELMETED)
(BARKS A LAUGH) With your blaster shaking like that?

FX: *A click of her blaster as she aims at him.*

QUIN:
Off the speeder. Slowly.

FX: *Marchion dismounts.*

MARCHION: (HELMETED)
We haven't time for this, Quin.

QUIN:
I would ask why you're here, but I could guess ... Boolan.

MARCHION: (HELMETED)
Where have they taken him? The medcenter? Is that where they've taken his cure?

QUIN:
And don't you just hate it? You've lost, Ro. Just like the rest of us.

MARCHION: (HELMETED)
You don't know what you're talking about. Let me pass.

QUIN:
You know, I was scared when I saw you on Waskiro. Terrified. But I'm through with being intimidated. I'm not much, little more than a reed-head in desperate need for a fix, but I *can* stop you. I can stop you from ruining everything. How do you like that?

MARCHION: (HELMETED)
I haven't time for this.

FX: He lunges at her. They fight.

QUIN:
(EFFORT) I'm not going to let you win, Ro.

MARCHION: (HELMETED)
Without a blaster?

FX: He slaps it out of her hand.

QUIN
(REACTS)

MARCHION: (HELMETED)
Somehow I doubt it.

FX: The struggle continues.

QUIN:
(EFFORT) Better this way. Who needs weapons to ride the Storm?

MARCHION: (HELMETED)
You do!

FX: Marchion deploys one of his hidden blades and drives it into Quin's side.

QUIN:
(GASPS) Hidden blade. That's . . . cheating.

MARCHION: (HELMETED)
(QUIET, CRUEL) I write my own rules.

QUIN:
(A RAGGED BREATH)

FX: She slides from his blade and slumps to the ground.

MARCHION: (HELMETED)
Goodbye, Quin!

LOURNA: (OFF MIC)
No!

FX: Whoosh of cape as Marchion whirls around.

MARCHION: (HELMETED)
What now?

LOURNA: (COMING UP ON MIC)
Get away from her!

FX: Blaster bolts stream in, followed by running feet.

MARCHION: (HELMETED)
Lourna!

FX: One of the bolts hits him, his armor absorbing most of the energy, but he's still knocked back.

MARCHION: (CONT, HELMETED)
(REACTS)

FX: Lourna runs past him.

LOURNA:
Quin! No, no, no, no, no.

FX: She drops to her knees beside Quin.

LOURNA: (CONT)
Let me see.

QUIN:
(WEAK) Just a scratch.

LOURNA:
A scratch? For stars' sake, Quin. I've seen those blades before. They're covered in toxins. (CALLING OFF MIC) Skoot! Get over here.

FX: SK-0T swoops over.

SK-0T:
Zep-zep!

LOURNA:
Go back to the *Overtone*. Grab a medical kit. Grab anything you can.

SK-0T:
Zup-zet!

FX: SK-0T buzzes off.

LOURNA:
He'll be back soon, Quin. Do you hear? And then we'll sort you out. Quin?

No response.

LOURNA: (CONT)
Quin!

FX: Marchion pushes himself up. His helmet has come off.

MARCHION:
(BREATHING HEAVILY) Out of my way, Lourna.

FX: Lourna stands.

LOURNA:
(FULL OF HATE) Not going to happen.

FX: Marchion activates his lightsaber.

MARCHION:
I won't ask again.

FX: Lourna draws her own sword, activating the energy that crackles around the blade.

LOURNA:
You won't be able to.

FX: Lourna swings around and strikes.

LOURNA: (CONT)
This is for Quin.

FX: Another attack and block.

LOURNA: (CONT)
This is for Waskiro!

MARCHION:
Waskiro? Like you care about them. What next? Tears for Valo? For Tanalorr?

FX: He lands a punch with his lightsaber hand.

LOURNA:
(REACTS)

FX: Lourna stumbles back. Marchion's lightsaber hums as he goads her.

MARCHION:
I don't know what game you're playing, siding with Avar Kriss, with the Jedi. Anything to save your miserable hide. It's pathetic.

LOURNA:
Says the man who hides behind a mask.

MARCHION:
Better than hiding behind a grav-crane. Do you think those supports will protect you?

FX: He slices through one of the thick supports.

LOURNA:
What are you doing?

FX: Above them, the structure groans.

MARCHION:
Finishing this!

FX: The swords clash.

LOURNA:
(REACTS)

MARCHION:
Finishing *you*!

FX: Marchion goes on the offensive, lightsaber blazing. Lourna is being pushed back.

LOURNA:
Marchion!

FX: He slices through another support. The crane creaks ominously.

LOURNA: (CONT)
You're going to bring this thing down on top of us.

MARCHION:
Not on me!

FX: He slices through her sword.

LOURNA:
My sword. That's ... that's not possible.

MARCHION:
What did you think it was? Beskar?

LOURNA:
Phrik. At least, that's what the Hutts told me.

MARCHION:
Never trust a slug.

LOURNA:
Takes one to know one.

FX: She pulls her blaster and fires at point-blank range. The bolts bounce off the supports.

MARCHION:
Blades. Blasters. They won't save you, Lourna. Not from me!

FX: He comes around and kicks her in the chest, the clang reverberating as the blaster clatters away.

LOURNA:
(REACTS, THE AIR DRIVEN FROM HER LUNGS)

FX: She slides to the ground. Above them, the metalwork continues to groan.

LOURNA: (CONT)
(STRUGGLING FOR BREATH) Marchion.

MARCHION:
(BREATHING HEAVILY, BUT VICTORIOUS) And here it comes . . .

FX: The grav-crane creaks above them. The lightsaber hums.

MARCHION: (CONT)
The bargaining, the pleas—"I was wrong, Marchion. Forgive me. I can help you. You can trust me."

FX: Part of the grav-crane breaks off and falls, crashing nearby.

MARCHION: (CONT)
I trust no one but myself. Not that it matters. You're nothing to me, Lourna Dee. Nothing at all.

FX: The lightsaber comes up, ready to execute her, and . . .

LOURNA:
(LAUGHS, QUIETLY, WRYLY)

MARCHION:
You find this funny?

LOURNA:
Your little speech or the tons of twisted metal about to drop on our heads?

FX: To prove her point, another part of the crane comes crashing down. The metal framework continues to creak ominously throughout the following exchange.

LOURNA: (CONT)
I'm not laughing at you, Marchion. I'm laughing at myself. Who have I been kidding all these years? Blaming you for everything. You, your father, everyone I've ever met. But it's never been you. It's me. I allowed this to happen. Allowed myself to be manipulated. Because I was scared. I still am. And you're right. It's pathetic. I yell my name at the galaxy, demanding respect. For what? All I ever do is run. From who I really am. Who I want to be. (TONE HARDENING) But I'm not running anymore.

FX: With a roar of defiance, Lourna launches herself at Marchion, knocking him back.

MARCHION:
Lourna!

FX: The lightsaber clatters to the ground. The blade shuts off.

MARCHION: (CONT)
The lightsaber! Where is it?

LOURNA:
(STRUGGLING TO HOLD HIM DOWN) Trust me. That's the least of your worries.

FX: Another part of the structure comes crashing down nearby.

MARCHION:
The crane! Lourna!

LOURNA:
You shouldn't have killed Quin.

FX: More groans from the metal. More crashes as the crane starts to collapse.

MARCHION:
(STRUGGLING) You don't understand why I'm here. I tried to tell Quin—

LOURNA:
You don't get to say her name. Not anymore.

MARCHION:
(STRUGGLING) Soon none of us will be able to say anything at all!

LOURNA:
What are you talking about?

MARCHION:
Boolan's cure.

LOURNA:
For the blight?

MARCHION:
It's anything but, Lourna. It's a virus. A plague. It's going to kill us all!

FX: The crane collapses. The structure crashes down on top of them both.

CUT TO:

SCENE 139. INT. PROTOBRANCH MEDCENTER. CORRIDOR OUTSIDE WARD—SAME TIME.

Atmos: As before.

FX: Avar approaches.

AVAR:
Has it begun?

KEEVE:
They're about to. Dr. Gino'le asked us to wait out here.

ELZAR:
It's understandable. The medical staff needs space.

TEY:
Tell that to Boolan. He's in there.

SSKEER:
To advissse.

AVAR:
And we think that's wise?

ELZAR:
He's unarmed. And you say that he is—

SSKEER:
(NOT SOUNDING SO SURE) Sssincere.

AVAR:
Sskeer?

FX: An energy field activates on the other side of the window, the same we heard from earlier.

DR. GINO'LE: (DISTORT/COMMS)
We are applying the first treatment.

AVAR:
On the Lasat patient?

KEEVE:
Yes.

TEY:
The kid's getting worse.

ELZAR:
Her turn will come, Tey.

DR. GINO'LE: (DISTORT/COMMS)
We have made the injection.

TEY:
I can't watch.

KEEVE:
Where are you going?

TEY:
I don't know. Anywhere but here. Anyone want anything? A cup of caf? A new set of nerves?

FX: Tey strides off.

KEEVE:
Tey.

ELZAR:
He'll be fine. Trust in the Force.

KEEVE:
If only it was that easy.

AVAR:
It is. It will be. How long will it take?

ELZAR:
We should know soon.

SSKEER:
(WARY) Ssshould...

KEEVE:
You feel it, too, don't you? An uneasiness in the Force. We *all* feel it, but we're not *doing* anything. Except for being too hasty. There should be more tests.

ELZAR:
There isn't time. Dr. Gino'le—

KEEVE:
Dr. Gino'le is under pressure from the chancellor to get this done. We all are, *especially* the Jedi Council.

ELZAR:
That is—

KEEVE:
What, Elzar? Not true? Something about this is not right. Trust in the Force? We're not *listening* to the Force. And we need to start.

CUT TO:

SCENE 140. EXT. PROTOBRANCH SPACEPORT. ALLEY BESIDE HANGAR—DAY.

Atmos: As before, but there's creaking as the collapsed grav-crane settles. There's also movement in the distance. It won't be long before people come to investigate the accident.

Wild track: Cries of "Did you see that?" and "What happened?"

FX: Lourna pushes herself up.

LOURNA:
(COUGHING) That was close... A centimeter to the left...

FX: Creak of metal as she pushes against the wreckage.

LOURNA: (CONT)
(EFFORT)

MARCHION:
Lourna...

LOURNA:
(BITTER LAUGH) You survived as well. The universe really does have a sense of humor. Anything broken?

MARCHION:
I'm trapped. The metal. It's too heavy.

LOURNA:
Could be worse. Should've been worse.

FX: She pushes wreckage off her.

MARCHION:
(PAINED) Careful!

LOURNA:
Excuse me while I don't give a flying manta.

MARCHION:
Remember what I told you . . . Boolan's virus!

LOURNA:
More lies.

MARCHION:
It's the truth. Boolan betrayed me. All that time working on a cure, and instead he was researching a pathogen that removes connection to the Force.

LOURNA:
Why should you care? You hate the Jedi.

MARCHION:
But it's impossible, Lourna. Don't you see that? There's no way it can work. Not without killing everybody. I told the galaxy I would save them.

LOURNA:
And suddenly you're a man of your word? I watched you destroy an entire planet because people saw you bleed. Why should you care if people die? You'll say anything to save yourself. Just like me.

QUIN:
(WEAK) But . . . what if he's not like you? What if he's telling the truth?

LOURNA:
Quin!

FX: Lourna clambers over the metalwork.

LOURNA: (CONT)
You're still with us. Don't move. Skoot will be back soon. We'll get you through this.

QUIN:
(WEAK) We can't be sure he's lying.

LOURNA:
He is. He can't bear to lose.

MARCHION:
Everyone will lose.

QUIN:
(WEAK) You need to warn them, the Jedi.

LOURNA:
(MAKING A DECISION) I need to do what he said. I need to finish it.

FX: Lourna gets up and walks back to the wreckage.

QUIN:
(WEAK) Lourna.

MARCHION:
What are you doing?

LOURNA:
Well, look at that.

FX: A scrape of metal as Lourna picks something up from the ground.

LOURNA: (CONT)
Just what you were looking for.

FX: Lourna ignites the lightsaber.

MARCHION:
You need to listen to me.

LOURNA:
I need to listen to myself.

FX: The lightsaber hums as she examines it.

LOURNA: (CONT)
It would be so easy. While you're trapped, while you're helpless.

FX: Another hum.

LOURNA: (CONT)
To drive the tip into your chest.

MARCHION:
You wouldn't dare.

FX: She brings the lightsaber up.

LOURNA:
Care to test that theory?

QUIN:
(WEAK) Lourna, please.

MARCHION:
Well? What are you waiting for? Do it! Take your victory!

LOURNA:
Gladly.

FX: Lourna growls and swings the lightsaber down. It slashes through metal.

MARCHION:
(GASPS)

LOURNA:
There.

FX: She extinguishes the lightsaber.

MARCHION:
What are you doing?

LOURNA:
I could kill you. But you're not worth the effort. I choose life.

FX: She tosses the lightsaber away. It clatters off metal in the distance.

LOURNA: (CONT)
Good luck finding that.

MARCHION:
(ANGRY) Wait! Lourna!

FX: Lourna clambers back to Quin.

LOURNA:
Quin? Quin!

Lourna checks Quin's neck.

LOURNA: (CONT)
Still got a pulse. (EFFORT AS SHE PICKS QUIN UP) You better be right about this, you beautiful mess.

MARCHION: (OFF MIC)
You can't leave me here!

FX: Lourna eases the unconscious Quin onto Marchion's speeder.

LOURNA:
(IGNORES HIM) That's it, easy now. Just don't die on me, do you hear?

MARCHION: (OFF MIC)
What are you doing?

LOURNA:
Borrowing your speeder. You won't be needing it, will you?

FX: She gets on the speeder. In the background, we can hear people running up.

Wild track: Cries of "This way" and "Bring medkits."

MARCHION: (OFF MIC)
(STRUGGLES, PANICS) You need to help me. I can't move! Can't get out!

LOURNA:
I cut the first girder. The rest is up to you.

MARCHION: (OFF MIC)
Lourna!

LOURNA: (OFF MIC)
Killing you would've been easy. This is more fun.

FX: The speeder roars off.

MARCHION:
Lourna! (SHOUTING AFTER HER) *Lourna!*

CUT TO:

SCENE 141. INT. PROTOBRANCH MEDCENTER. WARD—SAME TIME.

Atmos: As before. Energy field on.

FX: The door slides open. Keeve rushes in.

KEEVE:
Doctor. Doctor, you need to stop.

FX: Elzar chases after her.

ELZAR:
Keeve!

DR. GINO'LE:
This is intolerable. Clear the room.

KEEVE:
Don't inject her. Don't inject any more of them.

DR. GINO'LE:
I already have! (LOOKING OVER HER SHOULDER) Master Mann. Marshal. *Please.*

AVAR:
What is their condition?

DR. GINO'LE:
Stable.

SSKEER:
Are you sssure?

DR. GINO'LE:
Did you become a doctor on your travels, Sskeer?

BOOLAN:
(UNDER HIS BREATH) The Force will be free. The Force will be free. (REPEATS)

KEEVE:
He's not telling us everything. We were so quick to believe him because he helped Sskeer, but he's holding something back.

TEY: (DISTORT/COMMS)
Funny you should say that, Keeve.

CUT TO:

SCENE 142. INT. PROTOBRANCH MEDCENTER. LOBBY—CONTINUOUS.

FX: Tey is running through the lobby.

TEY:
Excuse me. Coming through.

KEEVE: (DISTORT/COMMS)
Tey? Where are you?

TEY:
Coming through the lobby, on the way to you.

KEEVE: (DISTORT/COMMS)
Why?

TEY:
Remember that wasaka plant that looked so good? I called in to the lab, and it's not looking so hot now. The blight's back and worse than ever. And that's not all.

FX: The comm fizzes.

TEY: (CONT)
Keeve? Keeve, are you still receiving this? (BEAT) Kriff!

RECEPTION DROID: (COMING UP ON MIC)
Oh dear. This is not good. Not good at all.

FX: *Tey stops, overhearing them.*

TEY:
Hey, droid. What's not good?

RECEPTION DROID:
Internal systems are corrupting throughout the medcenter.

TEY:
Comms?

RECEPTION DROID:
Security, central databases, everything is shutting down. Some kind of virus locking us out.

TEY:
Just like on the asteroid.

RECEPTION DROID:
Ee-Seventeen, disconnect your scomp link.

ASTROMECH:
(CONCERNED BURBLE)

RECEPTION DROID:
I mean it. You don't want to be infected.

FX: *The sound of a speeder bike approaching outside.*

TEY:
(NOTICING) I don't think that's what he's worried about, is it, Ee-Seventeen?

FX: *The speeder bike is closer...*

RECEPTION DROID:
Oh my. It's that dreadful Twi'lek. The one management forbade access. Ee-Seventeen, lock the doors. Lock the doors!

ASTROMECH:
(URGENT BEEPS)

RECEPTION DROID:
Well, do it manually then.

FX: And closer...

TEY:
Don't think that's going to help. Oh, Lourna. (SHOUTS) Down!

FX: Lourna flies her speeder bike through the glass doors.

RECEPTION DROID:
Oh my!

FX: The speeder slides to a halt, glass still tinkling down.

FX: SK-OT flies in after her.

TEY:
Skoot! You were supposed to keep an eye on her!

SK-OT:
Zep-zep!

LOURNA:
Sirrek, help me get Quin off the speeder.

FX: They get Quin off the speeder bike.

TEY:
What happened?

LOURNA:
Poisoned blade. Get her to a doctor.

TEY:
You've come to the right place. What kind of poison?

LOURNA:
I don't know. All of them, knowing Ro.

TEY:
Marchion Ro? Here? On Protobranch?

LOURNA:
Where's Boolan?

TEY:
Secure wards, level two.

FX: Lourna is already running.

LOURNA:
(CALLING BACK) Look after Quin.

TEY:
I . . . I will. I promise.

CUT TO:

SCENE 143. INT. PROTOBRANCH MEDCENTER. WARD.

Atmos: As before.

BOOLAN:
The Force will be free. The Force will be free!

SSKEER:
Communications are down across the entire facility.

KEEVE:
Doctor, we need to stop until we know what's going on.

AVAR:
She's right, El. You know she is.

BOOLAN:
You're already too late.

ELZAR:
What's that supposed to mean?

FX: Lourna runs in at full speed.

LOURNA:
(BREATHLESS) Exactly what he's been saying.

BOOLAN:
The Force will be free.

KEEVE:
Lourna.

LOURNA:
New intel. From a dubious source, but hey, so am I! The cure isn't a cure. It's a curse.

DR. GINO'LE:
In what way?

LASAT PATIENT:
(GASPS)

FX: An alarm on a medical monitor blares out.

LASAT PATIENT: (CONT)
(GASPS)

AVAR:
What's happening?

DR. GINO'LE:
The Lasat. He's suffering a reaction.

FX: Dr. Gino'le checks instruments.

DR. GINO'LE: (CONT)
But this doesn't make sense. It's not the blight. His... his entire body is breaking down on a subcellular level.

LOURNA:
The baron's cure. It's a trick, another experiment.

AVAR:
In what way?

LOURNA:
It's like the virus in the computer system, but this one doesn't target data. It targets your abilities to touch the Force.

ELZAR:
But that's... that's impossible.

BOOLAN:
We'll see, shall we? You wanted a cure, Master Mann, and I provided one. A cure for the Jedi. A cure for all who manipulate the Force to their own ends.

SSKEER:
Even if that was posssssible—

AVAR:
Which it isn't!

SSKEER:
How could you do such a thing?

BOOLAN:
You see why, don't you, my friend? All that pain you suffered after losing your connection to the Force? That torment. No one will have to endure that again. The Force will be free. And you will be free of the Force. The temptation to abuse its power will be gone forever. And with it, the damage you so selfishly inflict on the galaxy. The blight was a warning from the Force, a warning I alone heeded.

LOURNA:
What did I tell you? He's insane.

FX: Boolan takes a step toward Sskeer.

BOOLAN:
I thought you would understand, Sskeer. I even gave you back your abilities, for just a short time, before they were gone forever. A gift given freely.

LASAT PATIENT:
(RAGGED BREATH)

KEEVE:
Doctor, the Lasat. It's . . . it's horrible.

DR. GINO'LE:
There's nothing I can do. He's not responding to treatment.

LOURNA:
Like he's unraveling.

AVAR:
Dr. Gino'le, this patient . . . did he ever exhibit any particular affinity to the Force?

DR. GINO'LE:
It's hardly my area of expertise, but if you're asking whether he could do the things you can do, then no. Nothing in his record indicated any kind of sensitivity to the Force.

BOOLAN:
Then the cure should not affect him.

LOURNA:
Like it's not affecting you, Baron?

BOOLAN:
What?

ELZAR:
Your hands.

AVAR:
The same thing's happening.

BOOLAN:
But it can't. I cannot touch the Force.

KEEVE:
But the Force touches you. It touches every living being. Destroy its ability to dwell in us...

DR. GINO'LE:
(GROGGY) And you destroy... life.

KEEVE:
Jedi or not.

DR. GINO'LE:
(GROANS) So...

FX: The doctor collapses.

AVAR:
Dr. Gino'le!

KEEVE:
Don't touch him. Don't go anywhere near him or the Lasat.

BOOLAN:
(GROGGY) No... it was the Path... the Path showed me the way. (COUGHS WETLY)

LOURNA:
So you're saying we're all kriffed, whether we're Jedi or not.

KEEVE:
Unless it can be reversed. Is that possible, Boolan? Can you reverse the process?

BOOLAN:
(GROGGY) Yes... yes... but it will take time. Time...

FX: Boolan crashes down.

LOURNA:
And there goes our last hope. Dead to the world.

AVAR:
Not yet. This institute is the best in the galaxy. Geniuses wherever you look.

ELZAR:
We just need to give them time.

SSKEER:
The ssstasis fields. The doctor said we could use them in case of an emergency.

LOURNA:
I think this qualifies.

KEEVE:
Everyone needs to get out of here. We don't know how this is spreading.

AVAR:
The next ward is empty.

KEEVE:
Then that's where you need to go—you, Elzar, Sskeer. The Order needs you.

LOURNA:
And if they're already infected?

KEEVE:
One crisis at a time, Lourna.

SSKEER:
The Order needs you, too, Keeve.

KEEVE:
Maybe, but the galaxy seems to have other ideas. Look.

AVAR:
Your hand!

KEEVE:
The same lesions as the baron, as the doctor. You go. I'll set up the field generators.

SSKEER:
Keeve . . .

KEEVE:
Go! I'm not losing you again.

ELZAR:
Listen to her, Sskeer. You, too, Avar.

FX: Footsteps as they leave.

AVAR:
The Force will be with you, Keeve.

KEEVE:
You better believe it. (GASPS)

FX: She stumbles, barging into equipment.

KEEVE: (CONT)
You, too, Lourna.

LOURNA:
You're a better person than me, Keeve.

KEEVE:
You called me Keeve?

LOURNA:
There's no need to get sentimental.

FX: Lourna slams a door control.

AVAR:
Lourna!

FX: The glass door slides shut.

AVAR: (CONT, MUFFLED THROUGH GLASS)
Lourna, wait.

LOURNA:
Sorry, Marshal. Can't hear you through the glass.

FX: The door locks.

KEEVE:
You're on the wrong side of the door, Lourna. You shouldn't be in here with them, with me.

LOURNA:
Yeah, but we've seen how quickly this thing works, haven't we?

FX: Lourna crosses the room.

LOURNA: (CONT)
And I need you to tell me how to set up these damned stasis fields.

FX: She pulls out the first generator, the equipment heavy.

LOURNA: (CONT)
(EFFORT) The Yacombe first, Boolan last. Hopefully he won't make it.

KEEVE:
Lourna.

FX: She pulls the first generator toward the Yacombe child.

LOURNA:
A girl can dream.

KEEVE:
But what about you?

LOURNA:
Should be enough of these things to go around.

FX: Lourna connects a cable.

LOURNA: (CONT)
I'll go under last. (PITCHING UP VOICE) And you people out there better be right about an antidote. Do you hear me, Marshal?

AVAR: (MUFFLED, THROUGH GLASS DOOR)
You have my word. We'll find a way.

LOURNA:
(BREATH CATCHING) You better. I have someone out there I want to see again. Someone—(GROANS)—I hope will see me.

KEEVE:
(WEAK BUT HOLDING IT TOGETHER) Lourna Dee, savior of the galaxy.

LOURNA:
Don't push it, "Light of the Jedi."

FX: Beeps as Lourna presses buttons, priming the generators.

LOURNA: (CONT)
We have work to do.

FX: The first stasis field activates.

CUT TO:

SCENE 144. INT. STAR CRUISER—NOW.

Atmos: As before.

RHIL:
And they were right? There *was* an antidote?

LOURNA:
I'm here, aren't I?

RHIL:
As large as life.

LOURNA:
Some might say larger.

RHIL:
How did Keeve put it? "Savior of the galaxy."

LOURNA:
We don't know what would've happened if Boolan's "cure" had gotten out of the ward. It didn't. We contained it. And Avar's institute of genii made sure that we recovered.

RHIL:
Because you bought them time.

LOURNA:
With Trennis—(CATCHES HERSELF)—with Keeve. (COVERING) But it's all in a day's work for the mighty Jedi. Nameless, blight, even deadly pathogens—they never stop.

RHIL:
Sounds like you're a convert.

LOURNA:
Hardly. But I know how much your audience loves that crud.

RHIL:
If we can broadcast it.

LOURNA:
I thought it was what the chancellor wanted. And what the chancellor wants, she gets.

RHIL:
After extensive fact-checking.

LOURNA:
That's up to the powers that be.

RHIL:
Of course, some things we *can't* check. Like your account of leaving Marchion Ro trapped in the spaceport.

LOURNA:
The *Gaze Electric* appeared above Protobranch. That's in the public record.

RHIL:
And disappeared soon after.

LOURNA:
While I was still in stasis.

RHIL:
So you couldn't go back to finish what you started.

LOURNA:
I don't need to. And I hope it keeps him awake at night.

RHIL:
And what about your friends?

LOURNA:
Friends?

RHIL:
The Yacombe child?

LOURNA:
Still in stasis. They reversed the effects of Boolan's "cure" . . .

RHIL:
But the blight is still a threat.

LOURNA:
Unfortunately, yes.

RHIL:
And Keeve Trennis? The Jedi you risked your life to save?

LOURNA:
She saved me first.

RHIL:
Can I quote you on that?

LOURNA:
She would never let me live it down. But from what I hear, *for the record,* Keeve is doing just fine.

CUT TO:

SCENE 145. INT. PROTOBRANCH MEDCENTER. PRIVATE ROOM—THEN.

Atmos: A medical monitor beeps.

DR. GINO'LE:
If I could have a little room, please?

AVAR:
Of course. Sskeer?

SSKEER:
My apologies, Doctor.

FX: The doctor's cybernetic legs clatter as he moves nearer the bed where Keeve Trennis is lying.

DR. GINO'LE:
Not a problem. Not a problem at all.

FX: The hiss of a hypospray as he administers the treatment.

DR. GINO'LE: (CONT)
There.

AVAR:
It is done?

DR. GINO'LE:
The final treatment.

SSKEER:
Force willing.

KEEVE:
(COMING AROUND)

AVAR:
She's coming around. Keeve?

KEEVE:
(STILL GROGGY) Avar? (SEES HER FORMER MASTER) Sskeer.

SSKEER:
No, don't try to move. You're still weak.

KEEVE:
And you still have a face like the backside of a dewback.

SSKEER:
(SMILING) Yesss. But you'll get ssstronger.

FX: Keeve suddenly shifts, remembering.

KEEVE:
The kid? The doc?

DR. GINO'LE:
I'm here. I'm here. Not up to full strength, by any means... but recovering. As will you.

KEEVE:
Thank you.

DR. GINO'LE:
Thank my team. And yourself, for that matter, you and Lourna Dee both. If you hadn't put us into stasis... hadn't bought us time to develop an antidote...

KEEVE:
How long?

DR. GINO'LE:
Were you out? A month, give or take a few days.

KEEVE:
(TAKING IT IN) An entire month.

SSKEER:
But ssshe will be fine, won't ssshe, Doctor?

DR. GINO'LE:
I see no reason why not, after a period of extended rest and recuperation.

AVAR:
I'm afraid that might not be possible.

KEEVE:
Avar?

SSKEER:
If you could give usss a moment, Doctor.

DR. GINO'LE:
Of course.

FX: His legs clatter on the floor as he bustles off.

DR. GINO'LE:
Good luck, Master Trennis.

KEEVE:
And why exactly will I require luck? Avar, what aren't you telling me?

AVAR:
We can discuss everything on the flight home.

SSKEER:
We leave in a few hours.

KEEVE:
For the *Ataraxia*?

AVAR:
No.

SSKEER:
The Council has other planss for the flagssship.

AVAR:
You are to report to the *Gios,* where OrbaLin will be waiting.

KEEVE:
And the bond-twins?

SSKEER:
That has yet to be decided.

FX: Crinkle of fabric as Avar sits on the bed.

AVAR:
The chancellor is establishing a fleet on the border of the Occlusion Zone.

KEEVE:
But the defense coalition already *has* a fleet. Admiral Kronara—

AVAR:
Admiral Kronara's fleet has been stationed near Eriadu.

SSKEER:
Whereas yoursss . . . sssomewhat different.

KEEVE:
Mine?

AVAR:
We need to send a message to the people of the Republic, Keeve, especially those along the Stormwall . . .

SSKEER:
Those under consssstant threat of attack.

AVAR:
They need to know that they are protected. That someone is watching out for them.

This isn't just a military operation. Yes, the RDC will be there, but it's more than that. Planets all across the Republic are sending ships. Not because of political obligations or treaty stipulations, but because they want to *help.* And they're not alone. Private spacefarers, traders, even bounty hunters—they're all coming together to show the Nihil that we're not scared. That we can look after our own, even in the face of such adversity.

You should see the fleet coming together, Keeve, ship by ship, volunteer by volunteer. It's wonderful.

SSKEER:
But they need a marshal. Sssomeone to guide their way.

KEEVE:
Then it should be Avar. She was the marshal of Starlight. She's—

AVAR:
She goes where the Force leads her, and this is not her path. It's *yours,* Keeve. And I can't think of anyone better.

SSKEER:
Which is why Master Kriss recommended you to the chancellor.

KEEVE:
But I'm not ready. I'm . . . I'm not a commander!

AVAR:
You are a Jedi who has spent the best part of a year holding back the Hutts. A Jedi who led fights, liberated planets.

KEEVE:
A Jedi who disobeyed orders.

AVAR:
A Jedi who cares, who wants to do the right thing, whatever the cost. Do you remember what I called you before we left Coruscant?

KEEVE:
(STILL SLIGHTLY EMBARRASSED) The Light of the Jedi.

AVAR:
And we need that light more than ever. The *people* need the light. This is your chance to shine, Keeve, to shine *bright,* to be the beacon I know you can be.

SSKEER:
And you won't be alone. I will be with you. Every ssstep of the way.

KEEVE:
You will? As a Jedi?

SSKEER:
That... is for the Force to decide.

AVAR:
Oh, I think the decision has already been made.

FX: Avar produces something from her robes.

AVAR: (CONT)
You'll be needing this, Master Sskeer.

SSKEER:
My lightsaber.

KEEVE:
Take it, Sskeer.

SSKEER:
If you think... I am worthy...

KEEVE:
Oh, shut your face and light the thing.

FX: Sskeer does as he's told, igniting his lightsaber.

FX: The blade hums.

KEEVE: (CONT)
There.

SSKEER:
Better?

KEEVE:
The way it should be.

AVAR:
For light and life.

FX: *A rustle of robes as Avar stands.*

AVAR: (CONT)
Are you ready, Marshal Trennis?

KEEVE:
No, but I'll try to be. For all our sakes.

CUT TO:

SCENE 146. INT. STAR CRUISER—NOW.

Atmos: As before.

RHIL:
And what about you, Lourna Dee? Where are you going? What's next in your story?

LOURNA:
A new beginning.

RHIL:
As a bounty hunter.

LOURNA:
As the head of a guild. I have a lot of ... associates out there in need of—

RHIL:
Rehabilitation?

LOURNA:
Employment.

CUT TO:

SCENE 147. EXT. CORUSCANT. REPUBLIC DEFENSE COALITION SPACEPORT—NIGHT—THEN.

Atmos: Coruscanti air travel. Drilling RDC troopers.

FX: The Overtone *lands. The ramp lowers as footsteps approach: Elzar Mann and the Temple Guard.*

FX: Lourna Dee descends, flanked by Tey Sirrek. SK-OT buzzes nearby.

ELZAR:
Welcome back to Coruscant, Lourna, Tey.

TEY:
Laser Mann!

ELZAR:
Please stop that.

LOURNA:
Have to say, this is quite a welcoming committee. I wasn't expecting to see you in all your finery.

ELZAR:
The chancellor asked me to personally manage transportation of the prisoner.

LOURNA:
Transporting him to . . . ?

ELZAR:
The chancellor thanks you for your service, Lourna. Beyond that...

LOURNA:
It's none of my business.

ELZAR:
A business that is benefiting from a generous fee, from what I've heard.

TEY:
Not to mention a full pardon.

ELZAR:
Lina Soh is a woman of her word.

TEY:
(LAUGHING) Here's hoping Lourna's the same, huh? (NOTICING HER GLARE) Er. I mean...

LOURNA:
(ICY) We have a prisoner to deliver, Tey. If you would be so kind...

TEY:
You know I don't work for you, right?

LOURNA:
Of course you do.

TEY:
Right. Um. Of course. Give me a minute. The repulsor cell is at the top of the ramp.

FX: Tey runs back up to the open doors.

TEY: (CONT)
(CALLING DOWN) Won't be a sec!

ELZAR:
Your staff will need some work.

LOURNA:
I'm sure I'll find a way to lick them into shape. But while he's busy, there is one thing you may be able to help me with, Master Mann.

ELZAR:
Of course.

LOURNA:
As you said, Chancellor Soh has been ... generous. More than generous, as it happens, but I wondered if you could help me ... redistribute some of the funds.

ELZAR:
I'm not sure I'm the right person to talk to.

LOURNA:
But you'll know the right person. More than me. (BEAT) I'm talking about Dalna.

ELZAR:
Dalna?

LOURNA:
How does the head of a bounty hunter guild go about making a donation to the Dalnan relief fund? I assume there *is* a fund. It's how all this operates, right?

ELZAR:
All this.

LOURNA:
Civilization.

ELZAR:
You wish to donate?

LOURNA:
I hear there are tax breaks.

ELZAR:
You're going to pay taxes?

LOURNA:
Don't rub it in. But I think there will be enough, even after paying for the ship. Enough to repay a debt.

ELZAR:
Leave it with me.

LOURNA:
Thank you. But don't tell everyone.

ELZAR:
Of course not. You have a reputation to protect.

LOURNA:
Precisely.

TEY: (OFF MIC)
Ready?

LOURNA:
(CALLING BACK) I don't know what took you so long.

TEY: (OFF MIC)
Blame Skoot, fussing about like a mother hen. Bringing the prisoner down now.

FX: There's a buzz of a repulsorlift and the stomp of Tey's feet on the ramp.

BOOLAN: (COMING UP ON MIC, MUFFLED)
The work isn't finished. Oh no. The Force will be free. You'll see. You'll all see. The Force will be free. It will be free.

ELZAR:
Has he been like that all the way from Protobranch?

TEY:
Ever since he came out of stasis. Scrawling on the walls, muttering beneath his breath.

LOURNA:
We should have just deactivated his vocabulator. But he's your problem now, Master Mann. Yours and the Republic's. (SMILING SLYLY) May the Force be with you.

CUT TO:

SCENE 148. INT. STAR CRUISER—NOW.

Atmos: As before.

RHIL:
Is that something you believe in now?

LOURNA:
The Force?

RHIL:
The Force, the Republic, the common good.

LOURNA:
If it pays.

RHIL:
The same old Lourna Dee.

LOURNA:
It's the only way to be. (BEAT) Are we done?

RHIL:
I suppose we are. Although there is someone else I should ask about.

LOURNA:
There is?

RHIL:
You've told us what happened to Keeve Trennis and the baron. But you haven't said what became of Quin after she was stabbed by Marchion Ro.

LOURNA:
No, I haven't. (BEAT) This ship. Have I mentioned its name?

RHIL:
No. It was the *Overtone*. A name I assume you changed the moment it came into your possession.

LOURNA:
But changed it to what?

RHIL:
I would've thought that was obvious: the *Lourna Dee*.

LOURNA:
She's named after her captain.

RHIL:
As I said...

FX: The door slides open, and someone enters.

FX: Lourna turns in her chair.

LOURNA:
And here she is.

QUIN:
We've had a fresh batch of contracts arrive from Deltron of all places... (REALIZES THEY'RE NOT FINISHED) Oh, sorry. I thought you were done.

LOURNA:
Rhil, may I introduce the captain of the—

QUIN:
No! No, I've told you. We're not calling her the *Quin*. It's a ridiculous name for a ship.

LOURNA:
You have *so* much to learn.

QUIN:
We both do.

RHIL:
And what should I call it, then? The ship. In the final edit.

LOURNA:
Maybe you don't have to call it anything. It's not important, really. Not in the great scheme of things.

QUIN:
What's *important* is the guild.

RHIL:
The guild.

QUIN:
Open to anyone who longs to walk a new path, unshackled by the past.

LOURNA:
You're enjoying this, aren't you?

QUIN:
And you're not?

RHIL:
And does this guild have a name?

LOURNA:
(GRINS) Oh yes. Yes, it does. (BEAT) The Tempest Breakers.

THE END

Acknowledgments

Audio drama was where I began, twenty-five years ago, writing timey-wimey adventures for another franchise, and, a quarter of a century later, it's still my favorite medium. Why? Because it takes so many people to realize. Yes, it starts with a script, but it's more than that. It's the work of the actors, the sound engineers, the composers, the director, the producers. It's truly a team effort, and I thank each and every person involved, from Tom Hoeler (editor), Abby Duval (production editor), and Laura Jorstad and Laura Petrella (copy editors), to our amazing cast and crew.

There's our director, Kevin, who had the dubious "pleasure" of directing yours truly in a cameo; our producer, Nick, who gives the best hugs; the whole team at Lucasfilm, including Mike; everyone at Story Group; and our publishing coordinator, Isabel, who, by the time you read this, will have moved on to new pastures and will be sorely missed. And no High Republic acknowledgment section would be complete without a mention of my fellow THR creators, including the wonderful Ario Anindito, who first gave Lourna a face!

My family, as always, requires thanks for putting up with me as I wrangle a script, as do George Mann and Mark Wright (with whom I wrote my first audio script back in 2000) for cheerleading me every step of the way.

But there's another group that is essential for any drama, be it audio or otherwise: the audience. You. The listeners and the readers. As I type this, the end of *Star Wars: The High Republic* is in sight. Once this script book is finished, I have three comic book scripts to write and that's it—I'll be done. It's been an incredible experience, one not without dramas of its own along the way. But looking back, there is one thing I think I'll remember: the fans. From the excitement online during our launch in pandemic days to the thousands upon thousands of excited readers filling convention halls, you have been brilliant. And the creativity . . . oh, the creativity. Art. Costuming. Building props. Composing entire soundtrack albums! I have been in constant awe. You, to coin a phrase, are wizard.

Thank you for reading, listening to, and watching our story unfold. Thank you for supporting it every step of the way. For the theories. For the excitement. For everything.

We are all the High Republic.

For light and life. Always.

About the Author

The creator of *Godfather of Hell, Night of the Slashers, The Ward, Dead Seas,* and *Shadow Service, New York Times* bestselling author CAVAN SCOTT is the writer of *Star Wars: The Rising Storm, Star Wars: Dooku: Jedi Lost, The Patchwork Devil,* and *Anchor's Heart.* Scott is a lead story architect for Lucasfilm's bestselling multimedia initiative, *Star Wars: The High Republic.* His other work includes scripts for the Emmy-winning *Star Wars: Young Jedi Adventures;* numerous comic book series for Marvel, DC, Dark Horse, IDW, and *2000 AD;* plus original full-cast audio dramas for Audible and Big Finish Productions.

Scott lives in Bristol, UK, with his wife and daughters. His lifelong passions include classic scary movies, folklore, the music of David Bowie, and walking. He owns far too much LEGO.

www.cavanscott.com

About the Type

This book was set in Hermann, a typeface created in 2019 by Chilean designers Diego Aravena and Salvador Rodriguez for W Type Foundry. Hermann was developed as a modern tribute to classic novels, taking its name from the author Hermann Hesse. It combines key legibility features from the typefaces Sabon and Garamond with more dynamic and bolder visual components.